THE MOTHER

VALERIE KEOGH

B
Boldwood

First published in Great Britain in 2024 by Boldwood Books Ltd.

Copyright © Valerie Keogh, 2024

Cover Design by Head Design Ltd

Cover Photography: iStock

The moral right of Valerie Keogh to be identified as the author of this work has been asserted in accordance with the Copyright, Designs and Patents Act 1988.

All rights reserved. No part of this book may be reproduced in any form or by any electronic or mechanical means, including information storage and retrieval systems, without written permission from the author, except for the use of brief quotations in a book review.

This book is a work of fiction and, except in the case of historical fact, any resemblance to actual persons, living or dead, is purely coincidental.

Every effort has been made to obtain the necessary permissions with reference to copyright material, both illustrative and quoted. We apologise for any omissions in this respect and will be pleased to make the appropriate acknowledgements in any future edition.

A CIP catalogue record for this book is available from the British Library.

Paperback ISBN 978-1-80549-431-7

Large Print ISBN 978-1-80549-432-4

Hardback ISBN 978-1-80549-430-0

Ebook ISBN 978-1-80549-433-1

Kindle ISBN 978-1-80549-434-8

Audio CD ISBN 978-1-80549-425-6

MP3 CD ISBN 978-1-80549-426-3

Digital audio download ISBN 978-1-80549-427-0

Boldwood Books Ltd
23 Bowerdean Street
London SW6 3TN
www.boldwoodbooks.com

*For my grand-niece
Emma Fearon
With love*

For my grand-neice
Emma Lennox
with love

PROLOGUE

In prison, in the slow tick tock of minutes passing, in the dragging days and dreary weeks, there is time for thinking. And I had plenty of time – years when I'd be able to review every action, every word, and wonder if I should have done things differently.

Time to wonder too, if it is better, as the saying goes, to have loved and lost than never to have loved at all.

A stupid saying, quoted by fools who haven't a clue.

They have no idea. Because when you really love someone, you never give them up – ever – the loss would be unbearable.

Would it be better never to have loved at all?

No, because in these dark days, it is the memory of that love that keeps me from falling to pieces.

I was guilty of loving too much, others for not loving at all.

Each extreme, in their own way, led to disaster.

And to murder.

1

It was late Friday afternoon. Sarah was speaking to Nick about their weekend plans, her mobile pressed to her ear as she tapped on the keyboard with the fingers of her other hand. They'd been invited to a housewarming party that night by an old college friend of hers, Charlie, who had been gregarious, irreverent, and fun in college. He'd dipped in and out of her life in the years since, drifting from job to job, relationship to relationship, seeming never to grow older – or up. Sometimes, as she struggled with her studies and then the long hours as a junior doctor, Sarah had looked at him through a green-tinged lens.

That afternoon, exhausted after a particularly stressful week as a GP in a busy practice, she was thinking of him with irritation rather than envy. With his usual lack of discernment, Charlie would have invited all and sundry to his new rental apartment. The party would be a noisy, jammed occasion, full of people neither she nor Nick would know, and others she knew and didn't like. After a busy week, she'd have preferred to stay at home, order takeaway, and watch a good movie. She knew Nick would feel the same way.

He, after all, hadn't wanted to go in the first place. 'Charlie will flirt with you, as usual. Or if not him, one of his creepy friends will,' he'd said. 'Can't we give it a miss?'

She'd dug her heels in because, since they'd married, Nick never wanted to go out with friends. At first, she'd enjoyed the romantic dinners out *à deux*; Nick was attentive and charming company. It was only when the weeks drifted into months, when the attentiveness was starting to smother and she had messages from friends asking if she'd fallen off the edge of the planet, that she suggested they meet up en masse in their favourite pub the way they used to.

'I prefer to have you to myself,' Nick had said when she'd brought up the idea. He'd arrived home with a huge bouquet of flowers for her, so it would have been churlish to have insisted then. The following week, she managed to persuade him that it would be nice to meet up with some of her friends, get to know them.

'I'd do anything for you,' he said, kissing her on the cheek. 'But I still prefer to have you to myself. Anyway,' he added, 'I know Jade, don't I?'

Jade, Sarah's closest friend. He couldn't help but get to know her; she and Sarah had been friends forever. It was a shame Nick and Jade had taken an instant and obvious dislike to each other, though. It was a shame too that he hadn't taken to any of her other friends, regarding her male friends with blatant suspicion that had initially amused Sarah. Less so when Nick insisted on keeping a possessive arm around her whenever any of them approached.

'Don't you trust me?' she'd said.

'Of course I do,' he'd said, surprised. 'I don't trust *them*, though.'

Sarah wanted to laugh, to say it took two to tango and would have done had she not discovered, a few weeks after their marriage, that Nick didn't have much of a sense of humour.

She was only half-listening as he continued to bemoan their decision to accept Charlie's invitation. There was no point in her saying she no longer wanted to go; it would only make accepting the next invitation to join their friends more difficult. Once she got home, had a shower, and put her glad rags on, she'd be fine. She was still inputting patient details with one hand, and only switched her attention from the computer screen when she realised Nick had stopped speaking. She took her hand from the keyboard and tried to smooth away the lines that had corrugated her forehead all morning. Had she been cut off? Or had he hung up on her? 'Nick?'

'We need to talk.'

The silence was filled with anticipation, with dread. Four simple words, but put them together, say them in a tone of voice as filled with portent as Nick's was, and they were enough to take Sarah's breath away.

She could cut the connection, pretend she'd never heard. She was good at that. None so deaf as those who didn't want to hear, those who chose to ignore the difficulties life threw at them in a series of constant repeats rather than to face making difficult decisions. She'd been doing it for months. Ignoring the growing distance between them, the slowly dawning realisation that their marriage had been a mistake, that their relationship had run its course. Maybe it already had before their wedding exactly a year before.

They hadn't been together for long when Nick proposed, only a few months. She'd met him only weeks after breaking up with a man she'd been so crazy about that she'd hung on long after she should have given up. Clem had been unreliable, and probably unfaithful, during their three-year relationship.

It was probably why she'd fallen so quickly for Nick. He was reliable, attentive, kind, and made it obvious that he was totally smitten with her. He was a band-aid for her bruised ego, her cracked and bleeding heart. When he'd proposed, when he'd gone down on one knee in a smart, Italian restaurant, and said, 'Sarah, I love you, will you marry me?' she'd been stunned.

Her first instinctive reaction had been *no!* She'd looked at him, on one knee, a small box in his hand holding a sparkling diamond, a look of adoration on his face, and said, 'Of course I will,' with such exaggerated enthusiasm that Nick had never noticed the slightest of hesitations that had come before her answer.

2

The months between proposal and wedding had been filled with enough excitement to swamp any recurring doubts Sarah had. Telling both sets of parents had been the first step. She was gratified how delighted Nick's parents had been that their only child was getting married, and wasn't the slightest bit surprised at her mother's reaction: relief that Sarah was *settling down* with a good man. Friends were either surprised or excited about forthcoming celebrations, insisting on an engagement party and as soon as that was over, arguing where they should go for a hen party or stag do.

'I never have you to myself anymore,' Nick had said, more than once as the arrangements became increasingly complicated. 'Maybe we should simply elope.'

Sarah had laughed the first time, smiled the second, but by the time he'd said it for the tenth or twentieth time, she was irritated enough to ask, 'Are you regretting your proposal now? Because if you are, say so before it's too late.'

He'd rushed to reassure her. He was excited about being married; he just hadn't expected all the fuss.

'It's not fuss, it's tradition,' she'd argued. And in making all the arrangements, any hesitation that Sarah had, any doubt, was swept away along with everything else.

He mentioned moving in with her, but she'd laughed and waved a hand around her tiny apartment. 'It's barely big enough for me.' Seeing his disappointment, she'd given him a key to the front door. 'Here, you can stay some nights.' She'd meant an occasional night, at her request, but found it hard to complain when she arrived home to find him slouched on the sofa, watching TV and waiting for her. He'd jumped up and smothered her with kisses. How could she complain? Soon they'd be together every day. They simply needed a bigger place.

She'd thought they'd rent somewhere more suitable, but Nick had insisted that buying would be a better option. She was happy to agree until he said he wanted to find somewhere before they got married. It was all too much. The stress of trying to find, never mind buy a place, clashed horribly with the stress of arranging the wedding. Both combined to launch an assault on logical thinking of any sort. Add a busy job into the mix, and Sarah didn't know how she kept going.

When they'd looked at several small apartments in their preferred area and discovered the horrendous reality that they couldn't even afford the smallest and grottiest of these, she threw her hands up and refused to look at one more. 'There's no point,' she insisted. 'We can't afford to buy anything unless we go much further out.'

Even if she'd cancelled the ridiculously expensive wedding venue, the three-day hen party to Marrakesh, the wedding dress she'd fallen in love with that cost four times what she'd expected, none of the extra money would have made the slightest difference.

Two weeks before the wedding, tired after a busy day, she'd arrived home to find Nick had cooked her favourite dinner. Candles were lit, Spotify was playing her favourite songs. She'd sighed with pleasure, kicked off her shoes, curled her toes into the soft pile of the carpet, and took the glass of wine he handed to her with a smile. 'Just what this doctor ordered,' she said, reaching to plant a kiss on his cheek.

'I have some good news.'

He touched his glass to hers, a knowing grin on his face that irritated her. He liked guessing games, so did she on occasion, but after the week she'd had, ending with a day from hell, she wasn't in the mood. She supposed she should have been grateful he'd said *good* news, not merely news, leaving her to wonder whether she should back out the door, retrace her steps to the pub she'd passed minutes before, and this time give in to the temptation to have a quick one before heading home.

It wouldn't have been the first time. She knew the danger, the thin edge of the wedge she was using to counter the stress that stretched every day to breaking point. That's why she'd passed by that day, to prove to herself she could. Now she was sorry. Whatever news Nick had, be it good or bad, would be easier to bear with a double vodka inside.

She settled for almost emptying her wine glass in two long gulps that had Nick raise one knowing eyebrow. As if he in his cushy office job had the slightest clue what hard work really was. Luckily, the wine was absorbed quickly into a stomach that had seen nothing all day other than the piss-poor coffee they had in the surgery. She'd meant to stop for lunch – she always meant to stop – but she was a good GP and when her last patient of the morning had been a woman who needed more time, she'd given it. It had eaten into the thirty minutes supposedly set aside for a break, the afternoon list too busy to afford her time to start late. Instead of eating, she'd swallowed coffee and ran on fumes.

She'd emptied the last of the wine in a mouthful and put the glass down before reaching for the cheque being held out to her. After a quick look at the figure written on it, she'd looked at Nick's handsome face. It had beamed with a mixture of pride and excitement. Perhaps the alcohol had raced too fast into her bloodstream and had coloured her thoughts. Why else would her first reaction have been the terrifying feeling of being trapped? With a suddenness that made her stomach lurch, she got to her feet. She wanted to tell him she'd made a mistake, that she wanted out; instead, she handed back the cheque and conjured up a smile from somewhere. 'This is fantastic.'

'It's a loan,' he said, 'but a long-term one that we can pay back as and when we can over the years to come. Interest free. It means we can buy a decent apartment. Two bedrooms. Plan for the future.'

Sarah's smile became a painful grimace as the implications hit her that this was it. Her future was mapped out. For the next several years, it would be her career, marriage to Nick, living in London, paying off the loan.

This was what she wanted, wasn't it?

*　*　*

Sarah pressed the mobile to her ear, trying to drag herself back to the present and to Nick's unusually serious *we need to talk*.

'Sarah? You still there?'

She could hear a hint of anxiety in his voice. So typical of him. A blustering man, not a brave one, his courage always ebbed quickly. *We need to talk*. Maybe he'd found the courage to admit what she'd known for months: that their marriage had been a mistake. He wasn't brave, but she was a total coward, far preferring to go with the flow than to face the consequences of any decision she might make. It was part of the reason her life was in such a mess.

'Yes, I'm still here but I have to go; my next patient is waiting. We can talk later, or even better, over the weekend, okay?'

'Tomorrow night. I'll book dinner in Alfredo's.'

The restaurant where he'd proposed. It was a good choice. Tomorrow, they'd close that circle. Admit they'd made a mistake, part on good terms and go their separate ways.

3

Sarah was later than she'd expected leaving the surgery. The last two patients of the day had complicated health issues which took time. They were also both desperate to talk with someone who understood, who took the time needed to give holistic care, looking at them as people with needs rather than a condition or disease. Sarah kept her professional smile in place and when they hesitated, she offered encouraging words for them to continue. It was these moments when she remembered why she'd wanted to be a doctor.

As a child, she'd sat in front of the TV, glued to every episode of *Peak Practice*. She'd decided then she'd be a doctor when she grew up and that dream had never changed. What had was the location. Sometimes, when she looked around her office in the huge, sprawling medical clinic, she wondered what had happened to that dream of being a country GP.

No time for wondering anything that night. She checked her watch and frowned. Almost six. It would take twenty minutes to get home, twenty to shower and change into something suitable for one of Charlie's parties, another fifteen to get to his place. He'd said from seven. She and Nick had already agreed they'd arrive early and leave early before the party descended into raucous chaos fuelled by both drink and drugs.

A drink would, however, help to get her through the evening, so

Sarah did as she was doing with increasing regularity – she stopped in the small pub a short walk from the two-bedroomed apartment they'd bought with Nick's parents' help. The pub wasn't one she and Nick frequented; she was smarter than that. That she felt the need to be secretive about her drinking worried her, until the first mouthful of the double vodka hit and erased that worry spot.

Nick was ready and waiting when she pushed open the front door of the apartment a little before seven. The one double vodka hadn't been enough to ease the tension of the day, so she'd had a second. A third would have been perfect, but she wasn't that far gone as yet, not that stupid. The effects of two could be disguised as end of the week exuberance; the effects of three would have taken away all her filters and she might have said or done something stupid. She might even have pre-empted Nick's *we need to talk* and blurted out the truth in two blunt words. *It's over*.

'Sorry,' she said, bending to drop a kiss on his cheek. He was looking particularly well, the white shirt he wore setting off the tan he'd acquired on their recent holiday to Mauritius. He was a handsome man. A good one. It was just a shame she didn't love him. She wasn't sure she ever had. 'I'll have a quick shower, change into something suitably wild, and be ready in fifteen minutes, okay? You could order the taxi for...' She pushed back the cuff of her jacket to check the time. '...say seven forty-five to be on the safe side.'

'We were going to be there for seven,' he said grumpily.

'Well, now we'll be there for eight,' she said with a grin that she worried might be a little too cheerful, a little too alcohol fuelled. 'We can still leave early, don't worry.' She ruffled his hair, then vanished to their room. She'd already decided she was going to wear the black slip dress that showed off her figure and her sun-glowing skin. After a quick shower, she shrugged it over her head and let it settle over her curves.

Heavier make-up than she wore during the day, her long hair released from the work-day bun to curl around her neck, high stilettos that she'd probably take off after a few more drinks, and a wrap in case the mild evening turned chilly. She cast a critical eye over herself in the mirror. Her reflection was blurred. In soft focus, she looked younger than her thirty-eight years. *Soft focus* – she had stopped at two doubles, hadn't she? Or had she had that third?

She moved closer to the mirror, trying to see the truth in the blurred lines. If it was there, it wasn't obvious. With a grunt, she left the doubts in the mirror, turned away, grabbed her bag and left the room.

* * *

The party was exactly as they'd expected. Had they arrived at seven as originally planned, they'd have had a chance to speak to their host, but by the time they arrived just after eight, the modest apartment was already bulging with people and noise, and Charlie was nowhere to be seen.

'He'll be lucky if he's not thrown out,' Nick said, keeping his hand on Sarah's waist.

She muttered agreement. In rented apartments, parties were generally classified as a big no-no. 'Let's get a drink, find Charlie, say hello and make a quick exit. We could stop at Alfredo's, see if they have a free table. I could do with something to eat.'

Nick pulled her closer and pressed his lips to her cheek. 'No lunch again?'

'I had a banana.' It wasn't quite true; she'd peeled one. That had been as far as she'd got. His raised eyebrows made her smile. He was a good man; she hoped they could remain friends after they split.

They were on their second drink before they spotted Charlie pushing through the crowd towards them. Sarah didn't need twenty-twenty vision to see her friend was already high on something. His pupils were dilated to eerie black holes and he moved with a jerky, restless agitation. He pulled each of them into a hug, holding Sarah for longer than she liked, closer than she cared for, close enough to smell the distinct and telling stink of burnt rubber that screamed crack cocaine. She met Nick's eyes over his shoulder, her message clear. *Get me out of this.*

'How's it going, buddy?' Nick tugged on the arms wrapped around Sarah until she was finally released.

She wasn't flattered that Charlie was coming on to her. He always did; it was a game they played, amusing banter they both enjoyed. She'd tried to tell him that Nick didn't like it, but instead of stopping his flirtatious manner, he exaggerated it, enjoying Nick's annoyed, frustrated reaction. She'd told Nick to ignore him but didn't have much success there either.

But that night, Charlie wasn't coming on to her or being flirtatious. He'd simply been using her to keep from falling flat on his face. 'He's high,' she said, not bothering to lower her voice. If Charlie heard, he didn't appear to be offended.

'Good to see you both,' he said, lurching forward, stopping when Nick's hand tightened around his arm. He looked down at the hand, then reached up with his free hand to brush it away, missing and connecting with his own arm. 'Oops,' he said before pulling his arm free. 'Must mingle, have a good night.'

'We will.' Sarah grabbed Nick's hand. 'Let's scarper. He's not going to notice whether we're here or not.'

Out on the street, Nick used his mobile to check that Alfredo's had a table and call for an Uber. Within a few minutes, they were on their way to the restaurant.

In the taxi, Sarah shut her eyes and rested her head back. Not for the first time, she promised herself she would give up drinking. Or at least those slightly dodgy visits to the pub on her way home from work. Not that night, though. She'd have a few glasses of wine over dinner. It would help wash down the words she was sure Nick would want to have that night rather than waiting for the following day.

She turned to look at him. He was staring straight ahead, a slightly mulish look on his face. It didn't look as if he was going to wait until they got to the restaurant to have his say. Did he think she'd be upset? That she'd break down and beg him not to leave her? She reached a hand out for his arm, closed her fingers around it and squeezed gently. Offering him reassurance that their break up was for the best. For both of them.

He took her hand, held it in his, then turned awkwardly in his seat to face her. 'You probably know what I want to talk about.' He smiled. 'I've been dropping pretty unsubtle hints.'

Unsubtle hints? He'd been more distant than usual. Or maybe that was her. She'd been drifting recently. Half the time, she wasn't listening to him, letting him babble on about something or other – usually football. At least she could understand the game but when he started talking about cricket, she was lost. He never noticed her lack of contribution, carried away by his own enthusiasm.

'So, what do you think?'

What did she think? That the two glasses of wine she'd drunk at the party, on top of the vodka she'd had earlier, had turned her brain to mush. She tried to shake off the alcohol-induced stupor to answer. 'I think you're right.'

It was obviously the correct answer. He slumped in relief. 'I wasn't sure you'd agree. You've always said you weren't interested.' He lifted her hand to his mouth and kissed it. 'I'm the happiest man alive.'

How many drinks had she had? She was relieved that their split was going to be amicable, but this was going a little too far. She pulled her hand away, sat up straighter. The seat belt felt tight, restricting her movement, her breathing. She fumbled for the control to open the window, sucking in the gust of fume-laced air that slid in from the streets.

'You okay?' Nick's voice laden with concern.

She took another gulp of air before bringing the window up, shutting out the fumes and the noise. 'Yes, sorry, I'm fine.' Somewhere in a part of her brain, a little voice was screaming a warning. Perhaps if she'd been stone-cold sober, she might have understood what it was trying to say. As it was, all she could do now was to look at Nick blankly. 'You're the happiest man alive? I'm not sure I understand?'

And then he explained.

4

Sarah escaped from the house on Saturday, telling Nick she had a long-standing arrangement to meet her friend Jade for lunch. 'So sorry, I thought I'd told you. You don't mind, do you?' She knew he wouldn't. There was an important cricket match on that afternoon. He'd head down to their favourite pub and join the crowd cheering on their team.

'If you're finished early, why don't you join me?' he said. 'We're going to win; it'll be exciting.'

'I might do that,' she said, not having the slightest intention of doing so. Anyway, once she and Jade got together, the hours would quickly pass. There wasn't a long-standing arrangement but she'd sent her friend a quick message first thing that morning begging her to cancel whatever she'd planned and meet her. She'd stared at her phone until the reply came.

> Had planned a lazy day. Sounds serious. Come for lunch. We can drink wine and sort out whatever is ailing you.

Some of the tension eased as Sarah tapped out a reply.

> Best friend! See you around one.

Nick was still poring over the newspapers when she left. She stood in the doorway watching him. He really had no idea what he'd done to her. The chaos he'd caused. The shitstorm that was making her head throb. It was tempting to cross the room, grab the paper, shred it before his eyes and throw it at him. But she didn't. In the same way as she'd stayed quiet the night before when she should have spoken out – should have told him the truth instead of nodding inanely like a brainless idiot. She'd been numb. That was her excuse for saying nothing. Numb, tipsy, soon to be so drunk, she didn't remember the dinner, what she'd eaten, if she'd eaten. Didn't remember leaving the restaurant, or the journey home, just a vague memory of Nick helping her out of her clothes.

'I'll see you later,' she said, drawing his attention from the newspaper. 'Enjoy the game.'

As she knew he would, he got to his feet and crossed to kiss her goodbye. 'Have a good time, tell Jade I said hello. Don't forget to join me in the pub later.'

She moved closer, her cheek against his as she replied, 'Will do.'

Then she was gone.

* * *

Sarah's friend lived in a beautiful, terraced home a short Tube ride away. They'd been friends since their mid-teens when the Potter family had moved to London from Yorkshire. Jade worked for a pharmaceutical company and spent a lot of her time at conferences in various parts of the world, often away for days at a time. Sarah wouldn't hear from her for weeks, sometimes months when she was particularly busy, then she'd have a message saying Jade had some free time and demanding that Sarah meet and fill her in on all the gossip.

All the gossip! Luckily, Sarah was astute enough to see that what her friend really wanted wasn't more excitement, but a taste of hum-drum normality. And sadly, Sarah was able to give her that.

She smiled when the door opened and Jade stood there, arms held wide, a smile on her strikingly beautiful face. 'You're in trouble,' she said, folding Sarah into a tight hug. 'Let's see if I can help get you out of it.' She hooked an arm around her waist and led her into the house. 'Sit, I'll get the wine and you can tell me what's put those worry lines on your face.'

Sarah was happy to do what she was told, taking a seat on the comfortable sofa, her eyes going automatically to the window with its view over the garden.

'Here you go.' Jade handed her a glass of wine.

A very large glass: it was filled almost to the brim. Sarah gave a short laugh and shook her head before taking it and downing a few mouthfuls in quick gulps.

'Maybe I should have just put a straw in the bottle.' Jade sat on the sofa beside her and put a hand on Sarah's knee. 'It can't be that bad surely.'

Sarah still couldn't believe she'd got it so wrong. When Nick had told her what he claimed he'd been hinting about for weeks, she'd looked at him in absolute horror. That feeling had receded, leaving her slightly stunned. She put the glass down and twisted in the seat to meet her friend's inquisitive eyes. 'Nick wants us to have a baby.'

Jade had taken a mouthful of wine. She choked on it inelegantly, flapping a hand in front of her face. 'You trying to kill me?' She tapped the hand on her chest and coughed again. 'Bloody hell, this is a surprise. Last time we spoke, you seemed unhappy. I got the impression your marriage was in trouble. Did I read that wrong?'

'No, you didn't.' Sarah gave her a quick rundown of the previous evening. 'He said he wanted to talk, I assumed he was thinking along the same lines as me. He's been so distant recently.' Sarah snorted. 'He said he'd been dropping hints. Just shows how much I listen to him because I don't remember hearing anything about a baby. Not one fucking word.'

'So you told him it was a crazy idea, yes?' Jade waited a beat, then sighed. 'You didn't, did you?'

Sarah picked up her glass and held it to her mouth, pressing it hard against her lower lip.

'You didn't!' Jade sat back with a grunt of frustration.

Sarah shrugged. She hadn't said yes or no to Nick. She hadn't said anything. She couldn't. Stunned and inebriated, it was impossible to come up with anything sensible. Not with Nick holding her hand and staring into her eyes with a dopey grin on his face as the taxi swayed on its way. She hadn't said anything, but had she nodded? Or had he simply taken her silence as acquiescence because he'd sat back with a satisfied expression for the rest of the journey to the restaurant.

'When he'd said he wanted to talk, I assumed he wanted out, that he was unhappy in our marriage.'

'Like you are,' Jade said when Sarah stopped.

Was she? Sarah wasn't sure about anything any more.

'You said you didn't want children.' Jade laughed and wagged a finger. 'But then again, you said you never wanted to get married, and look at you now!'

Sarah nodded. There was no point in arguing. She'd tried to put on a brave face when her previous relationship had failed, tried to show the world that she didn't care, that she wasn't interested in marriage or children anyway. She'd spouted a deluge of crap. 'You know how cut up I was when Clem ended our relationship. I wanted to marry him, to have children with him, and suddenly there I was, almost thirty-eight and single, with nothing to show for the three years we'd spent together.' She'd been so hurt, and Nick had saved her. 'Nick's a good man who loves me. Children would—'

'What?' Jade interrupted. 'Make you fall in love with him?'

Sarah wanted to say she did love him, but she knew her friend would see through the lie. 'I think children would bring us closer. He's stupidly adoring; he'll make a great father. And I'm not getting any younger, tick tock, you know.'

Nick *would* make a great father.

It didn't matter that she didn't love him, did it?

She couldn't think clearly; she blamed the deafening sound of that damn clock. Tick bloody tock.

5

I had believed I'd never find love. Sex was a different bunch of bananas, that I had as often as I wanted, far more than I needed, but it was, like most pleasures, addictive. It was the stomach-tightening, pulse-racing, head-scrambling sort of love I'd never managed to find, so when it did come that one mesmerising, memorable day, it was as if my eyes had finally been opened, as if every sense had just been switched on. Colours were brighter, the world seemed happier, even the damn birds seemed to tweet more sweetly.

The funny thing is, I hadn't been looking. Usually, wherever I go, I scan my surroundings to look for possible companions. Not always for sex, sometimes simply to pass a pleasant hour or so. But that day, it had been raining heavily for hours and I'd discovered I had a hole in my shoe after I'd walked into a water-filled pothole while crossing the road. So I wasn't in the mood for anything when I pushed open the door into my usual lunchtime haunt, my mood further dimmed by seeing how jam-packed it was, every table and almost every seat occupied with people from nearby offices having their lunch.

They tended not to linger too long. I hoped by the time I'd ordered, I'd spy somewhere to park my weary, wet body. Unfortunately, there was a group of three in front of me, and when a table emptied, they grabbed it.

I had no choice but to depend on the charity of those already in possession of a table to allow me to share. I discounted the elderly couple who would probably want to engage me in conversation, and the two businessmen who had laid coats and briefcases on the two spare chairs at their table as if to say, *don't you dare.*

Just when I was thinking the elderly couple were my only bet, I saw two women gather their belongings and make moves to depart. I hurried over before I lost the place to someone else, smiling at the women who were leaving.

Not all of them, though – one stayed seated, her head buried in the book sitting on the table beside a half-finished cappuccino. She'd bent the cover of the dog-eared book back, keeping it in place with one long, unpainted fingernail. Assuming she wouldn't care if I took one of the vacated seats, I sat to have my lunch.

As I ate, with nothing else to occupy my mind, I watched as she turned page after page, her concentration focused and complete. I enjoyed a good book and wondered what it was that was keeping her glued to the words. She might shut it before she left and I'd get a chance to see the cover.

But when she did, when she closed the cover, she looked up with a rapt expression on her face that swept every thought from my head.

I never did discover the name of that book. It was tucked away in the tatty satchel she carried and I never saw it again. Much later, I learned she was an avid and avaricious reader capable of reading three or four books a week, devouring them like a true bookworm. But then, in that café, I was more interested in knowing about her. The flesh and blood, so-incredibly-alive woman with startling, light-blue eyes, a wide, generous mouth, heart-shaped face, shining, chestnut-brown hair. I think I was searching for something to bring me down to earth, but nothing did and I sat there like a child faced with their first Santa Claus.

'You can't beat a good book,' she said, dropping her bag to the floor.

I tried to think of something clever to say but quick-witted repartee wasn't my forte. Right at that moment, I'd have settled for the ability to say anything reasonably intelligent. My tongue felt huge and unwieldy in my mouth, tripping me up when I said the best I could come up with. 'It's h-hard, c-certainly.' Embarrassment swept its brush over my cheeks. I felt them burn. Knew it'd be obvious. My eyes flicked to the door. It'd be better to forget about my half-finished coffee and leave. The rain would sizzle when it hit my cheeks.

'Although a good cup of coffee comes close,' she said with a laugh.

I picked up my cup, tilted it towards her in acknowledgement of her remark and took a sip. It loosened my tongue and thoughts so I was able to answer her without sounding gormless. 'You're right, it does.'

She smiled, picked up her own, reached across and touched it gently against mine.

The tinkle of china hitting china hadn't faded before an intense, unbelievable thought hit me.

This woman was going to change my life.

6

That night, Sarah took out her packet of contraceptive pills and sat on the bed staring at it. She could of course lie: tell Nick she'd stopped but continue to take them. Tell him that Mother Nature had made the decision for them. She could, but Sarah was a very bad liar. What she should do was to tell him the truth: that she wasn't sure she wanted a child. Or should she be completely honest and admit she didn't want a child with *him*.

But there was that damn clock ticking away. She was thirty-eight. Already, she'd be classified as being AMA, advanced maternal age, a term which sounded far better than its predecessor *elderly primigravida*, but which boiled down to the same thing – she was old to be having her first child and wasn't getting any younger.

She tapped the packet against her palm in time to the music that was drifting through from the living room where Nick was sitting, a book in one hand, a can of Bud in the other. He was a good, kind man. Handsome too. A child of theirs was sure to be amazing.

He would be a good father; she would be a good mother.

She had a last look at the packet she held, then took aim at the bin in the corner. If it went in, she'd take it as a sign that she should stop taking the pill; if it landed on the floor, she'd keep going and worry about the consequences later.

So there it was, one of the most important, life-changing decisions she was likely ever to make was being made on the flick of a wrist. It was taking *going with the flow* to extremes, wasn't it? Or was she simply throwing herself onto the lap of the gods and allowing fate to take over.

Why not. She tossed the packet, her eyes following it as it sailed through the air. Which outcome did she want? If they had a child, would it make their creaky marriage better? Nick's love could be smothering. If he had a second person to shower it on, wouldn't that be better? When the packet landed, rattling inside the metal bin, she thought about rushing over to empty it onto the floor and pretend it had missed. But it seemed that finger of fate had made a decision for her.

The bin rattled louder when she kicked it so hard, it bounced against the wall and toppled over. But even then, it laughed at her and kept the pills tightly gripped inside.

The finger of fate, her biological clock, even the damn bin was in league against her.

* * *

She'd been on the pill for years. 'It might take months before my body readjusts,' she told Nick. 'Some women find it hard to conceive, you know; I might be one of the unlucky ones.' *Or the lucky one.* The thought pinched her and made her squirm. How could she be a good mother if she wasn't sure if she wanted to have a child or not?

She certainly thought she'd have a few months to get used to the idea and when she missed her period, she thought nothing of it. It was simply her body readjusting. That was all. She couldn't possibly be pregnant so quickly. Even when she felt nauseous for three mornings in a row, she blamed the fish they'd had at the weekend, the milk that had tasted slightly off, any bloody thing apart from the blindingly, bloody obvious. She was pregnant.

She took a test into the staff toilet during the morning, fingers on her free hand crossed, hoping it would be negative, swearing if it was that she'd speak to Nick and tell him it had been a crazy idea, that she wasn't mother material. She wasn't even wife material. They needed to part company, let each of them find what they really wanted. Nick would find someone else – he was such a lovely man – someone who'd keep house, have his babies, care for him. And she – perhaps she'd look for that country GP position she'd dreamt of when she was a child. There had to be more than this. She was still thinking about what she'd do, where she'd go, when the pregnancy test she was holding in a death-grip told her she wasn't going anywhere.

At least not alone.

She was going to wait another few weeks before telling anyone, even Nick, but the morning sickness increased in severity, uncomfortable nausea becoming full-out vomiting. On the second day of throwing up, on her knees in front of the toilet, holding her hair back with one hand, pulling at the roll of toilet paper with the other, retching and wiping her mouth, flushing, then retching again, she knew she wouldn't be able to keep the secret any longer.

Nick handed her a damp flannel. 'This is the second day you've been sick.'

She reached to flush the toilet again, took a deep breath and got to her feet.

'Is it...?' He was trying to look sympathetic but the underlying excitement won. 'Are you pregnant?'

'I might be,' she said, unwilling to tell him the truth: that she'd done a test and hadn't told him. 'Or I might just have a bug. Covid is still doing the rounds, you know.' She watched as he fought the disappointment to put an arm around her shoulders and pull her close to him.

'You should lie down for a while. I'll ring the clinic, tell them you won't be in today.'

She shook his arm away. 'No, it's fine. I'm fine, or at least I will be. Go make me a ginger herbal tea; that will help settle my stomach.'

Pleased to have something to do, he nodded. 'Sit down first, though.' He was reluctant to leave her, waiting until she sat, hovering over her until she managed an encouraging smile to send him on his way. Moments later, she heard the kitchen cupboard doors snapping shut as he opened one after the other searching for the ginger tea that was tucked there somewhere. She hoped it would help to ease the nausea. She was feeling ridiculously weak.

'Here you go.' Nick held the mug of tea out. 'I put a drop of cold water on top so you should be able to drink it down. I've put a couple of slices of bread in the toaster. I read somewhere it was good for morning sickness.'

She sipped the tea. It was the perfect temperature and she took a few mouthfuls, enjoying the warming feel of the ginger. 'You read it somewhere?'

'The last crime book I read, the wife of one of the detectives was pregnant. He was always making her toast or buying cream crackers.'

'I'd definitely pass on the cream crackers but a slice of toast might be just the thing.' She needed to eat something; she hadn't had anything since a small bowl of cornflakes early the previous day. If she was lucky, the morning sickness would pass in a few days... or weeks.

But she wasn't lucky. As it turned out she was one of the very unlucky ones whose morning sickness went on all day. Some days, she could hold nothing down. Not the ginger tea, or the slice of toast, not even the damn cream crackers that Nick had insisted on buying. When she'd been unable to keep anything down for three days in a row despite the anti-sickness medication she was prescribed, she was admitted to hospital for intravenous fluids.

She didn't need to be told the diagnosis. *Hyperemesis gravidarum.*

'Just like Kate Middleton had with her pregnancies,' Jade said when she came to visit.

'Yes, well she didn't have a job as a busy GP, did she?' Nor did she have a husband whose solicitousness was driving Sarah crazy.

'You'll have to take time off, won't you?'

What choice did Sarah have? She could hardly see sick patients, then ask to be excused because she needed to throw up. 'Hopefully, it'll improve as the weeks go by.'

'Can't they give you something to help. Anti-sickness pills of some sort?'

'I've been taking them, but they're only of limited use. I'll just have to adapt. Eat when I can. Drink to stay hydrated.'

'Not vodka, though.'

Sarah turned to glare at her friend. 'I haven't touched a drop since I discovered I was pregnant. I may be an idiot but I'm not going to risk harming my baby.' She didn't say how difficult it had been or admit how many times she'd walked into the pub on her way home from work, ordered a drink, took the tiniest of sips before pushing it away and leaving the remainder behind. Nor did she tell Jade how often she'd cursed her stupidity for getting pregnant.

She was sent home with a list of instructions. As if she didn't know exactly what she needed to do. Rest. Wait. Hope her condition would improve. At least enough for her to be able to return to work.

It did ease. Sticking to small meals, lots of dry, tasteless food, staying away from dairy, drinking water or juice and when she couldn't tolerate either, sucking on ice cubes. It was four months into the pregnancy before she began to feel a little better. Only a little. The nausea remained but at least she wasn't throwing up several times a day.

She was five months pregnant before she felt well enough to go back to work.

'Are you sure?' Nick said. 'You don't think you should stay home till the baby is born?' He'd arranged to work from home while she was unwell. She'd tried to be grateful, but every time she opened her eyes, he was there, either sitting beside her with his laptop open in front of him, or worse, standing looking down at her. The only place she was guaranteed privacy was in the bathroom.

'No, I'm fine. I'll be better off going back to work,' she said through gritted teeth. 'If I have to sit around one more day doing nothing, I won't be responsible for my actions.' In the previous week, she'd smashed two glasses against the wall, thrown a book so hard at the TV that it sent it crashing to the floor, never to work again, and burst into tears so many times that he'd rung her mother for advice, an action that had further infuriated Sarah when her mother rang her.

When Sarah hung up, she threw the phone at Nick. 'You rang my mother!'

'I was worried about you. I thought she'd be able to help.' He picked up the phone, put it on the table beside her. Then, he plumped a pillow up and put it behind her head and pulled the footstool over for her feet. 'I'll make you some herbal tea; it'll help you relax.'

She didn't want tea, didn't want his fussing. She definitely didn't want to feel like an overstuffed goose. Nausea swept over her and she gulped. Slow, deep breaths helped, as did the mug of ginger tea Nick brought her. 'Thank you,' she said, taking a sip. 'I'm sorry if it seems I'm being difficult. I'll be fine once I get back to work.'

'I don't think you're being difficult.' He sat beside her and laid a hand over her bump. 'You're pregnant with our child and I love you. I just want you to be happy, so if you want to go back to work, that's what you must do.'

He was being so kind, so reasonable; it was wrong that she wanted to slap his caressing hand away so she didn't. She should have done, because he kept at it, his fingers sneaking under the loose T-shirt she was wearing.

'If you want to go back to work, it's a sign you're feeling better, and if you're feeling better,' he got to his feet and reached for her hands to pull her up, 'it seems a shame not to make the most of it.'

They hadn't made love since early in the pregnancy. She'd been too nauseous or too sick and if she wasn't either, she pretended both. She wasn't sure if he realised. She looked into his eyes, but if the truth was there, it was buried beneath such blatant lust, it made her shiver. He seemed to take it as an indication of her desire because he laughed and led her into the bedroom.

She could deal with it, could put up with his lovemaking even when it was the last thing she wanted to do, because she felt so guilty for not loving him.

* * *

Being back in the clinic was hard, especially the first few days when all Sarah wanted to do was to go home and admit she'd made a mistake. About the job, about the blasted baby that was pressing painfully on her bladder during the day and competing for an Olympic medal in gymnastics at night.

She was cross, easily irritated, exhausted, tearful, totally fucking fed up. It was all part of the hyperemesis gravidarum. Nothing to do with the realisation that she'd made the biggest mistake of her life. Two mistakes if she was being pedantic – marriage and having a child with a man she didn't love, a child that would make it harder to cut loose.

In the last few months of her pregnancy, the nausea vanished. It didn't provide her with much relief, replaced as it was by increasing discomfort as she swelled like an overripe fruit. She didn't consider herself to be a vain woman but she was used to her body looking slim, elegant, used to being able to move with grace. By the last few weeks of the pregnancy, she felt like a baby hippo, and no matter how hard she tried not to, she waddled like a duck. A fat, ugly duck.

'You look beautiful,' Nick assured her when she'd told him how she felt.

'Beautiful!' She shoved a cushion behind her back and lifted her feet to rest on the footstool. Every movement was difficult, awkward, and uncomfortable. 'I'm a mountain. A bloody volcano waiting to erupt.' She ran a hand over the bump. 'Another two weeks. I can't wait to get it out.'

'It!' Nick laughed, then sat on the sofa beside her and took her hand in his. 'She is curled up waiting to join us, and I bet she'll be as beautiful as her mother.'

She. Sarah was finding it difficult to think of the entity living inside her as a person. When they'd been asked if they wanted to know the sex of the baby, she'd shrugged. Maybe it was the morning spent hanging over the toilet bowl, but she'd found it difficult to get anyway excited about something she'd no possibility of changing. She was about to say exactly that when she'd seen Nick's shining eyes and open mouth. 'I suppose it would be nice to know,' she'd said trying to inject some enthusiasm into her voice.

'It's a little girl,' the sonographer had said, beaming at them.

Sarah had looked down at the shining dome of her belly. 'Not little enough.'

Nick had laughed before leaning forward to kiss her cheek. 'I hope she has your sense of humour.'

The sonographer had smiled, but Sarah had caught her guarded look, as if she was weighing up this mother-to-be and was unhappy with what she was seeing. No doubt she'd made a note to that effect, underlining it in red to warn her colleagues to keep a close eye. They'd no need. Sarah planned on being a good mother. After all, it wasn't the baby's fault that she was feeling increasingly trapped.

When the baby arrived, she was sure to have a change of heart and love it.

It.

7

The last few days of the pregnancy would have been mind-numbingly boring if every moment wasn't spent trying to find a position that was in any way comfortable. Nick, with his constant assurances that she was looking beautiful, that when their daughter was born, they were going to be so happy, that it would all be over soon, grated the few nerves that weren't already raw and worn to a bloody pulp.

All well and good for him, he wasn't the one whose body was straining to contain the brat, it wasn't him who'd have to eject it kicking and screaming into the world through a hole that was designed, she firmly believed, by a masochistic male god.

'When you hold your baby in your arms, all the discomfort will be forgotten,' her mother said.

'That's a conspiracy to keep us breeding,' Sarah replied, but maybe she would have forgotten the discomfort of pregnancy if her labour hadn't stretched over twelve agonising hours. After the first two, she begged the nurses to get the baby out by any means. After another three, she was threatening to sue if they didn't get it out *now*. And at the end, exhausted, red-eyed, weary, she'd have crawled across the floor, grabbed a pair of scissors and cut the child out herself if Nick hadn't been there, holding her hand, telling her how amazing she was and stopping her from making that leap.

And then it was out, on one final, agonising, screaming push where she was sure her body was being torn in two, wrenched apart to allow a giant to materialise between her splayed legs.

'She's beautiful.' Nick's voice was filled with awe, wonderment, absolute joy. Wary of touching the scrunched, pink mess that the nurse had placed on her chest, he kissed Sarah instead. 'It's a miracle.'

She looked down at the baby and waited to be filled with the glow of maternal love, hoping her mother was right and that the painful hours would be forgotten and she'd be filled instead with all-consuming love for this child she and Nick had produced. The crinkled, pink body was light and warm where it lay on her breast. She reached up and felt the incredible softness of newborn skin, used the tip of her finger to brush the dark, soft tendrils of hair, and waited for that rush of emotion that would mark her as a mother and bind her to this scrap of humanity forever. But it didn't come. She looked at it and thought of the agony she'd endured to bring the little scrap into the world. There was no hatred, no resentment towards it, but no love either. Nick reached out to uncurl the tiny fingers, oohing and aahing in awed delight. She turned to look at him, recognising the adoring love in his eyes and in the same dopey smile he used to give her, and felt the first surge of emotion – angry disbelief that it was coming so easily to him. She looked back at the child lying curled on her and willed herself to feel something, anything rather than total apathy.

Fake it till you feel it. She'd no idea where the thought had come from. Something she'd read somewhere, perhaps. It would do. 'She's so beautiful,' she said, looking up to meet Nick's eyes. 'Our gorgeous daughter.'

'We never discussed names.' He looked at her hesitantly as if afraid to upset her after her ordeal.

Damn right too. Sarah rested a head back, relieved when the nurse lifted the baby away with a few muttered words she didn't bother acknowledging. They could take the baby away for good for all she cared.

'I was thinking about Kaya.' Nick's voice was hesitant.

Kaya. Sarah opened her eyes and turned to look at him. 'That's a name?'

He leaned closer, picked up her hand and held it to his chest. 'It's Dutch. It means pure.'

'Pure?'

'I thought, as in purely gorgeous, you know?'

Kaya? Why not? Nick's maternal grandmother, who'd died when he was a baby, had been Dutch. No harm in naming their baby in her memory. It was better than the 'it' that was in Sarah's head. 'Yes, that's a great name, well done.' She saw the worried lines fade from his forehead, guessed she must have done a good job of faking enthusiasm for the name. No point in telling him he could have suggested Medusa for all she cared.

When, a mere twenty-four hours after having her body almost torn in two, she was told she could go home, Sarah looked at the nurse in horror. 'Home?'

Nick was sitting by the baby's cot, staring into it with the same stupid grin he'd been wearing since he'd first seen her. He turned to look at the nurse. 'That's good news.'

For who? Not for Sarah, who'd been assisted out to the toilet an hour before and who'd wondered if she'd ever be able to walk unaided again. 'I'm not sure I'm ready.'

'The doctor says everything is as it should be with you and little Kaya,' the nurse said, as if that was the end of the discussion. It must have been because she smiled and left the room.

Sarah managed to drag out her departure for another couple of hours but that was it. Nick had gone home for a few hours' sleep. He was supposed to have brought fresh clothes back with him, but he'd forgotten.

'I was so anxious to get back to you, it went out of my head,' he said, pressing a kiss on her forehead, then her lips. 'Back to my two beautiful girls.'

She felt a long way from beautiful. There was clean underwear in the small case she'd brought in with her, but she was stuck with wearing the clothes she'd worn when they arrived the day before. Her hair was greasy, the clothes not particularly clean. A brief glance in the small mirror in the en suite told her what she already knew. She looked an absolute mess. She hadn't slept well in days; dark circles ringed her eyes, hormonal eruptions blighted her chin and forehead.

When she went back into the room, Nick was holding the baby in his arms, staring down at it. 'She's so beautiful,' he said. 'Just like you. We're going to be so happy together. The three of us. A happy family.'

A happy family? He had absolutely no idea that she felt like death and viewed the concept with absolute horror.

As she sat into the car, and waited while he fixed the car seat into the back, the thought running through her head was not how she was going to manage, but how she was going to get out of this.

8

After two weeks, Sarah was still faking it. Every morning, she woke and hoped this would be the day where she'd feel the way a mother was supposed to feel for her baby.

She tried not to say, or think, *it*, failed miserably and caught strange looks directed her way by her mother and friends. She wasn't sure Nick noticed. He was totally besotted with the child. But if Sarah had hoped that having two people to love would dilute some of Nick's overeager attentiveness, she was wrong. He adored the child, but if Sarah picked her up, he was there, beside her, keeping a hand on her arm, or thigh, or some damn part of her anatomy.

He was being supportive. Had taken paternity leave to be there for her. And it was driving her crazy. Sex was off the cards. She'd told him bluntly it would be weeks.

'Four to six,' he'd nodded. 'I know, I googled it.' He'd reached for her, pulled her close and rubbed his erection against her until she wanted to throw up. 'I'm hoping it'll be only four weeks.'

She'd just pushed a seven-pound baby out. The thought of letting anyone put anything back inside, ever, made her want to cry. 'I'm sure.' She accompanied the vague, meaningless words with a smile. It must have looked more sincere than she'd meant because he pressed his mouth to hers, his tongue invading. Determined to get inside her somehow.

She tried to push away but he persisted. Only when his mouth moved down her neck was she able to speak. 'I need to go, Nick; Kaya is due a feed.'

'She can wait a bit.'

'No.' Sarah pushed him away. 'She has a routine.' She was surprised when his expression darkened, but then with a shrug, he let her go. 'Sorry. It's just that I miss you. Us.'

A needy adult, a needy child: suddenly it looked as if Sarah had two to care for.

***

Nick went back to work after two weeks paternity leave. 'I'll miss you,' he said, hugging Sarah so tightly, she was unable to breathe.

'I'll miss you too,' she lied. It would be a relief to be able to shut her eyes without wondering if he was staring at her. To be able to pick up Kaya without him feeling the need to form a tactile threesome. Perhaps, when it was just the two of them, mother and daughter, she'd be able to bond with Kaya.

That didn't happen, and she was weary, sad, and frustrated when Nick burst through the front door that evening, excited to hear everything Sarah and Kaya had done that day.

What they'd done? The same as every other day for the past two weeks. Kaya did fuck all, apart from eat, shit, and pee, while Sarah munched through biscuits, bars of chocolate and drank mugs of milky coffee. No wonder she'd put on pounds since the birth.

'You should have breast fed,' her mother said during one of her visits, looking at Sarah's waistline with disapproval. 'You'd get back into shape faster.'

The very thought had made Sarah quiver in distaste. 'I'll get back into shape when I'm back to work.'

It was the thought of getting back to the clinic when her compulsory two-week maternity leave ended that kept her sane. She'd thought it would be easy to get a place for the baby in some creche or nursery, but the ones she'd contacted wouldn't take a baby so young. She found one, not too far away, that would accept the baby when it was six weeks old, but they'd no places available.

'You're entitled to fifty-two weeks maternity leave,' Nick had said. 'Why don't you relax, take the lot and enjoy being with Kaya.'

'We could share it. Take a few weeks off each.' Sarah was excited about the idea. Nick was good with the baby. Far better than she was. It was a perfect solution. She could get back to work. She looked at him, excitement making her eyes shine. 'What d'you think?'

'I don't think it would work. Finance is a dog-eat-dog world. I was already getting dirty looks for taking the two weeks paternity leave.'

'You were entitled to it!'

'Yes, and I could talk to them about taking more time off but,' he shook his head in what looked like genuine regret, 'the older partners won't understand and think I've lost focus. The younger financiers will understand, but they'll also be the ones whispering that they could take over some of my accounts if I wasn't coping.'

So it was all down to her. Sarah felt anger sizzle through her as she turned away. She finally found a place for Kaya in a nursery. It wasn't the most convenient, or the cheapest, but the only one that had a vacancy – and not for another month. So Sarah had to keep on faking it. She pasted on the painfully false grin that she'd practised in the mirror until she felt it bore some semblance to the smile a real loving mother would give.

Out of desperation, she went to a mother and baby group and sat with the other mothers as they oohed and aahed over their babies. She listened to their banal, baby-centric talk, wondering if they noticed her eyes glazing over or her less than enthusiastic contributions. When they mentioned meeting up for coffee at other times, she made an excuse. She had a list of them. Excuses to her friends, to her mother, to Nick.

When her mother called around unexpectedly one afternoon to find Sarah unwashed, in her pyjamas, and the baby crying loudly, she picked

Kaya up, frowning to discover the sopping wet nappy. Mrs Hopper shot her daughter a worried glance before taking the child away to change and comfort. 'You've a touch of the baby blues,' she said when she returned with the child sucking on a bottle.

Sarah pushed a lock of greasy hair back with one hand, holding it there as if to stop her head exploding. This was all she bloody well needed: her mother butting in with her take on life. It was better to put space between them before she screamed. 'I'll make some tea.' She tucked her hair behind her ears. 'Or would you prefer coffee?' She'd prefer a drink herself. Through the pregnancy, she'd steered clear. It was the least she could do for the child she'd been increasingly reluctant to carry. So far, she'd resisted the temptation to hit the bottle and allow alcohol to steer her rocky progress through life, but she had taken to having a drink in the afternoon once Kaya had gone to sleep. And sometimes in the morning when the day stretched too long before her.

It was tempting to suck a glug of vodka now while she waited for the kettle to boil. She might have done if she hadn't wanted to keep her wits about her to deal with her mother and her pseudo-psychological assessment of Sarah.

Leaving the tea to draw, she raced up to her bedroom, pulled off the grubby T-shirt and pyjama bottoms and slipped on a cotton dress. There wasn't much she could do with her hair apart from dragging it back and pinning it into a bun. A lick of mascara and lipstick made her look almost human.

She put a bounce in her step and a smile on her lips when she carried the tea tray into the lounge where her mother was still sitting on the sofa feeding the baby. 'Do I look better?'

Her mother gave her a glance and an almost imperceptible nod. 'A little. Are you feeling okay?'

'I had a bad night and went back to bed for a rest while Kaya was sleeping. She'd just woken up when you arrived.' If you told a lie with enough confidence, most people were fooled. Even her mother, usually the most perceptive of people, was taken in by it. Sarah saw her expression relax and the worried look of concern fade.

Determined to cement the lie firmly in place, she poured the tea and spent the next hour chatting and telling her mother stories of every gurgle Kaya had made.

Making out like she was the world's best, most besotted mother.

That she loved her.

9

Love at first sight doesn't exist. Of course it doesn't. It's simply an intense physical attraction. But if you're lucky – as I was – it can develop into more.

By the time we left the café that day, we knew we wanted to see each other again. And then again.

It wasn't until our third or fourth date that I knew she was the woman I'd been waiting for all of my life. That it was true – there is someone for everyone.

I tried to keep my love under control, not to swamp her with it, perhaps scare her away with my slightly obsessive behaviour.

'I love you,' she said.

'I adore you,' I replied.

And it was always so. No matter how much she loved me, I loved her more. My every thought, every goal, was to make and keep her happy. 'I'd do anything for you,' I'd tell her. Words lovers often use, true, but I really, really meant it. I'd have done anything to keep her happy, to keep her loving me, to make sure she'd no reason to leave me.

Anything?

Absolutely anything.

10

Sarah and Jade had been friends since primary school. Their paths had diverged for a few years: different universities, cities, choices. It might have been months, and on one occasion two years, before they met, but they'd stayed in touch by phone calls, emails, text messages and when they physically met, it was as if they'd never been apart and there was lots of laughter and soul-baring.

There was a time – after Sarah's relationship with Clem had ended – when they'd become even closer, a closeness that had almost tipped over into something more. Jade hadn't hidden her feelings, as she'd never hidden that she preferred her romantic attachments to be of the female variety, and for a moment, Sarah had been tempted. Still stinging from Clem's rejection, it would have been so easy to fall into the arms of someone who would have loved her and treated her well.

Nothing happened for two reasons – first, she loved Jade too much as a friend to use her as second-best, and second, Nick had come into her life and roped her in with his obvious admiration, then his quick declaration of love, and finally, his willingness to commit.

'He's different,' she'd explained to Jade, quickly looking away from the glassy sheen of disappointment she'd glimpsed in her friend's eyes.

'It's rebound. Three weeks ago, you were madly in love with someone else!'

'Maybe.' Sarah had shrugged. 'But there's no harm in giving him a chance, is there?'

'No harm at all.' Jade had agreed but seconds later had complained of a headache and left. It was a couple of weeks before Sarah saw her again.

Messages to Jade had received short replies but she was never one to bear a grudge and when they met up again, Sarah was enveloped in a quick hug. 'You look happy,' Jade had said, pushing her away and looking into her eyes.

'I am.' Sarah had grinned like a Cheshire cat. 'I think I'm in love.'

Jade waved to the waiter. 'Let's order before you give me the grisly details.'

'Grisly!' Sarah barked a laugh. 'I'm not sure that's the appropriate word.' When no riposte came from her normally smart-mouthed friend, Sarah buried herself in the menu. She hadn't meant to hurt Jade or damage their friendship.

Sarah had managed to steer their relationship back onto the familiar path it had been on for years, and Jade was still her best friend, the one she bared her soul to.

* * *

Sarah left Kaya with her mother and arranged to meet Jade in one of their favourite pubs. She was early and managed to snag a booth. Pulling off her jacket, she tossed it onto the seat opposite before pulling her mobile from the bottom of her bag and sending Jade a message.

> Here early. Sitting at the back.

Then leaving her jacket to conspicuously lay claim to the booth, she crossed to the bar. 'A bottle of Chardonnay and two glasses, one with ice, please.'

She drummed her fingers on the bar while she waited. A drink would relax her. Something needed to. 'Thanks,' she said. Tapping her credit card against the reader to pay, she grabbed the bottle and glasses and returned to the booth. A twist of the cap, then the glorious glug glug as she filled her glass almost to the brim.

It was half empty before she spotted Jade coming through the door. Sarah lifted her arm and waved even as her friend was walking in her direction. She hadn't realised how much she needed her till that moment. 'It's so good to see you,' she said, as Jade pushed Sarah's jacket out of the way and slid into the seat opposite.

Jade raised one eyebrow, then nodded towards the almost empty glass. 'How many of those have you had?'

'Just the one.' Sarah reached for the bottle and poured wine over what was left of the ice in Jade's glass before refilling hers. 'Believe me, I need this.'

'Trouble in paradise?' Jade lifted her glass and swirled the ice cubes before taking a sip. 'Nice wine.' She continued to swirl her drink as she looked across the table. 'Go on then, what's got you looking so stressed?'

Sarah was less stressed sitting there, chatting with her friend, drinking wine. Like it used to be. She sighed. 'I'm going crazy stuck at home with the baby.'

'You should have listened to me.' Jade swigged her wine and put the glass down with a snap that sent the ice cubes rattling. 'If you had, you wouldn't be sitting there looking like death.'

Sarah shut her eyes. What her friend had suggested had never been an option for her. Jade had been the first she'd told about the pregnancy, even before Nick. Sarah had held the pregnancy test in one hand, her mobile in the other. 'I'm pregnant.'

'So you went ahead with it?'

'I didn't think I'd get pregnant so quickly.' She'd hoped she wouldn't get pregnant at all. How pathetically stupid she'd been.

'You stopped taking the pill, Sarah; what did you think was going to happen? Honestly, for a doctor, you can be pretty thick.'

It wasn't the time to explain that she'd made a mistake. Two mistakes. She should never have married Nick, never have agreed to have a baby. She blamed the double vodkas she'd knocked back that night for weakening her defences. But she couldn't blame them for tossing the pill into the bin. That had been simple, stone-cold stupidity. 'What am I going to do, Jade?'

'Get rid of it.'

Jade's blunt, almost callous words had made Sarah blink. She'd tossed the pregnancy test into the bin and sat on the toilet seat. 'I can't do that.'

'Why not?'

Because she'd taken an oath to do no harm. Didn't that apply to this baby growing inside her? 'I just can't,' she'd said. As arguments went, it was up there with *I don't want to*, but with the shock of discovery it was all she could come up with.

And now, here she was again asking for advice, hoping this time it was some she'd be able to take. 'Kaya is beautiful, and she's a good baby. It's me. My fault. I can't feel anything for her and I'm beginning to hate her for tying me to the house, to this life I'd never wanted.'

'You sure you're not suffering from post-natal depression or something?'

Baby blues, post-natal depression. Everyone was offering their diagnosis of what was wrong with her. Sarah wished it were that simple, that it was something she could get help with, that this feeling would ease and she'd wake up one day and realise she was being silly, that of course she loved her baby. It wasn't that simple, though.

'I don't want her,' she said quietly, her fingers twiddling with the stem of her glass, afraid to look up and see Jade's expression, the shock she was sure to see there. A hand wrapped around hers, Jade's strong fingers pressing gently forcing her to look up. All she could see was sympathy, no judgement, and she wondered again what she'd done to have such a good friend.

'Does Nick know how you feel?'

Sarah shook her head. 'He adores Kaya, assumes I feel the same.' She smiled sadly. 'I'm doing a good job of pretending.'

'I don't know what to say.' Jade took her hand away, picked up her glass and sat back. 'What are you going to do?'

A group of young women burst through the door, short dresses, wide smiles, loud voices. Their joy was infectious, causing other customers to glance their direction and smile. 'Do you remember when we were that young? We thought life would always be good, fun, exciting. Where did that faith in our lives go?'

Jade was never one for introspection. 'We grew up.'

Sarah stared at the young women for a little longer before dragging her eyes away. Jade was waiting for an answer, but she wasn't sure she had one. No, she was sure she *didn't* have one. She sighed. 'What am I going to do? I have no idea. Keep going. Maybe buy myself one of those irritating signs that say *Keep on keeping on*. It fits perfectly, doesn't it?' She could see her friend wasn't impressed with her attempt at humour. 'I don't know, Jade. If you're worried about Kaya, don't be. I've no intention of harming her. She gets the best of everything and as I said, Nick adores her. I simply don't love her the way a mother should.'

'I wish I could help.'

'You listened to me. You've no idea how much it means that I can speak honestly about it to someone.' She waved a hand around as if to encompass the rest of the world. 'With everyone else, everywhere I go, it's one big pretence.'

Jade reached for her hand again and squeezed it. 'I hate to see you looking so unhappy. If there was anything I could do, I promise you I'd do it.'

Sarah turned her hand and gripped her friend's. 'I know you would. You've no idea how much that means to me.' She just wished there was something Jade could do, but there wasn't.

If she wanted to sort out the mess that was her life, Sarah had to take care of it herself.

11

It had been Sarah's idea to go away for a weekend. Nick had raised an eyebrow when she'd mentioned Lynton. 'Couldn't we go somewhere a bit closer?'

Of course they could, but she wanted to go to Lynton. 'I'd really love to take Kaya to places my parents took me when I was a child,' she'd said, dropping her voice to the soft, wheedling tone she knew he couldn't resist.

'It'll be a long drive. Four hours at least, and that's if we don't get stuck in traffic.'

'I thought maybe you could take a half day, then we could get on the road before the worst of the Friday-afternoon traffic. I managed to get us a sea view room in a nice hotel. We could go for long walks, get lots of fresh air. We wouldn't need to leave till late Sunday so we'd have two days there to enjoy. And the weather,' she smiled as she added the final persuader, 'it's set to be warm and sunny for the weekend and there's nowhere more beautiful than Devon in the sunshine.'

He gave in as she knew he would. He constantly said he'd do anything for her; she shouldn't feel guilty for taking him at his word.

And as she also knew he would, he took a half day off on the Friday and they arrived at the hotel just after six. Kaya slept most of the journey, waking as Nick lifted her from the car. He looked after her as Sarah checked in at reception. It was Nick who fed and changed her as Sarah put away the few clothes they'd brought and unpacked the ridiculous amount of stuff needed for the baby.

Sarah had booked dinner in a restaurant only ten minutes' walk from the hotel. Nick carried Kaya, once again sleeping peacefully in the infant car seat that was proving to be worth the money they'd paid for it. In the restaurant, he fixed it to a chair and gently touched her cheek.

'Don't wake her, for goodness' sake!' Sarah hissed. Opening the menu, she scanned it quickly then raised a hand to get the attention of a waiter hovering nearby. 'We'll have a bottle of the Sancerre, please.' When he didn't move, she frowned. 'If you could get that while we're deciding on the food, that would be good.'

Determined to make it a weekend to remember, she put herself out to be chatty and cheerful, not the petulant, unhappy woman she'd become in the last year. She had the next day planned. They'd walk down to Lynmouth, then along the Lyn River to Watersmeet to have a cream tea. Back to Lynmouth, then maybe have an ice cream or a drink at one of the pubs before catching the cliff railway back up to Lynton. It was going to be a good day; she'd make sure of it.

It was a perfect, blue-sky day when they set out the following morning. Almost everywhere in that part of Devon was stunningly beautiful, but the walk down the zigzag, steep pathway to Lynton, then on to Watersmeet following the course of the Lyn River, was particularly nice with dappled shade above and gurgling water below. The walk to Watersmeet had been a firm favourite with her parents and she'd visited many times as a child. She wasn't as fit as she'd been then, and she found herself getting breathless when the twisting path climbed steeply upward. Luckily, Nick was carrying Kaya in a sling across his chest. When Sarah stopped to catch her breath, he stopped too, waiting patiently while she sucked in air.

It was a little over two miles to the National Trust café at Watersmeet. It was, as always, busy with people who'd arrived from various directions. A mixed bag: serious walkers with backpacks and wide-brimmed hats; casual walkers trailing children and dogs; couples, singles, and family units.

The café had, in its heyday, been a lodge of some sort. Now, along with serving food, it housed a small shop selling maps and expensive souvenirs. The only seating was in the large garden to the front: round, wooden tables encircled by attached benches requiring a certain amount of dexterity to swing one leg at a time over to sit. Closer to the café, on a rough stone veranda, there were smaller, wooden tables and 'proper' chairs. All looked to be occupied and Sarah looked around in frustration.

'There.' Nick indicated a group of people who were in the first stages of departure. The woman gathering various items of clothing, the man peering at a map, the two children jostling one another and squealing.

Some people might have been embarrassed to have stood too close, afraid to appear intimidating. Sarah had no such qualms and hovered a mere two feet away, afraid someone else would swoop in and pinch the seat if she didn't stand close enough.

But when the seated woman looked up with a frown, it was Nick who shrugged. 'I'd take your grave as quickly,' he said with a laugh. Then he kissed Kaya's head. 'She's surprisingly heavy for one so little.'

What woman could resist such a sight? She got to her feet and moved closer to get a better look. 'She's gorgeous. How old is she?' A finger moved to tentatively touch the skin of the baby's cheek. 'You forget how deliciously soft they are.'

'She's a little over three weeks,' Nick said.

'Gorgeous,' the stranger said again, then returned to her own flock. She didn't sit again, gathering her children and husband, herding them away with a smile and nod towards Nick.

'That was well spotted,' Sarah said, immediately moving in to take possession. She sat, facing outwards, and watched Nick undo the sling to take Kaya out, moving the child into the crook of his arm.

'It pays to keep your eyes open.' He rocked the baby gently. 'Do you want to take her and I'll go and get us something to eat?'

Sarah shook her head. 'No, you sit, I'll go.' She indicated the café with a jerk of her chin. 'There's a queue. It doesn't look to be moving fast and you know how you hate waiting in line.' It was always a source of friction between them. They'd be somewhere on holiday, she'd want to visit an attraction, he'd see the snaking queue and shake his head. Sometimes, she'd take a stand and insist; usually, she didn't bother because any pleasure in whatever it was would be spoilt by the resentful, sullen-faced man who'd stand beside her with his arms crossed and huffing a long, loud sigh every couple of minutes.

Queuing never bothered her. She'd stand patiently, lost in her thoughts, or make conversation with the people around her. If they were abroad, she'd read her guidebook, fascinated to learn the history behind whatever she was going to see. It fascinated her that Nick had no interest. On dark days, she admitted that they'd little in common. The same dark days that seemed to be consuming her recently.

'D'you want a sandwich or a cream tea?' She got to her feet, waiting as he lifted one and then the other leg over the top of the bench, tucking his legs under the table and balancing Kaya on the edge of it. 'There you go, baby girl,' he said to her before turning to Sarah with a smile. 'A cream tea sounds perfect.'

'Right.' She left him to entertain the baby and headed across to join the slow-moving queue. She looked back to where Nick sat. He was pulling funny faces at the baby. She'd told him it was too soon to get any response from her but he kept going. 'One of these days, she's going to smile at me.'

'It'll be wind if she does.'

Sarah didn't try to communicate with the baby. She fed her, changed her, kept her clean. She never held her close or pressed her lips against the soft pink cheeks. It was Nick who did that, he who rushed to pick her up if she cried.

Sarah looked at Nick, and at the baby in his arms, and hated both of them.

12

We'd been living together for a year. The house I'd rattled around in for a long time suddenly felt like a home. I'd finally stopped expecting the bubble to burst and dump me back into an existence I hadn't realised was lonely and miserable until she'd opened my eyes.

Happiness was a tangible thing that wrapped itself around me whenever I was near her. Only someone who loved completely, absolutely, would understand what I mean.

I was so in tune with her that I knew without her saying if something was making her unhappy. Knowing, however, didn't necessarily tell me why her eyes had dimmed, and the corners of her wide mouth drooped rather than curved upward.

It was only when she opened the kitchen cupboard and reached for the analgesia she kept specifically for period pains that I knew the cause. A stab of pain pierced my happiness. I waited till she'd dry-swallowed two pills, then filled a glass with water and gulped half down, before I crossed the room and took her into my arms. 'Next time,' I said.

She pulled away and looked at me, her expression unusually serious. 'We said that last month and the month before. I think it's time we find out if there's a problem.'

There was, of course, an insurmountable one that made Meg weep and cling to me. Once all the results of all the horrendously intimate and invasive tests came back, the doctor explained in great detail. She sat us down in her office and went to great lengths to explain why Meg couldn't get pregnant, why she couldn't ever carry a child. Some unusual, possibly congenital defect in her uterus. She could suffer the mess and the pain of monthly periods but nature was having a cruel laugh at her expense – she could have the blood and the agonising cramps, but not the baby.

Of course, we refused to accept it – cue more tests, all to no avail. Some things weren't fixable and poor Meg's uterus was one of those things.

She sank into depths of self-blame; telling me I should leave, find another woman. 'A working one,' she said.

'I love you. I don't care about children; you're all I want.' I wasn't lying; I'd never thought about having children. This was her need, not mine.

'I wanted to be a mother,' she sobbed. 'I've always wanted a child.'

I held her as she cried, felt her tremble as the sobs wracked her body, saw her fade over the next few weeks as the reality of her childless state continued to haunt her, saw the light in her eyes dim, her beautiful mouth becoming fixed in a tight line of despair, and I knew I had to do something.

13

'Here you go,' Sarah said, placing the laden tray on the table. While she'd been gone, Nick had raised the parasol, providing welcome shade from the midday sun. 'Luckily you didn't go up; the queue was crazy slow.' She sat, swung her feet over the bench and started to unload the tray. 'Shall I add jam and cream to your scone?'

'Yes, please.' Nick was holding Kaya with one arm, rocking her gently.

She was awake but she was quiet, staring ahead as if she was taking in her surroundings. Or was she staring at Sarah, wondering why her mother was so distant, so unloving. Sarah pressed clotted cream into the scone with such force, it split in two. She stopped, took a breath, a moment to listen to the birdsong, the background gurgle of the river, the pleasant chatter from others making the most of the lovely day.

'You okay?'

She smoothed cream onto the other half of the scone, added jam and slid the plate towards him. 'I was just having the usual mental debate whether to put the cream or jam on first.'

'Either works for me.' He picked up the laden scone and bit into it.

Sarah licked jam from her fingers before pouring the tea and adding milk to both cups. Picking up one of the broken pieces of scone, she popped it into her mouth. 'They're good. Maybe I should have got two each.'

Nick finished his last mouthful. 'No, that'd have spoilt it.' He lifted his cup and drank. 'This was a good idea. It's a long way, but it's worth it.'

Sarah finished her scone, filled up their cups with the end of the tea, then sat back with hers cradled between her hands. The beautiful setting was in contrast to the dark thoughts racing through her head. Not even the sight of Nick cooing at Kaya could lighten them. How could it? She hated the ease at which he'd bonded with their daughter. Hated how easily, how enthusiastically he loved – her, their child, their life.

And Sarah... hadn't she once loved the same way? Why was it so difficult to remember that time? It had existed. She was sure of it. Love, laughter, happy days. She had had them. They were just hidden behind a fug of dreary, dismal thoughts.

It was her: Kaya. If she hadn't had her, she could have left Nick. Started again with someone else. Somewhere else. Maybe follow her childhood dream and be a country GP somewhere. In Scotland maybe, or Wales. It was impossible to leave Nick now. If she did, her friends, her family, everyone would look at her askance. What mother walks out on her child? She'd be criticised, despised. She'd lose her friends, her self-respect.

She couldn't leave without her; she couldn't take her with her. How could she when she'd no feelings for the child? She might not love her, but Kaya deserved better than that. She deserved better than this.

Sarah's sigh was lost in the sounds of happiness drifting from other tables and the gurgle of the Lyn as it rushed over boulders on the riverbed. Nick had finished his tea and had moved Kaya from the crook of his arm to rest on the edge of the table, cooing stupidly at her. He blended in well with the family scenes that surrounded them. It was Sarah who stood out. She swung her legs over the bench, startling him.

'We're going?'

'No, I just thought I'd walk to the bridge and take a couple of photos.' She brushed a finger over Kaya's cheek. 'You stay here with her; I'll be back in a few minutes.'

Nick didn't argue. When she glanced back, seconds later, she saw he was once again engrossed in their daughter. Sarah waited till a straggling group of adults crossed the bridge, then she moved to the centre of it and leaned over the rail. Below, the river bubbled and foamed over rocks. There had been a lot of rain in the previous couple of weeks and the water was deep, fast flowing. Hypnotic. Would this be an easier choice? Leaning forward, she rested her elbows on the rail, fixed her eyes on the swirling, gushing water below.

She turned to look at the path that followed the course of the river on the far side. She could take it, keep going, never come back. Vanish and leave Nick and Kaya with a mystery. The police would search for her, so would members of the public. But there were miles of countryside to get lost in. If she really wanted to. It worked in books and movies; it even happened in real life.

A group of women crossed the bridge, stopping beside her to take photographs.

One of the women turned to Sarah with a smile. 'Would you mind taking one of us?'

'Sure.' She took the mobile, waited till the women squashed together and smiled before taking a couple of shots. 'Here you go. Enjoy your day.'

'How could you not enjoy being in such an amazing place,' the woman said, taking her mobile back with a nod of thanks.

How could you not indeed. Sarah leaned on the bridge and looked down at the river. No, she couldn't take her own life because, desperate as she was, she hadn't yet sunk to that awful depth of despair. Nor could she simply vanish. How could she justify putting Nick and her parents through that? Anyway, she had a plan, didn't she?

More voices dragged her back to the present. Groups of people approaching from both directions this time. It was time for her to move on. With a final look at the river, she headed back to join Nick and Kaya.

It would be okay. She'd do what she'd planned. Make this a happy weekend, one to remember when bad days returned.

As they would.

14

The walk down the zigzag path from Lynton to Lynmouth was fun, the walk back, murder. Instead, they took the easy way and hopped on the funicular cliff railway that trundled up and down between the two towns.

'Where are we eating tonight?' Nick asked when they'd reached the top and were walking the short distance along the road to their hotel.

'The Post Office. It's a pub.'

'A pub?'

His surprise was understandable. She'd never been an advocate of pub grub despite the improvement in quality over the years. 'It was a favourite of my parents; we used to go there a lot when we came here. I'd like to go back to it for old times' sake. You don't mind, do you?'

'No.' The word was dragged out. 'You sure there'll be space for the baby?'

'I'm sure there will,' she said dismissively. Nothing was going to spoil her plans for that weekend.

* * *

'Ready to go?' Sarah cradled the sleeping Kaya in her arm. 'She's had her bottle and I've changed her nappy.' She nodded to the infant carrier. 'We can take her in that and hopefully she'll stay asleep until we've eaten.'

Nick picked up the carrier, holding it by the handle as Sarah slipped the baby gently inside. 'There,' she said standing back. 'She should sleep for a few hours.'

Nick tucked a light blanket over the baby. 'Right, let's go, that walk has given me an appetite.'

The Post Office pub was in the centre of Lynton, only a short distance from the hotel. They walked slowly, the carrier swinging from Nick's hand, his other clasped around Sarah's. 'It was a good idea to get away, even for a couple of days.'

Sarah felt his fingers tighten around hers. He was a good man. It should be easy to love him. She wasn't sure why she didn't. It would have been nice to have blamed the arrival of Kaya, but that would have been unfair. The change had occurred before his rogue sperm had encountered her stupidly welcoming egg. Around the time when she'd begun to find his love and commitment smothering rather than adorable.

A couple of smokers hanging around the entrance to the pub moved out of their way as Sarah and Nick reached the door.

'Hi,' she said, greeting them because this was Devon; it was what you did.

Their muttered responses floated on a mouthful of exhaled cigarette smoke but Sarah and Nick had already pushed through into the pub. It was a noisy, bustling space. Nick frowned, lifted the infant carrier, and held it protectively in front of his body. 'Not sure this was a good idea, Sarah; it's pretty jammed.'

'Pessimist,' she said, thumping his arm lightly. 'Leave it to me; I'll find us somewhere to sit.'

The bar took up the far corner of the space. Round tables and chairs filled the centre of the room; square tables around the edges had chairs to one side, banquette seating to the other. Every seat looked to be taken. Those who hadn't been lucky stood in groups, drinks in hand. Sarah stretched to peer over their heads to the far corners of the pub, then turned and put her mouth close to Nick's ear. 'I see a space, follow me.'

She didn't wait for his answer, leading the way through the crowd, leaving Nick to follow behind her, the baby carrier bumping against people forcing him to continuously mutter 'sorry'. Sarah stopped at a table where two women were sitting opposite one another. The woman seated on the banquette was resting one elbow on a rucksack that took up the space beside her. The chair beside the other woman was empty apart from a denim jacket draped over the back. 'Hi,' Sarah said, resting her hand on the chair. 'Is this one free?'

'Sure.' A slim hand with short, scarlet nails reached over and grabbed the jacket. 'There you go.'

'Thanks.' Sarah pointed to the banquette. 'Would you mind awfully if I squeezed in beside you, then Nick can sit here with the baby?' She flashed her best, most winning smile at the older woman sitting opposite. It wasn't returned. Instead, sharp, dark eyes glanced over her shoulder to where Nick was standing.

'Doesn't look as if we have much choice in the matter really, does it?' The rucksack was hauled up and dropped on the floor to the other side.

'Thanks so much.' Sarah squeezed through the gap between the tables and sat. 'We didn't expect it to be so busy.'

'It always is this time of year.' The woman opposite waved her red-tipped hand as she spoke. Younger than her friend, her face was pleasant rather than pretty, her eyes large, almost Bambi-like, her hair tied back in a ponytail. As if to make up for her friend's less than graceful remark, she turned to give Nick a welcoming smile and shuffled her chair further away to give him more space.

The space would have been fine for him, but not for him and the infant carrier. He sat with it balanced awkwardly on his lap, blocking Sarah's exit. They had seats at a table but no way to get to the bar to order either food or drinks. There were only a few inches between her and the man seated at the next table, but on the other side of the woman, there were several inches free. She was about to risk another request when she was saved by another swirl of those red-tipped nails.

'Budge over, Andrea, and give them space for their baby.'

The request was greeted by a loud, long-suffering sigh.

'It's fine,' Nick said. 'I think we'd be better off going elsewhere, actually.'

'No, no!' This time the red-tipped fingers fluttered to land on his arm. 'Please, you won't get a seat in any restaurant without a booking on a Saturday night; you're better off staying here. Andrea can move over a bit, then there's loads of space for your baby.' She leaned forward to peer into the carrier as she spoke. 'A little girl! She's lush!' Her eyes were sparkling when she looked up. 'You should see her, Andrea; she's like a little doll. Go on, move over, then they can prop the carrier on the seat. It'll be safer, and you can have a look for yourself.'

With obvious reluctance, Andrea shuffled over.

'That's brilliant, thank you.' Sarah waved at Nick to hand over the carrier and set it beside her. She saw the woman's sideways glance as she looked at the baby and she'd swear she saw a softening of the rather grim expression. Babies and dogs, they always worked.

She waved to catch Nick's attention. 'I'll have a large Chardonnay, please, and if you could grab some menus while you're up there, that'd be perfect.'

The bar was busy and there only appeared to be two staff serving. Sarah guessed she'd be waiting a while for her wine, and even longer for her food. It might have been better to have ordered a bottle of wine. She wasn't driving, after all. If Nick would only take his mobile with him, she could send him a text but he never saw the point in bringing it when he didn't need to. She glanced to where Kaya was still sleeping peacefully. It would only take seconds to dash across and tell him. Nothing could go wrong in seconds.

Her dilemma must have been written on her face because the woman opposite leaned towards her. 'You okay? My name's Meg, by the way. Can I help?'

Sarah smiled. 'Thanks, Meg. Actually, I've changed my mind about what I ordered and was wondering if I could dash across to tell Nick.' She put her hand on the handle of the carrier. 'It's really handy but awkward in crowded spaces.'

'No problemo, tell me what you want and I'll go tell him for you.'

'Oh that would be kind. Thank you. It's so busy that I thought I should order a bottle of wine rather than a glass, that's all.'

'A bottle, not a glass. Easy message.' She grinned. 'And a sensible one too. The two behind the bar are nice but slow.' She pushed her chair back noisily and got to her feet. 'Back in two ticks.'

Sarah watched her as she dodged around other customers to get to the bar where she caught Nick's attention with a hand on his arm, laughing when he turned to her, pointing back to where Sarah sat, laughing again, before nodding and returning to the table.

'There you go, all done,' she said, taking her seat again.

'That was very kind of you, thank you.'

'No problem. You just here for the weekend?'

'Yes, we came down yesterday evening, heading back to London tomorrow.'

'A long way for a short break.' It was Andrea who spoke, drawing Sarah's eyes.

'We like this part of the world. We did a lot of walking today and we'll do some more tomorrow before we leave.' She shrugged. 'I used to come here a lot when I was younger; I wanted to take Kaya here.'

Andrea looked into the carrier and raised an eyebrow. 'I'm not sure she knows where she is.'

There didn't seem to be any point in arguing, especially since Sarah agreed. She gave a tight smile, then concentrated on watching Nick, hoping he wouldn't be long.

'I think babies absorb far more than we think,' Meg said. 'They say they can hear and even learn while they're still in the womb so why wouldn't they be able to when they're with us? Absorbing experiences, seeing colours, shapes, things like that.'

'Exactly,' Sarah said although she wasn't sure she agreed. Meg was obviously the earth-mother type; she probably had a clatter of children at home. Sarah didn't want to get into a conversation swapping experiences. She hoped her one-word answer would bring the baby talk to a halt.

It might have done if Kaya hadn't decided to join in.

15

When Kaya began to grizzle, Sarah adjusted the angle of the carrier so the baby could see her.

'She okay?' Nick asked, arriving back with a bottle of wine in one hand, two wine glasses in the other and a menu tucked under his arm.

'She's fine, don't fuss.' Sarah took the bottle of wine from him, twisted the cap and poured into the glasses. 'You didn't get a beer?'

'No, I'll be fine with wine.' He handed her the menu. 'I've already had a look and I'm having the fish and chips. Decide what you want and I'll go and order. They aren't the speediest behind the bar.'

The menu, a single, A4-sized card sticky from use, listed the usual high-fat pub grub that made Sarah's coronary arteries spasm. The only nod to those who were calorie and health conscious was a chicken Caesar salad. 'I'll have that,' she said pointing it out to Nick. 'With the dressing on the side, please.'

He gulped a mouthful of wine before getting to his feet again and heading back to the bar.

Relieved that the two women were engrossed in a quiet conversation, and Kaya seemed content to sit staring at nothing in particular, Sarah sat back with her wine and let her thoughts drift. She was so lost in them when Nick returned, he clicked his fingers to get her attention. 'Sorry,' she said with a faint smile. 'I'd zoned out.'

'Obviously.' He made a point of leaning over to check on Kaya, brushing a finger over one of her hands. 'She's taking it all in, isn't she?'

Sarah reached for the wine bottle, topped up Nick's and refilled her empty one. 'Did they say how long the food would be?' She put the half empty bottle down and wished she'd asked him to get a second.

'A few minutes.'

It was almost ten before a hassled-looking waiter crossed to their table with two brimming plates. Sarah was annoyed to see they'd poured the dressing over her salad and shot Nick an irritated glance. Had he forgotten to ask? She lifted two of the more heavily dressed leaves out of the way, but before she could start to eat, a plaintive mewl came from the carrier. Kaya's face was creased, her lower lip trembling in that way she had before crying. And then there it was, a high-pitched cry, loud and sharp enough to pierce the surrounding hubbub, and have faces turn in surprise.

'Fuck's sake!' Sarah put her cutlery down with a snap.

'Give her to me,' Nick said, pushing his plate away.

Sarah unstrapped the baby and picked her up.

'I'll take her outside,' Nick said, reaching for her. 'If I walk around for a bit, she'll fall back to sleep.'

Sarah shook her head. Cold fish and chips were no fun. 'My Caesar salad will be just as good in ten minutes; I'll take her. You stay and eat your dinner while it's hot.'

'Why don't I take her out?'

Nick and Sarah both turned in surprise to look at the young woman.

'Honestly, I'd love to,' Meg said. 'We've finished our meal. I could walk up and down with her if you think that'd help.' She pointed to the fish and chips. 'I can vouch for that; it's what I had. It'd be a shame to spoil it by letting it go cold.'

Sarah rocked the screaming baby a little frantically. It wasn't making the slightest difference to the level of sound coming from her. 'We couldn't possibly ask you to take her.'

'You didn't ask; I volunteered,' Meg said reasonably.

Sarah could see reluctance on Nick's face; he was going to say no. 'That's terribly kind of you,' she hurried to say. She stood and passed Kaya into the waiting hands.

Sarah was relieved to see Nick's worried expression easing a little when he saw Meg holding Kaya with confidence that said she'd handled babies before. 'It's not long since she's been fed and changed. It might simply be the noise in here that's unsettling her.'

'Right.' Meg stood with Kaya held tightly against her shoulder. 'I'll take my jacket. It can get chilly this time of night.' She smiled at Andrea. 'I'll be back in a few minutes and we can head home then. Don't look so pissed.'

The older woman merely shrugged.

'It's very good of her,' Nick said as Kaya's cry receded and the usual level of hubbub was restored.

'She's kindly given us a bit of peace to eat our meals so we should get on with it.' Sarah was more than content to have someone else take care of their daughter while they ate, but she could tell from Nick's frequent glances towards the exit that he wasn't so happy. When he'd eaten half his meal and Meg hadn't returned, his concern became more pronounced. 'I thought she'd be back by now.'

'She's probably sitting on a bench outside, singing to the baby,' Andrea said. 'She's good with kids.'

He looked towards the door again. 'Maybe I should go and check that she's okay.'

Andrea sighed. 'If it's bothering you so much, I'll go and get her.' Without waiting for his reply, she got to her feet. She lifted her rucksack from the floor and put it on her vacated seat. 'If you'd keep an eye on this for me, we'll be back in a jiffy.'

'Honestly, you could look a little grateful,' Sarah said, scraping dressing off a piece of chicken with the edge of her knife. 'At least you were able to have your dinner.'

'I am grateful.' He finished the fish. 'This was really good.' He picked up a chip with his finger and dipped it into the remainder of the tomato ketchup he'd squirted onto his plate. 'Good chips too.'

'Have some more wine.' Sarah filled his glass, then topped up her own. 'We should have got two bottles.'

Nick took a sip, then put the glass down and looked anxiously towards the door. 'They're taking their time coming back, aren't they?'

'Maybe Meg walked further than she'd thought. They'll be back any moment.'

But they weren't.

16

'I'm going to go and look for them,' Nick said, getting to his feet and hurrying across the pub to the exit. He was back within seconds. 'There's no sign of them.' He sounded scared.

'Stop being so dramatic, for goodness' sake. It's only been a few minutes since Andrea left. This part of Lynton is a maze; she's probably wandering around looking for Meg.'

'And Kaya, or have you forgotten she has our daughter with her?'

'Stop being an asshole.' Sarah picked up her glass, drained it and reached for the bottle. 'D'you want some more?' When he shook his head, she emptied the bottle into her own glass. 'Good, more for me.'

'Aren't you even a little concerned?' He hissed the words at her, then pulled the chair out and sat, twisting around to keep the exit in view.

Her eyebrows rose into her hairline. 'Why would I be? What, you think they've kidnapped Kaya?' She jerked her head towards the huge rucksack. 'Swapped her for that, maybe?'

Ignoring her, Nick continued to stare at the doorway.

'They'll be back any minute,' Sarah said. 'Why don't you get yourself a pint?' When he didn't reply, she shrugged and lifted her glass. 'Suit yourself.' She sipped her wine and tried to relax. Everything was going to be fine. He was being ridiculously suspicious.

When several minutes passed with no sign of the two women, Nick turned back to Sarah. 'Something's wrong. They should've been back by now.'

She saw the lines of stress scrunching up his face. He looked like Kaya did before she started her godawful screaming. Feeling the first twinges of sympathy for him, she put her almost-empty glass down. 'Why don't you go out, have a walk around? I bet they're sitting somewhere nattering and haven't noticed time passing.'

Nick grasped at that, his expression lightening a little. 'Yes, like when you and your friend Jade get together.'

'Hours can vanish,' she agreed.

'Right, I'll go and have a look around.'

It was almost ten minutes before he came back, his mouth downturned, a deep frown between his eyes. 'There is no sign of them.' He didn't sit; instead, he moved to the banquette, lifted the rucksack onto the table and reached for the buckle to open it.

'What are you doing?' She tried to pull the bag away. 'Andrea doesn't look like the kind of woman who'd appreciate you going through her stuff!'

He pushed her hands away. 'They have Kaya!' He struggled to undo the buckles, then pulled the rucksack open. His eyes widened in horrified surprise. 'Shit, Sarah, look!' He dragged the edges down to show her the contents. 'It's filled with crumpled newspaper.' He dug his hands in, pulled the crushed balls of paper out and tossed them about willy nilly, drawing surprised looks from those sitting nearby. When he'd emptied the main compartment, Nick searched the smaller pockets to the front. 'They're empty.' He looked at Sarah, his mouth hanging open, the colour draining from his face to leave it a sickly grey. As he staggered under the weight of reality and sank onto the banquette, he cried out, 'They've taken her! They've taken Kaya!' His voice rose as he spoke, drawing more attention, whispers circling them.

Sarah swallowed the hard lump that had formed in her throat. Usually, it was Nick who remained calm while she was the one to panic, but he was frozen, his hands gripping the straps of the rucksack as if they were stopping him from drowning. She looked towards the exit:

still no sign of Andrea, Meg, or their daughter. How long had it been? Fifteen minutes? Maybe twenty since Meg had taken Kaya?

There was only one thing to do. Taking out her mobile, she pressed 999. 'Police,' she said, when asked which service she required and then, as calmly as she could, when every part of her wanted to scream out the words, she said, 'Someone has taken our baby.'

17

It didn't take long for the news of Kaya's disappearance to be passed from mouth to mouth. Within minutes, the pub was buzzing. The two men behind the bar may have been slow to serve, but as soon as they heard the rumours, one came over to Sarah and Nick while the other moved to the only exit. He stood there with his arms crossed, waiting for the nod from his partner. When it came, when the rumour was confirmed, he quickly locked and bolted the door.

The first barman, introducing himself to Sarah and Nick as Roger, stood on the banquette beside Nick and waved his hands until a hushed silence fell over the room.

'Someone has taken this young couple's baby. The police are on their way and until they get here, I'm afraid everyone is going to have to stay where they are, okay?' He didn't seem to expect an answer. 'The bar and the kitchen are still open so we'll keep serving for the moment.'

He jumped down and faced the couple. 'I don't know what to say; this isn't something I've dealt with before.' He nodded towards where his colleague still stood at the door. 'All I know about crime I've learnt from watching TV programmes. The nearest Devon and Cornwall police station is in Ilfracombe about seventeen miles away. With the roads the way they are, I can't see them getting here for at least twenty minutes. You probably don't want another drink, but can I get you some tea or coffee?'

Sarah pressed her lips tightly together to stop them trembling. *Kaya was gone.* She would have liked a drink. Something stronger than wine. Maybe a neat vodka, or a whisky. She glanced at Nick. He seemed to have sunk into himself, his face ashen, tears streaming from his eyes. He would probably benefit from a large brandy. But they were going to have a tough few hours ahead; wafting alcohol fumes over the police when they did arrive wouldn't be the best. 'Coffee would be good, thank you.'

Before he left, Roger had a quiet word with the people in the tables immediately surrounding them. With a lot of noisy shuffling, and curious glances, they moved tables and chairs so that within minutes, there was a moat around the table where Nick and Sarah sat.

Roger returned with the promised coffee. A pot of it that he left in the middle of the table surrounded by cups, a jug of milk, a bowl containing sachets of white and brown sugar and packets of sweetener. All so normal, apart from the eyes that were staring at them. Sarah could feel them. She didn't have to see them to know they'd be filled with pity, shock, disbelief. And she knew that every one of them who had a young child was thinking, *thank God that's not me.*

For a few minutes after Roger addressed the room, there was an uneasy silence broken only by the odd hushed whisper. Eventually, these became murmurs which increased in volume until the room was once more filled with sound.

Nick sat silently, his face a picture of shocked disbelief. Sarah leaned closer to grab one of his hands. 'It'll be okay,' she said. 'There'll be a reasonable explanation. Maybe Meg got lost or something.' The straws she was clutching were fragile and broke without much effort. Even if Meg had got lost, Andrea would have returned by now. Sarah released the hand she was holding and reached for the coffee pot.

Pouring a cup for Nick, she added milk and sugar and pushed it towards him. 'Drink it. You might need the caffeine.'

She certainly did and downed one cup in a few mouthfuls before filling it again and sipping slowly this time, her eyes fixed on the door, waiting for it to open. For an apologetic Andrea and Meg to push through with Kaya clasped safely in their arms. Or the police. The sense of waiting was unnerving, unsettling. She shuffled in her seat, sipped more coffee, glanced towards Nick, then quickly away. She couldn't handle the look of sheer misery on his face without breaking down herself. One of them had to hold on and it looked as if that was going to be her. It was okay. She could do it. As a GP, she'd learned to be stoic in the face of misery. 'Drink your coffee,' she said. 'The sugar will give you some energy.' She refrained from adding that he might need it to get through the hours ahead.

Roger must have been keeping an eye on them because as soon as she poured the last of the coffee into her cup, he appeared with another pot.

She couldn't find the words to say thank you. That lump had reappeared in her throat. But he seemed content with a nod and slight smile. 'I'll keep it coming,' he said. As if coffee was the answer to the world's woes.

She was relieved to see Nick finally move to pick up his cup. It trembled in his hand, and rattled against his teeth but he drank it, emptying the almost-cold coffee in a series of frantic gulps.

He turned to look at her, his eyes wide and blank. 'I don't understand; why would they have taken her?'

'Some kind of mix-up. Maybe Andrea found Meg and they both got lost, couldn't remember which pub they'd been in.' She nodded as if suddenly certain this was the reason. 'There are a few pubs within a short distance. They're probably sitting in another one wondering where we are.'

He looked hopeful for a second before his expression returned to the fearful one he'd been wearing since he'd opened the rucksack. 'That doesn't make sense.' He banged his hand down on the banquette, disturbing a small cloud of dust. 'How many pubs have seating like this, eh? Plus,' he tugged at the rucksack, 'they left this behind on purpose to make us believe everything was okay, that they were going to come back.'

'It might—'

He reached out and grabbed her hand. 'Don't try to explain this away, Sarah; someone has stolen Kaya. Someone has taken our daughter.'

18

A loud bang on the door startled both Sarah and Nick. It was loud enough to silence the conversations in the room, and everyone turned to stare.

'I told you,' Sarah said quietly. 'It was all a big mistake. Here they are now.'

But it wasn't them, of course. The second bartender unlocked the door, then opened it to peer around the edge before standing back to allow two people to enter. They were little and large: a plain-clothes officer with wide shoulders and a belly that stretched the buttons of his short-sleeved shirt, and a medium-height, slim officer in uniform. They stood for a moment in the uneasy silence. It was the bartender who leaned forward to whisper into the man's ear, then point deliberately to where Sarah and Nick sat staring.

They were still staring, unmoving, when the two officers crossed the now silent pub towards them.

The plain-clothes officer pulled out a chair and sat, leaving the uniformed constable to stand slightly behind. 'My name is Detective Inspector Andrew Maxwell and this,' he jerked a thumb over his right shoulder, 'is PC O'Farrell. You told the call handler that two women had taken your daughter, is that right?'

'Yes.' It was Nick who answered, the one word blurted out in anxious frustration. 'Can you get out there and look for her? Put an alert up or something. It's been almost an hour now; they could have got miles away.'

Maxwell held a hand up. 'We have a search in progress already. Three officers are out on the streets looking for any sightings of them. But you can help us by giving us more details.' He looked around the pub. 'I think we can probably dispense with the audience.' He stood and leaned down to speak into O'Farrell's ear.

Sarah watched as the officer muttered something in reply, then moved towards the groups of people sitting nearer to the exit.

With a 'give me a minute' addressed to Nick and Sarah, Maxwell went to the nearby tables.

Sarah was able to hear most of the questions he asked, a list of what would probably be classified as routine. Names, addresses, contact details, whether they had seen anything, if they could describe the two women who had been seated beside Nick and Sarah. She guessed from the many shrugs and head shakes that most had nothing useful to contribute.

She was conscious of Nick's rising frustration. He wanted them to be doing something. No, she reconsidered; *he* wanted to be doing something. When she reached for his hand, she wasn't sure she was doing it for his benefit or hers. Was this really happening? She felt numb, detached, as if she was floating above all the chaos. As she hadn't done since long-ago childhood, she prayed that Kaya was safe and being well looked after. Meg had held her closely, almost lovingly, Sarah didn't think she was likely to hurt her.

Within ten minutes, most of the other customers had left the pub, some stopping as they passed the table to wish Nick and Sarah the best of luck, some of the women with tears in their eyes. Sarah stopped saying thank you after the first few, realising how stupid it sounded.

It wasn't until there were only a few left that DI Maxwell took the seat opposite again. 'PC O'Farrell can sort the last few out,' he said. He stretched a hand to pat the side of the coffee pot. It was still warm. Roger must have been keeping a close eye because almost immediately, he was over with another cup.

'I can make a fresh pot,' he said, putting the cup in front of the detective before tilting the milk jug to check there was enough.

'No, this is fine.' Maxwell filled his cup, took a few noisy slurps then put it down and took a notebook from his pocket. 'Right,' he said, clicking the top of his pen. 'You'd better tell me everything from the time you arrived here this evening.'

PC O'Farrell saw the last of the customers out and joined them, taking the seat beside Maxwell. Whereas he was a restless man, shuffling in his chair, playing with the handle of his coffee cup, clicking the top of his pen – in out, in out – she sat with her hands on her thighs, fingers splayed, and looked first at Nick then at Sarah. When Maxwell began to speak, her eyes flicked between them as if watching for any untoward reaction. It was unsettling and Sarah found herself mirroring Maxwell's shuffling.

Nick was telling them the details, his voice harsh, the words clipped. Sarah waited to slip a word in if required but she didn't need to; he gave a flawless, minute-by-minute account of what had occurred after they'd arrived at the pub.

Maxwell scribbled in his notebook, flicking page after page. 'Right,' he said when Nick had reached the end. 'And you'd never seen these two women before?'

'Never.'

'But you handed your three-week-old daughter to them?' It was the first time the PC had spoken. Her voice was soft, the tone neutral, it was her expression that gave her away: tight lines of disapproval across her forehead, her lips pressed tightly into a slash of condemnation.

'Kaya had started to cry,' Sarah said. 'Like most babies, she can – for a little thing – make a lot of noise. We were conscious of disturbing other customers and we were going to take her out—'

'We?' O'Farrell interrupted. 'You were both going to leave?'

Sarah blinked, her mouth open as she tried to remember and put it into words. How had it gone? 'No, Nick was going to take her out, but his fish and chips had just arrived; I was having a cold meal so I said I'd take her, then Meg – she was the younger of the two women – volunteered to take her outside. It seemed harmless and I could see she was good with Kaya from the way she held her.'

'And what about you?' Maxwell looked at Nick. 'Were you happy with this arrangement?'

He hadn't been. She remembered he'd looked confused, and then concerned when Sarah had said it was a great idea. He'd eaten his dinner but he hadn't relaxed, his eyes constantly flitting to the door.

'Yes,' he said. 'It seemed to make sense.'

Sarah loved him for the lie, but she could see it for what it was, and she guessed the police officers had seen it too.

'How long was this Meg gone before you became concerned?'

Both of them shrugged. 'We were eating and chatting,' Sarah said. 'It might have been ten minutes. No longer.'

'And when you began to voice concern, the older woman,' his eyes flicked to his notebook, 'Andrea. She said she'd go and look for them, making a point of lifting her rucksack onto the chair and asking you to keep an eye on it, is that correct?'

'Yes.' One word said in unison.

'And it was another five minutes before you decided to go out in search of them?'

'Yes,' Nick said. 'When I came back, that's when I decided to look in the rucksack and found it was filled with rubbish.'

'Hmmm.' Maxwell flicked through his notebook again. 'So from the time Meg left with your daughter to when you made the phone call to the Devon and Cornwall police, we're talking twenty minutes, is that about right?'

Nick looked to Sarah for confirmation, but she'd no more idea than he of exactly how long it had been. 'It's hard to say, but about that,' she answered.

'Can you describe both women, please. As best you can.'

The detective was looking at Sarah, as if she'd have a better chance of describing them. It was probably true. 'Meg, I'd say, is mid-twenties.

My height, so around five-seven.' Sarah lifted her hand and made a chopping motion near her neck. 'Brown hair about this long. Slim. Nice looking without being anyway remarkable. Ordinary looking.'

'Eyes?'

Sarah wanted to make a joke, say that yes, she'd had them. Inappropriate humour in times of stress, they'd probably understand. 'I didn't notice what colour they were. She was wearing shorts and a sleeveless top, and she had a jacket.' She drew a sharp breath. 'She picked it up as she was leaving, said it might get chilly. But she'd no intention of coming back, did she?'

'And the other woman?' Maxwell asked, ignoring her question.

'Older, maybe mid-thirties. Long, dark hair pulled back in a band. Quieter than her friend; she barely spoke to us and wasn't particularly friendly when she did. Meg, on the other hand, was quite chatty. It was she who told Andrea to budge over to give us room.'

'Why did you choose this particular spot to sit?'

'When we came in, the place was jammed and it was the only space free. We hadn't booked anywhere and we were desperate to get something to eat after walking all day.'

'Was there a particular reason for choosing this pub?' O'Farrell asked.

She was looking at Nick, but it was Sarah who answered. 'We used to visit here a lot when I was a child. I wanted to bring Nick and Kaya to places I remembered. Revisiting old haunts, I suppose you'd say.'

'Right. Can you describe what your daughter was wearing?'

'Of course I can.' Sarah was offended both by the question and the officer's obvious disapproval of her. Of course she could remember what Kaya was wearing; she wasn't that bad a mother. The pretty pink dress that Sarah's mother had bought because she'd seen it in M&S and couldn't resist it. It had come with matching knickers, the bottom layered with ruffles. It had short sleeves so Sarah had slipped on a fine pink cotton cardigan. 'A Barbie baby,' she'd said when she'd dressed her, lifting Kaya high to show her off to Nick. He'd taken a photo with her phone. 'There's a photo,' she said. Reaching for her mobile, she found it and held it out to show them. 'Here, see, see how gorgeous she looks.'

Maxwell took it, looked at it, then passed it to O'Farrell.

'She is beautiful,' the officer said, looking up to meet Sarah's eyes. 'No gender-neutral clothes here, eh?'

'I like pink,' Sarah said sharply. She wanted to say it wasn't the time for such a conversation. But maybe it was. Maybe it was why those women had taken Kaya. In her pink outfit, she was such a flagrantly pretty girl-child.

O'Farrell tapped a few keys on the mobile before handing it back. 'I've sent that to our officers. It might help.'

Maxwell's mobile rang. He lifted it from the table and crossed to the far side of the pub to take the call.

O'Farrell glanced after him, then got to her feet as if unable to sit looking at them without his support. 'I'll ask Roger for more coffee.'

When they were alone, Sarah turned to Nick. 'You okay?' His sudden tightened expression told her it was an insensitive, stupid thing to ask. Of course he wasn't okay. 'Sorry. I don't know what I'm saying.' She squeezed her eyes shut, feeling hot tears building. 'It's all so unbelievable, and my fault. Despite what you said to the police, you didn't want that bitch to take Kaya. It was me, being stupid, selfish, thinking of my dinner. Fucking chicken Caesar salad.' She laughed at the absurdity of it all, heard the hint of hysteria creeping around the edges and brought it to a quick halt.

Nick reached for her, pulling her into his arms and resting his chin on her head. 'Neither of us are at fault. We're just too trustworthy, that's all. They played us. But they won't get far. The police will find them, bring our little girl safely home and we can put this whole horrid episode behind us.'

It was a few minutes before either Maxwell or O'Farrell returned, the latter with a pot of coffee and four clean cups that she carried awkwardly and put down with a clatter. Maxwell sat heavily and accepted the coffee she poured for him.

'Well?' Sarah said, shaking her head to the offer of a drink.

'My officers have called to every pub in the area and have stopped everyone they met to ask if anyone saw one or two women carrying a baby. Unfortunately, they've drawn a blank.'

Sarah, still wrapped in Nick's arms, gasped. 'But they have to be somewhere! They can't simply have vanished; you have to find them.' She pulled free and leaned across the table. 'My baby! You have to find her!'

19

Sarah and Nick spent an hour with a police specialist, trying to make an accurate, computer-generated, facial composite of Andrea and Meg.

'It's as close as I can get,' Sarah said. 'There was simply nothing particularly memorable about them. Apart from Meg's red nails.'

'It'll give us something to work with,' Maxwell said, staring at the computer screen. 'That's all you can do for now; you should try to get some rest. If anything turns up in the next few hours, don't worry, we'll let you know.'

'Shouldn't we stay here, in case…' Nick didn't finish the sentence.

'There's nothing you can do here, Mr Westfield; you're really better off trying to get some sleep. Tomorrow will be a long day.' Maxwell stood up. 'I promise you; if anything turns up, we'll be in touch.'

Nick didn't move and it was Sarah who got to her feet. 'Right,' she said putting a hand under his elbow and tugging until he got up. 'Come on, love, we'll see if we can get a little rest. Kaya will soon be back with us; we need to be ready.'

PC O'Farrell brought them the short distance to the hotel by car. She walked them to the door of the hotel which opened silently at her push. 'I know it won't be easy but do try to get some sleep. I'll return in the morning to take you through what happens next.'

'But they will keep searching, won't they? DI Maxwell mentioned an alert...' Sarah's voice faded as she sought for the name.

'The Child Rescue Alert, yes, so the search isn't just local any more. Every police force in England, Scotland, and Wales have now been notified. There are already alerts on social services and on the radio. The likeness of the two women will be shared where we can, including on late-night TV news. Tomorrow, with your help, we'll do an appeal.'

The officer sounded so calm, so rational. All in a day's work. Sarah wanted to scratch her eyes out. No words would come; there weren't any anyway. Side by side, she and Nick trudged up the wide staircase to their first-floor room, the infant carrier dangling from Nick's hand a sad testament to their loss. Both were feeling numb, dazed... bereft.

Bereft. She'd thought she didn't love Kaya. Had she been wrong? Had she made a colossal mistake? They'd left the room in a hurry and some of Kaya's things were spread across the bed. Sarah crossed to pick up a Babygro and pressed it to her face. It had been washed and smelt of washing powder, not the baby scent she'd expected and she tossed it down with a groan of dismay. 'She might be hungry and crying for her bottle. For us.' She turned and sank onto the bed. 'Why would they do such a thing? Take our baby.'

Nick stood inside the door. He turned to shut it, then crossed to sit beside her. 'They'll find them. And Kaya will be safe. You said yourself, Meg handled her like she knew what she was doing. Maybe she lost a child and that's why they took her. Perhaps Kaya reminded her of her own baby.'

'You make it sound like a Hallmark movie.' Sarah pushed his arm away and got to her feet. 'What if the police don't find her?' She pressed her clenched hands against her lips with such force that it hurt, but it stopped the tremble and the scream that was waiting to be released. 'What if we never get her back?'

Nick walked over and gathered her in his arms, pulling her back against him, holding her tightly even when she tried to escape. 'We have to stay strong. For Kaya's sake. Falling apart isn't going to help her or us. I'm here for you. I'll always be here for you.' He kissed her cheek and whispered in her ear. 'The two of us together, we can get through this, whatever happens.'

Sarah tried to pull away again, but his embrace tightened. She felt trapped by his grief, trapped by the loss of their daughter. *Trapped*. She wanted to pull from his arms, run away and never look back. But how could she leave him now?

20

It was two weeks after baby Kaya Westfield went missing. PC Zoé-Lee O'Farrell was sitting in the small kitchen of the home she shared with her husband, Tom, and their fourteen-month-old daughter, Raven. 'Here you go.' She held a spoon of baby food to the child's mouth. 'Open for Mummy.'

But it seemed Raven was more interested in wearing the food than eating it. Deliberate or not, her little fist knocked against the spoon to send the contents flying into the air and landing with a plop on the table of her baby seat. For a moment, she looked surprised, then she gurgled a laugh, showing off her few teeth. What could Zoé-Lee do but laugh, scoop the food off the child's T-shirt and start again?

'She being a monkey?' Tom asked, coming through the door with a folded newspaper in one hand. He tossed it onto the table and bent to snuggle a kiss on his daughter's neck, ignoring the sticky hands that immediately grabbed his hair. She laughed when he blew raspberries into her skin.

'If you get her too excited, she'll never eat,' Zoé-Lee complained. 'Then you'll be left with a cross child to care for while I'm out making the world a better place to live in.'

He took the spoon from her unresisting hand. 'Go, get ready, me and Raven will be fine.'

They would be, of course, but as she stood by the door, Zoé-Lee felt the twinge of guilt she always did when she left the two of them. And although it had been almost three months since she'd weaned Raven, she still felt that weight in her breasts, an ache that didn't seem to be fading with time. She knew how lucky she was. A job she loved, and a husband who worked from home who was as good with their daughter as she was. *Maybe even better.* It wasn't the first time that little voice in her head taunted her. She swatted it firmly away. 'I might be late home; we're heading to Minehead to follow up a sighting of the two women in the Kaya case.'

Tom looked up in surprise. 'How come the Avon and Somerset lot aren't looking into it?'

'Maxwell had a word, thinks it's better if I go since I've spent so much time on the case in the last couple of weeks. They were only too happy to hand it over. I'm guessing they think it's a wild-goose chase, like all the other sightings have been, otherwise they wouldn't have been so quick.'

'At least you won't have the baby's parents haunting you.'

'No, I won't.' Zoé-Lee had complained to him that almost every time she walked into the station, they were there, waiting to ask if there was any news. And if they didn't come in person, they were on the phone several times a day. She'd liked to have said yes, liked to have been able to tell them that their heartbreaking TV appeal had borne fruit, that the two women had come forward with their child looking hale and hearty. But life was never that simple. There had been dozens of reports, but not one had led them any closer to the two women who'd walked off with Kaya Westfield.

The parents had come into the station in Ilfracombe the previous day. DI Maxwell wasn't available so it was Zoé-Lee who had been called to speak to them. When she opened the door of the interview room, they'd looked at her, and despite knowing there wasn't any new information – they'd been on the phone to the station first thing – Zoé-Lee had cringed to see hope flicker in their eyes. It was dying faster day by day, soon it wouldn't flicker, but unless they found Kaya, or at least found out what happened to her, a relic of it would always be there.

They'd both lost weight in the two weeks, Nick Westfield in particular looking frail and haunted. 'You wanted to see us,' Zoé-Lee said, taking a seat opposite.

'Yes. To let you know, we're going to head home today. Back to London.'

It was Nick who spoke, his voice hoarse and raspy as if he'd been screaming for hours, maybe howling. Zoé-Lee thought of her daughter and wouldn't have blamed him if he had. Her eyes flicked to the more composed wife. When it came to couples, it was often the case that they'd take turns to fall apart, but every time Zoé-Lee had seen them – and that was at least twice a day, sometimes more, for two weeks – it was he who was barely hanging on, and Sarah who was holding it all together.

The police officer wasn't sure whether to admire her strength or criticise what struck her as unnatural composure. She'd never been able to get over the fact that she'd handed over her baby to a complete stranger.

'I think you're being a bit harsh,' Tom had said when she'd mentioned it a few nights before over a glass of wine in their tiny back garden. 'You don't know that behind closed doors it isn't the other way around: she's falling apart and he's holding her together. She's a doctor, you said; maybe she's used to portraying a neutral face for the public.'

'Maybe,' Zoé-Lee had said, but she didn't really believe it. She hadn't wanted to waste more of their me-time talking about work.

The previous day, after promising for the hundredth time to keep them informed of any developments, she'd walked the Westfields to the door of the station. There was no point in telling them that they probably wouldn't see her again. Since the Child Rescue Alert had been instigated, their case was under the aegis of the National Crime Agency. In future, since the Westfields were heading back to Islington, they would liaise with the Metropolitan Police rather than the Devon and Cornwall police.

Zoé-Lee had friends in the Met; she'd hear what was happening through them.

Meanwhile, she'd keep following up leads when they happened in their jurisdiction, or in the ones bordering Devon and Cornwall.

* * *

It was a nice day and the drive to Minehead was a pretty one, the road twisting and turning through the countryside. Zoé-Lee got stuck behind a caravan on a two-mile stretch of bendy road. There was no possibility of overtaking so she relaxed and turned the radio up.

She was meeting a PC Lin Perrett in the station in Minehead. 'You'll never find the house on your own,' she'd said when she'd rung the previous night to arrange for Zoé-Lee to come to assist. 'I don't know why we couldn't handle this here, seems a bit weird dragging you all the way.'

'It's just this missing baby case,' she hurried to reassure the officer. 'No criticism of the Avon and Somerset police was intended. It's simply that I've been liaising with the parents since it happened. DI Maxwell thought it was better to keep it that way till they leave our jurisdiction.'

When she pulled up outside the station, twenty minutes later than she'd promised, the officer was waiting, a bored look on her face.

'Really sorry,' she said, getting out and crossing to the officer with her hand extended. 'I got stuck behind a caravan, and then a tractor.' Her genuine apology seemed to melt the other officer's ice.

'Always the same this time of year.' Perrett pointed to where a police car was parked haphazardly. 'We'll take mine; it'll be easier. Park yours over there.' She indicated a space behind.

A minute later, they were pulling from the car park and heading back out of Minehead. 'It's not far,' Perrett said, 'just awkward to find if you don't know the area.' She glanced towards Zoé-Lee. 'So you've been involved in this since the beginning.'

'Yes. Two weeks now and no sign of the child. We're following up every lead, so are officers in different parts of the country, but so far, they've all been dead ends. In the beginning, we hoped we'd find the baby alive and healthy but now...' She sighed. 'You know the story. A tiny, three-week-old baby is way too easy to hide, dead or alive. They could be anywhere.'

'There was an All Ports Warning put in place immediately though, wasn't there?'

'Sure, but they were looking for two women and a baby. What if they travelled separately or hid the baby in a carrier bag of some sort? It's too easy to do.'

PC Perrett negotiated the twisting road silently but when it straightened out, she flicked a glance towards her passenger. 'It sounds like the women went there intending to take a child, doesn't it? I'm thinking of the rucksack filled with rubbish.'

'It does seem that way.'

'And you don't think the parents are involved in any way?'

Zoé-Lee smoothed a hand over her neat hair, checking her bun was still in place, no strands escaping to soften the look. It was her thinking mannerism. 'We've considered every option, of course, but there's no evidence the parents were involved in any way, and their grief seems honest and proportionate.' Nick Westfield's anyway. She still wasn't sure about the mother. 'Our working hypothesis is that the two women went out with the intention of taking a child, but...'

'But?' Perrett asked when the silence dragged out.

Zoé-Lee sighed. 'If that was their intention, did they simply get lucky the first time they tried? We've had officers ask in every pub, café, and restaurant in our patch but nobody reported seeing a couple matching their description.'

'Not the easiest time of the year. Lots of people walking about with rucksacks, hard to remember two unremarkable women.'

'Yes, and that seems deliberate too. You've seen the composite we made based on the couple's description, haven't you?'

Perrett snorted. 'I did; they could be anyone.' She indicated and pulled into a driveway. 'This is it. It's a rented cottage. The neighbour next door rang to say a couple arrived last week with a baby. *A couple of women.*' Perrett looked at Zoé-Lee with a shake of her head. 'That was her exact intonation. I'm guessing she's not a lover of same-sex couples. She hastened to add that she wasn't saying it *was* them, but I could tell she was hoping it was.'

'Well, it would be nice if the old bigot was right, wouldn't it?' Zoé-Lee grinned and pushed open the car door.

21

Zoé-Lee felt a rush of excitement when the door of the cottage was opened. The description the Westfield's had given them might fit a number of women – it certainly fit this one. More interesting was the agitation coming off her in waves, and she was jittery, glancing behind her, then back to them. Zoe-Lee felt Perrett tense beside her and knew she was thinking the same. This could be it. The end of the search.

It was Perrett's patch so Zoé-Lee let her take the lead. 'I'm PC Perrett, and this is PC O'Farrell. Is it possible to come inside, Ms...'

Another glance behind, a shuffle of bare feet on the polished floorboards of the tiny hallway. It didn't look as if the woman was intending to reply. Then, as Zoé-Lee was wondering what their next step should be, the woman heaved a huge sigh. 'It's Phillips, Katie Phillips.'

'Ms Phillips,' Perrett said, her voice gentle but firm. 'I think we need to come inside, don't you?'

Looking slightly dazed, Katie looked behind her again, then took a step backwards to allow the officers to enter.

The hallway was so tiny as to make the three bodies a crowd. It was Perrett who opened the door into a cluttered, bright room overlooking the rear garden. It was an odd space full of angles and corners, obviously created by knocking down older, smaller rooms and adding an extension. It was this addition that drew both officers' eyes. A baby's cot was oddly positioned in the middle of the floor surrounded by a smattering of clothes, toys, and toiletries.

Ignoring the officers, Katie moved to one of the mismatched chairs that were set around the small kitchen table. She sat with weary resignation, propped her elbow on the table and rested her forehead in her hand. 'I'm sorry,' she said.

Zoé-Lee wanted to pump the air in sheer pleasure and relief. She looked at Perrett, saw the same expression on her face.

'I thought you were Carina,' Katie said, lifting her head. When she looked their direction, her eyes glistened with tears. 'We had a big row this morning; she walked out and hasn't come back.'

The second woman. It was a relief to know she wasn't going to come barrelling down the stairs.

Perrett looked at Zoé-Lee and with a jerk of her head, indicated she take care of the child, while Perrett, since it was her patch after all, made the arrest.

Happy with her part, Zoé-Lee crossed to the cot. The child was asleep, long eyelashes like spiders' legs on soft pink cheeks. Yellow-clad arms were extended to each side, small fists curled. Closer, she could see a dirty nappy rolled up on the floor the far side of the cot. They'd obviously interrupted Katie while she was changing the baby. A clean, open nappy sat at the bottom of the cot.

The blanket that had been draped over the baby had been kicked to one side, exposing its naked bottom half. Zoé-Lee straightened from her hunched position. 'PC Perrett, I think you'd better see this before you say anything else.'

'I don't understand,' Katie said. 'Why are you reading me my rights? I haven't done anything!' Her voice rose as she spoke, the tears now flowing freely.

Perrett, hearing the tone of Zoé-Lee's voice, joined her and looked down at the child in the cot. 'That can't be Kaya.'

'Nope, that's most definitely a boy child.' The blanket was straightened and tucked in around the sleeping baby.

'We're sorry,' Perrett said, returning to the mother.

'I don't understand, what's going on?' Katie wiped away her tears and stood. 'You come in here. Read me my rights like I'm some kind of criminal. As if I didn't have enough to worry me.' It seemed to take all her energy to get the words out because she sank onto the chair again and sobbed.

The officers exchanged glances but it was Perrett who spoke. 'You've probably read about the missing baby, Kaya.'

A loud snuffle followed. Zoé-Lee looked around, spied a roll of kitchen paper and grabbed it. She pulled a few reams from it and handed it to the crying woman.

Katie wiped her eyes and blew her nose before finally, calmer, she looked from one officer to the other. 'Of course I did. Who hasn't? But what's it got to do with me?' Before the officers could answer, a soft cry came from the child in the cot. Immediately, Katie got up and went to him, put on the fresh nappy, and picked him up. With him in her arms, she sat and said, 'Well?'

'We were following up a report that two women had moved in here with a young baby.'

Katie barked a laugh that startled the child and made him squirm in her arms. 'Shush,' she said, pressing her lips to his cheek. 'I can guess who reported us. That old bat next door. The day we arrived, I was carrying the baby in when she stopped me to say hello. Right curious she was, wanted to know how long we were staying, where we were from. When she asked if my husband was around, I told her my wife was coming down later. You should have seen her expression! Ha!'

Katie was right to be annoyed, of course, but nosy, curious neighbours had solved cases for the police before. 'We've been asking for everyone to be vigilant, Ms Phillips, so I think we must excuse her this time. Somebody knows where Baby Kaya is. Her parents, as you can understand, are distraught.'

'Of course they would be.' Katie kissed the top of her baby's head. 'I hope you find her.'

'Sorry again for the misunderstanding,' Perrett said. 'I hope you and your wife can work things out, for your baby's sake.'

'Thank you. Carina has a fiery temper but she loves me. She'll be back.' Katie walked them to the door. 'I don't know what I'd do if anything happened to Charlie. But then I wouldn't hand him over to someone I didn't know either.'

Back in the car, Perrett sighed. 'The neighbour looks down on her for being a lesbian; she looks down on Sarah Westfield for being a bad mother.' She shook her head. 'Everyone's a critic.'

Zoé-Lee rested her head back and stared out the window as they made their way back to the station. She too was critical of Sarah for handing her baby over to a stranger, but did that make her a bad mother? Zoé-Lee wasn't sure. What were the criteria for being a good mother anyway? She refused to give that any further thought; she mightn't like the answer.

22

Zoé-Lee was only back in the station a few minutes when DI Maxwell came over and perched on the edge of her desk. He was looking unusually genial. It put her immediately on guard. They had a good relationship, worked well together, but she knew his tricks. When it was something he thought she mightn't want to do, he assumed that genial, butter-wouldn't-melt expression.

The disappointment of earlier was still sticking in her gut and she wasn't in the mood to be conciliatory. Or even polite. 'Whatever it is you want, the answer is no.'

'Tetchy, aren't we?' He rarely took offence. Unless it suited him.

'Well, I'm not sure about "we",' she twirled her index fingers to make quotation marks in the air, 'but *I* definitely am.' She gave him a rundown on the tip-off they'd been given in Minehead. 'The woman fit the description perfectly, which goes to show how fucking useless it is.'

'One of these days, one of these tip-offs is going to yield results.'

She thought the Minehead one had. She remembered the sense of euphoria as she'd crossed to the baby's cot, expecting to see Kaya. Was her disappointment because she hadn't had the glory of returning the child to its parents? Maybe her photo in the newspaper as she did so? Was she that much of a career-hound? *You know you are*, that irritating little voice in her head said, making her voice even sharper when she spoke to Maxwell. 'What is it you want? Because I know it's something and I'm not in the mood for games.'

'This is such a high-profile case, our friends in the National Crime Agency are eager to keep the Westfields happy. They're concerned that because the officers of the Met don't know them, that there might be some...' He made a mental effort to search for a politically acceptable phrase. 'Let's call it communication issues.' He smiled, pleased with himself. 'Yes, that about sums it up: communication issues. I'm not sure why they feel this way. Maybe there's been some argy-bargy between the Met and the National Crime Agency. It wouldn't surprise me. A tricky lot, those civil servants.' He raised a hand and batted away his musings. 'Anyway, to prevent such issues occurring, they've requested an officer from Devon and Cornwall go to London for a few days to provide a smooth transition between the forces.' He grinned. 'That's the way those National Crime Agency folk speak, seriously.'

She didn't care if they spoke Chinese and she was bored with Maxwell's one-man crusade to end acronyms and initialisms, thankful that he at least deigned to use the abbreviation Met rather than saying the Metropolitan police every damn time. She knew why he was wearing his favourite arse-licking expression. This was a big ask. 'You want me to go?'

'Who better? You've spent a lot of time with the Westfields since the night their baby was abducted. You know them better than anyone.'

She did. She had tried to make her reports as detailed as possible but how could she account for the feeling that things weren't quite as straightforward as they appeared? The reports were for facts, proven details, not gut feeling.

'You're judging her for handing her baby over to a total stranger so she could have her dinner in peace,' Tom had said, when she'd once again mentioned her reservations about Sarah. 'I think you're being a little unfair.'

Perhaps he was right. Or maybe it was simply that she didn't take to the woman. Zoé-Lee was empathetic by nature and normally had to rein in her feelings for victims. She felt genuine sympathy for Nick Westfield;

it was only Sarah she struggled with. Good mother or not, what woman in her right mind would hand their baby over to a stranger? She sighed. Tom was right. She'd been a little unfair and judgemental. Maybe even very unfair; after all, Nick had been in the pub too. Wasn't he as deserving of criticism as Sarah?

Maxwell was still in persuasive mode. 'It'll be for two, three days tops. You'll meet the Met officer, go through the case with them, then introduce them to the Westfields. Then you ease yourself away and leave them to it.'

Two or three days in London, working with the Met. She felt a buzz of excitement at the thought before reality kicked her in the stomach. 'It will mean leaving Raven for two or three days, though.'

'Tom looks after her, doesn't he? Why would that be a problem?'

Of course it wouldn't be. Tom would manage perfectly fine. He knew how much her career meant to her and would be encouraging. As for Raven, would she even miss her mother? Zoé-Lee doubted she'd even notice her absence. 'No, that's okay, it won't be a problem. Since the Westfields have already left, I assume you want me to go as soon as, yes?'

'No point in hanging around, is there?' He looked at his watch. 'It's only eleven. If you head home now to pack and drive to Exeter, you can pick up the London train and be there late afternoon.' He smiled as if he was bestowing a great adventure on her.

Zoé-Lee wanted to punch him.

* * *

'And that,' she said to Tom when she got home, 'was that.' She was packing some essentials into a small suitcase. 'I'm sorry, it really didn't look as if I could turn it down.'

'Even if you'd wanted to?' He stood in the doorway, a smile on his face, his eyes warm and reassuring. 'Admit it, even though you've never taken to the mother, you were still disappointed when the Westfields headed home to London.'

She nodded, then shook her head. 'I was, but it does make my life easier without them haunting me for information every day. Now they can haunt their local police instead. The crime happened in Devon; it's still officially ours. The NCA are only involved because they manage the CRA.' She saw him frown and sighed. 'You're as bad as Maxwell – the Child Rescue Alert.'

Tom shrugged. 'I'm on Andrew's side. Initialism is designed to confuse.'

Zoé-Lee raised her eyes to the ceiling. She was pleased that Maxwell and Tom got along so well but it irritated when they ganged up against her.

'Stay in London as long as you need. You might as well reap the benefits of me working from home.'

She shut her case with a snap. 'I'll miss you.' She felt him behind her, his hands creeping around her waist, pulling her against him. He was her rock. She wasn't sure she could do her job if she didn't always have him at her back. 'You and Raven. I couldn't live if anything happened to either of you.'

'Nothing is going to happen to us,' he said, kissing the top of her head. 'We'll be waiting for you when you get home from solving the mystery of what happened to little Kaya.'

Zoé-Lee laughed and turned in his arms. 'All that's going to happen this trip is that I'm going to hand over the liaison role to the Westfields' local police station. While I'm there, I'm planning to pop into our friends in the NCA but I'm not expecting to hear anything new.'

'You don't think you're going to find Kaya, do you?'

'Every day that passes makes it more unlikely. There have been so many reports but not one has brought us any closer to knowing who took the baby or where she is.' She reached a hand up, held it against his cheek. 'But I'm not giving up.'

Two hours later, she was sitting on the train bound for London Paddington. Lost in her thoughts, she stared through the window ignoring the scenery as it changed from a blur of green to one of grey. She hadn't wanted to admit it to Tom, but she really didn't think they were going to find Kaya, not without a huge amount of luck.

23

Sarah and Nick pushed open the door of their apartment. She was carrying the suitcase with their clothes. Nick, the baby carrier, and the Moses basket filled with Kaya's things. They'd barely spoken on the drive from Lynton. Truth was, they'd barely spoken in days. What was there to say that they hadn't said a million times since Kaya was taken?

How many times had Sarah said she was sorry? How many times had Nick said he didn't blame her – his attempts to convince her he didn't becoming more irritating by the day.

'I love you,' he said. 'We're in this together. Me and you.' And he'd kiss her and hold her tight, and it made her want to scream.

They hadn't told their respective families or their friends that they were coming back that day. Neither wanted to deal with their well-meaning intrusion and Sarah certainly didn't want to listen to the criticism – it would probably stay unsaid, true, but it'd be clear in every eye, every twisted mouth and rigid expression. *How could she have handed Kaya over to a total stranger?* Sarah had seen it in that police officer's expression, in her sharp little eyes. She was glad she'd left PC O'Farrell behind and wouldn't have to see her stupidly judgemental face again.

'I'll put Kaya's things into the spare bedroom,' Nick said. When he returned, she was still standing there. 'I'll put the kettle on for a cuppa.'

A cuppa! She'd have liked a stiff drink, whisky or brandy, wine at a push, but she hadn't had breakfast or lunch that day, and had eaten little the day before. In fact, she wasn't sure when either of them had eaten a full meal last. She left the suitcase in the hallway and followed him into the kitchen.

When Nick's mobile buzzed, he pulled it out and took a deep breath before looking at the screen. 'My mother,' he said, looking at Sarah with a half-smile. 'I'd better take it.' He walked from the room as he did so, leaving Sarah alone.

She stood by the counter, staring at the kettle as it did its thing, then made two mugs of coffee, leaving Nick's on the counter. The murmur of his voice drifted through. His mother had rung every day since she'd been told about Kaya. She'd wanted to come to Lynton and was only prevented from doing so when he'd assured her, at Sarah's insistence, that they'd be heading home any day. 'I couldn't bear it if she came,' Sarah had said. 'She'd blame me.'

'Of course she won't,' Nick had insisted.

But Sarah knew better. His mother doted on her only son and was an adoring grandmother. She'd be genuinely upset but she was the type of woman who'd look around for someone to blame and that arrow would hit Sarah right between the eyes. Why wouldn't it? Sarah blamed herself too.

Now that her darling son was back in London, no doubt she'd descend upon them. The thought made Sarah want to cry as she crossed to the living room. A pretty room, she'd pored over several style magazines before decorating it in various shades of grey with teal accent colours. On the balcony, she'd planted pots of white cosmos. They were in flower now, their heads swaying in the breeze. She'd been pleased how it had all come together but now, looking around, it seemed cold and heartless. The only things that were giving it life were the few things belonging to Kaya that lay scattered about. A baby-pink blanket, a rattle she'd never got to use, a small, plush teddy bear. Sarah's fingers tightened around her mug of coffee. Then with a cry of despair, she gathered Kaya's things with one hand. Using the toe of her shoe, she opened a cupboard door, shoved them inside and kicked the door shut.

When she'd finished her coffee, she'd make some phone calls, let people know they were back. There was no point in putting it off but it didn't mean she wanted to rush into picking up her mobile. She sipped her drink slowly, her eyes flicking to the doorway now and then to see if there were any sign of Nick appearing. 'Your coffee is getting cold,' she called out eventually. If he heard, he wasn't rushing to answer.

Finally with a reluctant sigh, she put her empty mug on the floor and picked up her mobile. Her parents first, her anxious mother answering the call; then her sister, less anxious, more critical; down through the few friends she had, thanking them for all their messages of support, each getting a version of the same conversation: *we're back in our apartment. No, there's no news. Yes, we're doing okay.*

There was still no sign of Nick. Sarah picked up her mug, got to her feet, took Nick's unwanted mug, and dropped both noisily and carelessly into the sink. The undrunk black coffee splashed upward. She looked down as mocha spots appeared on her white shirt and couldn't bring herself to care.

All the calls had left her mouth dry. That was her excuse for opening the fridge and taking out a bottle of wine. Later, she'd order a takeaway. For now, she'd have a glass of wine and make one more call.

Kicking off her shoes, she sat back against the cushions and rang Jade. At least with her, there'd be no criticism. They'd known each other forever, or near enough, and there were few secrets between them.

'Hi,' Sarah said when the call was answered almost immediately, as if Jade had been waiting for her to ring.

'You're back?'

'Yes, only just. Feels odd being here without Kaya. Sorry I haven't rung before—'

'Don't be daft, I didn't expect you to,' Jade butted in. 'I only sent messages so you'd know I was thinking of you.'

'Thank you, it meant a lot.'

'Would you like me to come over? I could be there in twenty minutes.'

'No, thanks, maybe tomorrow or the next day. We're both shattered to be honest and will probably have something to eat and head to bed.'

'If you're sure.'

'I am, but thanks, Jade.'

'I hate to ask, but I'm assuming there's no news?'

As if Sarah wouldn't have started with that if there had been. As if she'd leave good news as a postscript to their chat. She took a mouthful of wine and used it to wash down her irritation. Jade was being nice. 'No, there's nothing. The police say they're following up every lead but to be honest, I'm guessing they haven't a clue who took Kaya or where she might be.'

'I don't know what to say. I can't begin to understand what you and Nick are going through but I'm here for you, okay?'

It's just what Sarah needed, what she'd expected from her best friend. No judgement, just unconditional support. 'Thanks, Jade. Listen, I'd better go, I'll give you a ring tomorrow, okay?'

'I'm here for you whenever. Give Nick my love.'

Sarah put the mobile down. The murmur of voices from the bedroom had increased in volume. She hoped it was Nick arguing for his mother to stay away. If she came, it would definitely be classified as the straw that broke the camel's back. Sarah took another gulp of the wine, then rested her head back. When she felt her eyelids getting heavy, she put the glass down. Maybe sleep would come, give her brain a rest.

It wasn't to be. She heard the bedroom door open and shut, Nick's slow footsteps across the wooden floor of the hallway. They stopped and she pictured him standing in the doorway, staring at her. If she opened her eyes, would she be able to tell from his expression how the conversation with his mother went? She'd have laid the blame for Kaya's disappearance firmly at Sarah's feet. Nick would have defended her, she knew he would because, despite everything, there had been no let-up in his love for her.

She wished there had been. It was driving her crazy.

24

Sarah thought Nick would see she was asleep and leave her be, so she was surprised when he spoke.

'Did you say you'd made coffee?'

A wave of irritation swept through her again. It was impossible to keep her emotions in check. Hormones were still in the process of resetting following Kaya's birth. That and the stress, the surges of anger, the weight of the guilt. All were making her behave irrationally.

Jumping up from the sofa, she swept across the room to the kitchen, flicked the switch on the kettle without checking there was water in it, then flicked it off again when it hissed its displeasure. 'I made a mug ages ago, threw it out when it got cold.' She kept her eyes on what she was doing, conscious of him standing not far away. She wanted to ask what his mother had said, but she knew it would be critical and didn't want to add to the guilt that was already pressing her down. She made the coffee and handed it to him. 'There's no milk.'

'That's okay, I can drink it black.' He took it from her, lifted it to his mouth, blew on it, then slurped. 'Tomorrow, I'll go and get some stuff. Tonight, I thought we could order a takeaway.'

'That sounds good.' She crossed to the sofa, picked up the remote and switched on the TV. The solemn tones of a newsreader filled the room. It was automatic to brace herself for any mention of their case. There hadn't been in days, even the dramatic and awful theft of a baby eventually slipping down in importance.

'I'll order an Indian, shall I?'

She didn't care. 'Fine.'

A minute later, she felt the sofa creak as he sat beside her.

'It'll be here in a bit,' he said.

'Fine.' She reached down to pick up her glass. 'I fancied something stronger than coffee; you want a glass?' She turned the volume of the TV down, then twisted to look at him. His eyes were red-rimmed, his face pale and drawn. Once again, guilt swept over her in a toxic wave. She wanted to move closer to him, to tell him that everything would be all right but she couldn't because she wasn't sure they would be. How could they be? Even their future together was uncertain. She lifted the glass to her mouth, swallowed half the contents, hiding her face in it. Uncertain? No, it wasn't. Without Kaya to keep them together, she knew where her future lay, and it wasn't with him.

Neither ate much of the Indian takeaway when it arrived. They pushed the food around their plates and nibbled with little enthusiasm. When they were finished, when they both threw their cutlery down, there was almost as much food as when they'd begun.

'I'm going to head to bed,' Sarah said as she carried her plate to the kitchen. She scraped what she hadn't eaten into the rubbish bin, then put the lids back on the half-full containers of food they hadn't touched. There was enough to do them for the following day. She put them in the fridge and shut it, leaning against it briefly as a wave of weariness hit her. When it passed, she crossed to the living room.

Nick was staring at the TV. She doubted he was watching the wildlife documentary that was showing. 'You coming to bed soon?' She was hoping he'd say no, that he'd stay watching the TV until much later, until she was asleep or at least until she could pretend she was.

He'd been incredibly needy the last week, clingy like a child during the day, all over her as soon as they were in bed. She saw it for what it was – a need to bury the grief of loss under something life-affirming – so, sooner than the four weeks recommended after giving birth, and far,

far sooner than she wanted, they resumed their sex life. Sarah did her bit with what she hoped was well-disguised reluctance. Guilt, she decided, was a rough, unforgiving taskmaster.

'I love you so much,' he'd whispered as he held her afterwards.

She lay there, crushed in his arms, and knew he was waiting for her to respond, to say *I love you too*. She felt, or imagined she felt, his arms tightening further while he waited. She wanted to tell him he was hurting her, that she couldn't breathe. It would embarrass him; he was a gentle man who didn't know his own strength. 'Me too,' she lied eventually, relieved when his arms immediately relaxed enough to allow her to take a deep breath. He kept them loosely around her though, clamping her to his side, and it wasn't until he fell into a deep, post-coital slumber that she was able to squirm from his embrace. Hugging the furthest reaches of their bed, she tried to find sleep herself. On the drive home, she'd mentioned moving into the spare room. 'I'm so restless these nights, I know I'm disturbing you.'

'Of course you're not,' he said. 'I couldn't bear it if you weren't there beside me when I woke in the morning.' He gave a sad, self-deprecatory laugh. 'Honestly, I'd think someone had crept into the bedroom and kidnapped you, and it would kill me.'

He'd looked so sad, so grief-stricken at the thought that she couldn't bring herself to insist it would be for the best.

Soon though, she'd have to make it clear.

That night, when she woke, it was midnight and Nick wasn't stretched alongside her. She reached for the bedside lamp and switched it on, then stared at the ruffled sheets on his side. Exhaustion paired with the wine had knocked her out and she hadn't heard him coming to bed. Had he tried to wake her? She wasn't sure; a wispy fragment of a memory drifted through her head, a seeking hand that she brushed away unceremoniously. Had that really happened? The line between dreams and reality seemed fragile.

The bedroom door was open just a crack. Enough to hear the faint sound of a kitchen cupboard door opening and shutting. A minute later, the low murmur of Nick's voice drifted through. Who could he be talking to at midnight? She lifted her head and came up onto her elbows as she strained to hear.

But if he'd been speaking to someone on his mobile, he'd stopped. Maybe he'd simply been talking to himself. She nodded and collapsed back on the pillow. That's what it was. She'd caught herself doing exactly that recently, asking herself if she was going crazy, answering back that she must be.

Louder voices drifted through. This was easier. Nick had switched on the TV. He'd taken to watch the news on various channels, as if hoping one of them would have the news he wanted to hear, that Kaya had been found. As if this was how they were going to find out, as if the police, or social services wouldn't be hammering on their door to return Kaya to them. To return her, or to tell them they never would.

She curled onto her side, squeezed her eyes shut and tried to make her mind go blank. 'Blank, damn you,' she whispered, dragging the pillow over her ears. All she wanted was a few hours free of guilt. She wanted to believe that wherever Kaya was, she was happy. Safe. Being loved – as she never had been by Sarah.

Never had been.

So why did she feel this ache inside, as if a part of her had been wrenched away?

25

Nick didn't return and Sarah drifted in and out of sleep for the rest of the night. When she finally woke, she pulled on a robe and went into the living room to find him lying on the sofa. He woke immediately and looked at her with the lopsided smile she'd found so endearing when she'd first met him. She wasn't sure when it had become irritating.

'Did you sleep?' he asked, swinging his feet to the ground.

'A bit. What about you?'

'On and off.' He got to his feet and stretched. 'I'll head out and get some milk so we can have a decent cup of coffee, or would you like to go out for breakfast?'

Sarah shook her head. 'Get some bread while you're out, will you?'

'They do nice croissants; I'll get a couple.'

Yes, because that would make everything okay. 'That'd be nice.'

She waited till he'd gone before switching on the kettle. Black coffee was better than nothing. Certainly better than her first choice – a glass of wine. She might have had one if she wasn't afraid Nick's mother would appear. Imagining her sour face creased in disgust to see Sarah hitting the bottle at eight in the morning was enough to make her snort with amusement. It might almost be worth it.

The kettle coming to the boil made the decision for her. She made coffee and leaned against the counter with the mug cupped in her hand. The day stretched ahead of her, empty, useless.

Later, she'd ring the clinic and tell them she'd be back to work on Monday. If she could bury herself in the work she loved, she might just survive. They might be horrified that she'd want to return, but what did they expect from her? That she'd put the rest of her life on hold because someone took Kaya? To stay sane, she needed something in her life. After all, she was no longer a mother; soon, if she had her way, she'd no longer be a wife. All she had was being a doctor.

Her eyes filled and a lump lodged in her throat. Coffee wasn't helping. Perhaps she should have gone with her first choice and had a glass of wine. Or maybe a dollop of brandy in the coffee. She was still contemplating that decision when the doorbell rang.

Nick! She slammed the mug down, then crossed to the intercom. 'I suppose at least you were quick,' she said.

'Sorry?'

A female voice. Not Nick having forgotten his keys yet again. 'Who is this?'

'It's PC O'Farrell, Devon and Cornwall police, with DS Kate Lyn from the Metropolitan police. May we come in, Mrs Westfield?'

Sarah wasn't surprised to have police officers on her doorstep, but she was astonished to find *that* woman there. She thought she'd left her behind in Devon. The officer had never said anything overtly judgemental, of course, she was too clever, too professional for that, but it was there in her tight expression, the sharp eyes that pinned Sarah in place like a particularly interesting bug.

The thought that they might be coming with good news didn't cross her mind. That event would be heralded by the arrival of more senior officers than a mere police constable and detective sergeant. They were there to liaise with her, that was all. To keep her in the loop. To be seen to be doing the right thing. To be dotting every fucking i and crossing every bloody t.

'Mrs Westfield?'

Where the hell was Nick? Fucking typical that he wasn't there when she needed him. Her anger was unfair. He'd only been gone about ten minutes and the shop he was heading for was at least a fifteen-minute walk away. She could tell them to go away and come back later. What the hell were they doing knocking on her door at – she checked her watch – eight thirty in the morning? Ridiculous.

'Mrs Westfield, are you there?'

'Yes, sorry, come on up, fourth floor.' She pressed the buzzer to release the front door. There was no point in putting it off. She'd see them, hear their usual, and repetitive, *we're following every lead* then tell them to run along and leave her be.

She opened the apartment door and waited for the lift to arrive, then stood back to allow them to enter. It was tempting to speak to them in the small hallway. Tempting but foolish and unfair. They were doing their best. 'If you'd like to go into the living room,' she said pointing to one of the open doors. 'Nick isn't here, I'm afraid.' She didn't explain where he was. 'I'm assuming you've no new information about Kaya.'

'I'm afraid not,' PC O'Farrell said. 'This is really just a courtesy call to introduce you to DS Lyn who will be your police liaison here in London. I'm here to make sure the transition is seamless.'

'You sound like a civil servant,' Sarah said. 'Please take a seat. Can I get you some coffee or tea?'

'No, thank you,' the two officers spoke in unison. Like a comedy act. They did, however, take a seat.

'I've gone through your notes with DS Lyn,' O'Farrell said. 'She'll be your point of contact from now on, unless you return to Devon.'

'I doubt we will,' Sarah said, taking the small, leather tub chair opposite. 'It's unlikely whoever took Kaya is going to hang around there, isn't it?' She wasn't surprised when neither officer replied. 'Have there been any new leads or are the police still floundering in the dark?' It was almost amusing to watch the interplay between the officers as each wondered who best to reply. Sarah would have guessed it would be O'Farrell and gave herself a mental tap on the back when that officer spoke.

'There are still calls coming through from concerned members of the public that we're following up, as are police forces throughout the country. All ports of departure from the country are also being monitored. We are still hopeful of finding your daughter.'

Sarah noticed the absence of the pertinent word, *alive*. She wasn't sure the officer was even aware of it herself. 'Kaya was only three weeks old. A little scrap. She'd have been easy to hide. Wait till she was asleep, drop her into a large holdall. She could be anywhere. Any country. It's long past, what d'you call it...' She frowned, trying to remember the term she'd heard on a crime show she'd watched aeons ago. 'The golden hour or something?'

It was O'Farrell who spoke again and it was obvious she was choosing her words carefully. 'The first twenty-four hours are critical in any investigation, that's true, but that doesn't mean we give up hope or that we don't have success in solving cases in the days and weeks that follow.'

'That's a pretty photo of you and your daughter,' DS Lyn said, pointing to a framed image on a shelving unit in an alcove. If her aim had been to reduce the tension in the room, she should have stopped at that. Instead, she looked around the room, then back to Sarah with a cold light in her eye. 'There's nothing else to indicate a child has ever lived here. You've a very tidy home.'

It wasn't a compliment. Sarah wanted to jump to her feet, wave to the exit with an outstretched hand and pointed finger in a melodramatic Victorian style and tell them to leave. She could have crossed to the cupboard beneath the shelving unit and pulled out the things she'd shoved in the day before. Proof that Kaya had lived there. She could have taken them into the spare bedroom, showed them all the toys and clothes, the flat-pack crib waiting to be assembled. Or have taken them into her bedroom, pointed to the Moses basket beside their bed where it had been since they'd taken Kaya home from hospital. The empty Moses basket that was awaiting their daughter's return.

She could have jumped to her feet and clawed their mean, judgemental eyes out.

O'Farrell had never taken to her. Sarah knew that. She'd seen the quickly hidden appalled expression when Sarah had admitted handing

Kaya over to a stranger. It seemed her dislike had rubbed onto DS Lyn, who was looking at her in the same judgemental way.

A sudden, horrifying thought crossed her mind. Maybe it was more than that. Perhaps they thought there was something more to the story. That she had, in fact, had a hand in Kaya's disappearance. There'd been a crime series on the TV a couple of years before where a child had disappeared. It turned out in the end that the child had died and the parents were trying to cover it up. Could they be thinking that the same thing had happened here?

She frowned, trying to remember if other customers of the pub had mentioned seeing Kaya. They'd have seen the infant carrier, but had they seen the baby inside? Kaya had cried, and she did remember people turning to look, but had they actually seen her? It would have been easy to have used a recording on her mobile. In the noisy, jam-packed pub, it would have fooled people.

Sarah wanted to jokingly ask if she was under suspicion but she was afraid to hear the answer.

26

It had worked out exactly as we'd planned. Ridiculously easy, in fact. I looked across the room to where Meg sat with the baby in her arms and felt happier than I'd ever been in my life. Ever. This was exactly what I'd always wanted.

'You're sure about the name?' I asked, crossing to sit beside them. Her emphatic nod sent a strand of her hair falling over her eyes. I reached a hand over and swept it back. 'Well, if you're sure, I'm happy.'

'It'd be bad luck to change her name,' she insisted, leaning forward to plant a kiss on the baby's head. 'Anyway, I think Kaya suits her, don't you?'

I worried about it being so unusual that it would stand out, that someone might connect it to the missing baby, but Meg was happy with it, and that's what counted.

She turned to look at me, shooting me a sweet smile. 'I'm still in awe of it all, having such a beautiful little girl of our own.'

Sliding an arm around her shoulder, I pulled her a little closer. 'I've two beautiful girls of my own, so I'm twice as lucky.'

I had everything I'd ever wanted.

And it had all come so easily in the end.

Too easy?

That's what I was afraid of. That was the thought giving me sleepless nights.

What if it was all too easy – would it turn out to be a case of easy come, easy go? Would the happiness I'd waited for so long to experience vanish as quickly as it had come?

Puff!

I kissed Meg's cheek and brushed my free hand over our child's head.

Our child.

Nothing, nobody was going to change that now.

27

Zoé-Lee and DS Lyn left the Westfields' apartment block and walked the short distance to where Lyn's car was parked.

'Fancy stopping for a coffee?' Lyn asked, nodding to a café across the street. 'I missed breakfast and the coffee in the station is pretty dire.'

'Sounds like a plan.'

A few minutes later, they were sitting at a table, Lyn with a breakfast bun clamped between her hands, Zoé-Lee with the chocolate muffin she couldn't resist. She broke a piece off, popped it into her mouth and chewed slowly, enjoying the rush of sweetness. 'So what'd you think of Sarah?'

Lyn had taken a bite of her breakfast bun and she hurried to catch the runny egg that was threatening to drip onto her skirt. 'I think there's something a bit off with her, and that scarily tidy apartment didn't look like a place that would welcome a baby.' She put the bun down, took the top half off, then pulled the fat from the bacon, before reassembling and picking it up again. She regarded it with pleasure before sinking her teeth into it.

'None of the customers in the pub got a clear look at the baby, you know,' Zoé-Lee said, breaking another, bigger piece from her muffin.

'Although a couple of people who were sitting nearby said they thought they'd heard a baby cry.'

'The place was jammers, wasn't it? And I'm imagining noisy too.' Lyn polished off the bun and licked her fingers. 'That was just what I needed.' She picked up her coffee. 'So what're you thinking? That the Westfields planned it all? In that case, if those two women had nothing to do with it, why didn't they make themselves known, eh?'

Zoé-Lee shrugged. 'They don't want to get involved with the police for some reason, or they're off the grid and haven't seen any of the appeals.'

Lyn nodded. 'There was a TV series a few years back with that Jenna Coleman in it. It was called the...' She clicked her fingers as she tried to remember the name. '*The Cry*, that's what it was called. Did you see it?'

Zoé-Lee had. She'd thought it was terribly far-fetched. 'The Jenna Coleman character had post-natal depression and had killed the baby by accident, wasn't that the way it went?'

'Yea, so her husband helped her to cover it up by saying the baby had been kidnapped.' She put her coffee down and leaned forward, her expression bright with excitement. 'Maybe that's why Mrs Westfield comes across as being a bit cold and distant, a bit on edge. Maybe *she* has post-natal depression. The baby died somehow, and they took their cue from that series.'

Zoé-Lee couldn't help but smile at her enthusiasm for the far-fetched idea.

'You're laughing at me, but I know you've been considering if she's guilty yourself.'

'We're always told to keep our options open,' she said pedantically, then laughed and raised her hands in surrender. 'Okay, I'll admit, I've been trying to think of a way they could have done it. My DI, Andrew Maxwell, thinks I have it in for her because she handed over the baby to have a quiet dinner.'

'It was an odd thing to do. But there's the rucksack the couple left behind to account for.'

Zoé-Lee sipped her cappuccino, then wiped the froth from her lips with the back of her hand. 'The Westfields could have brought it with them. It could have been stuffed into that baby carrier thing, squashed down, then fluffed up to make it look bigger. They could even have brought the newspaper separately, rolled it up and stuffed it into the rucksack while they were sitting in the pub.'

'You have given this a lot of thought, haven't you?'

'I have a daughter, Raven; she's fourteen months. I keep imagining what it would be like to lose her. How devastated I'd be.' She sighed loudly. 'Sarah Westfield is so calm, so detached. There's something off about her.'

'Maybe she's simply putting on a brave face? Like I bet you did when you had to leave your daughter behind to come to London for a few days.'

Zoé-Lee opened her mouth to agree, then shut it on the lie. She hadn't been upset leaving Raven; she'd been excited about the trip to London and working with the Met. Anyway, there had been no reason to be upset; Raven was with Tom. Safe and well-cared for. 'It's not the same thing,' she said dismissively. The coffee was drained in a mouthful. 'We'd better go. You never know, maybe we'll get back to the station and they'll tell us they've found Kaya.'

28

Sarah paced the floor for several minutes following the visit by the two police officers. 'Pair of bitches,' she muttered. Where was the sympathy for the victims, eh? The thought that she might be under suspicion came to her again. Surely not? It was clear cut, wasn't it? Those two women. Their empty rucksack. Clear as mud, someone had set out to take Kaya.

There was no sign of Nick. What was keeping him? She could have done with his particular brand of reassurance, even if it did entail getting too up-close and personal for her liking. Perhaps he was right, and sex would put everything out of her mind. The thought made her shiver. It was over between them; she just needed to get around to telling him.

The thought that the police were suspecting her – them – of a hand in Kaya's disappearance worried her. She had to do something.

When another thirty minutes passed without any sign of Nick's return, she bit down her frustration, pulled on her jacket, grabbed her keys, and headed out. She'd get the damn milk herself.

There was a small convenience store only a few minutes away. Nick preferred the other, not because it was any better, but because he and the manager chatted about cricket, which bored Sarah to bits.

The convenience store was as usual, very busy. It was a small business; there was little room for pushchairs of any sort. If a parent was alone, they'd no choice but to try to negotiate the narrow aisles. Most tried to leave it outside accompanied by an older child.

That morning, there were two pushchairs parked end to end. There was no sign of the respective mothers, but three older children, standing nearby with their head buried in their phones, were obviously in loco parentis.

Sarah approached the first pushchair. An older baby, perhaps four months old. Moving to the second, she reached down and brushed a hand along the cheek of the sleeping baby inside. A girl-child, only a few weeks old. Sarah glanced around at the three children. They were oblivious to her presence. Giving little thought to what she was doing, she pulled back the light blanket that covered the child, gasping to see the large K on the front of the child's sleepsuit. It was a sign. She picked the baby up, turned so it was hidden by her body and walked swiftly away.

When she pushed open the door of their apartment, she could hear the hum of the shower. Nick was home. He liked to spend a long time in the shower when he could. She guessed she had at least an hour before he came out.

An hour. It was probably enough. She laid the baby on the sofa, tucking cushions around her to keep her safe while she went to the spare room for the carrycot. 'There you go,' she said, settling the baby into it a moment later. 'Look at you, back where you belong!' She sat on the sofa, staring down at the sleeping child. When she stirred, little fists jerking, Sarah leapt to her feet and hurried to the kitchen.

There was formula, she needed to check it was in date. It was. Sarah smiled in relief, then hummed as she made up a bottle. She was feeding the baby when the door opened and Nick came through. He was rubbing a towel over his damp hair so didn't notice at first. When he did, he staggered backwards, the towel dropping to the floor, the look of disbelief on his face changing to one of absolute horror. 'How... who...?'

'It's Kaya, she's back,' Sarah said with a happy smile.

Nick sat on the sofa beside her, reaching out to push the bib Sarah was using out of the way to see the child's face. 'She's beautiful,' he said. 'But this isn't our baby, Sarah, you know it isn't. Where did you get her?' He sat back and ran a hand over his face, dragging his skin down. 'You have to tell me,' he said, his voice gentle. 'It can't be that long ago. I can try to make things right, explain to the mother. People will understand.'

'What's to explain? Someone took Kaya, now we've got her back.' Sarah removed the teat from the baby's mouth then leaned her over her hand and rubbed her back. 'She was hungry, but she'd been well taken care of. A mother knows these things.'

Nick got to his feet, walked away, then returned to kneel on the floor beside her. 'This baby's mother is going to be frantic, Sarah; remember how you felt when our baby was taken? You wouldn't want to put another mother through that, would you?'

Sarah smiled at him. 'I don't know what you're talking about, Nick. Honestly, you should be pleased Kaya is home instead of making a fuss about nothing and worrying about strangers. Now, if you got the milk, I wouldn't mind a decent cup of coffee.' She settled the child back into the crook of her arm and proceeded to give her the rest of the bottle.

She could hear him behind her, could almost hear his brain trying to work out the best thing to do. He'd eventually realise he'd no choice. It took longer than she expected. The bottle was finished and the baby back in the cot sleeping peacefully before he returned with a tray laden with coffee and two packets of biscuits. 'I bought your favourite,' he said, placing the tray on a table and dragging it within reach. 'Why don't you relax, have your coffee and a few biscuits. I need to make a phone call, okay?'

Of course he did. He was doing exactly what she'd expected him to do, just a little slower than she'd predicted. The poor mother would be frantic. Hopefully, it would teach her not to leave the poor baby with children too young to bear that responsibility. She snorted – it was definitely a case of the pot calling the kettle black.

She tore open the packet of biscuits and knocked a few onto the tray before picking up the mug of coffee. She dunked one of the biscuits as she heard the murmur of Nick's voice. So serious. Poor Nick, he didn't have a clue. The biscuit, immersed in the coffee for too long, collapsed, its bottom half floating on the surface. She used a spoon to fish it out and eat it, then dunked the next more carefully. Always a good idea to learn from mistakes.

'The coffee okay?' Nick asked, returning to take the seat beside her.

She was amused. It was instant coffee, what was there to say about it? Bless, he was trying. She'd miss him a little when they split up, not enough to reconsider, but enough to cause her a twinge. A very little one. 'It's fine,' she said, taking a sip as if to prove it. 'And thanks for the biscuits. You were right, they are my favourite.'

He looked ridiculously pleased. A good man, he would make some woman very happy some day. She was truly sorry it wasn't her. It would have made life easier, but you couldn't make yourself love someone. She'd tried, hadn't she? And it hadn't worked.

Nick shuffled closer. He reached for her hand, took it in his and held it tight. 'That baby isn't Kaya, Sarah. I think you know that, don't you?'

'You're being silly.' She tried to pull her hand away. 'Of course that's Kaya. She's wearing that sleepsuit we bought her with that appliquéd K on the front of it. Remember the first time she wore it? It was far too big for her and we laughed and said she'd grow into it. And look, she has.'

Nick released her hand and got to his feet. He disappeared from the room, returning a few minutes later with something in his hand. She knew what it was before he laid it on her lap. 'This is the one you bought, Sarah. We put it away for when Kaya was bigger, and when she's back with us, we'll dress her in it, look back on these days and realise how lucky we are. But, darling, this baby isn't ours.'

The buzz of the doorbell prevented Sarah from answering. Nick rose to cross to the intercom. He pressed the buzzer to release the main door without asking who it was, then left to open the apartment door.

Sarah heard him speaking to someone. Low, urgent voices. Two people, maybe more. She hoped the mother wasn't there, unsure if she could face her anguish, or the look of relief when she saw her baby was safe.

'She's in here,' she heard Nick say. As if they lived in a bloody mansion rather than a small apartment.

She supposed she should have expected the same two officers who'd visited only hours before, but stupidly she hadn't and was taken aback when they walked into the room. She hid her face, bending down to look into the cot where the baby was sleeping soundly. A beautiful baby. Of course she knew it wasn't Kaya. Did Nick really think she'd get confused, that she wouldn't know her own baby as soon as she saw her pink, chubby cheeks?

'Mrs Westfield, it's PC O'Farrell and DS Lyn again. We were here earlier.'

Did they think she was stupid? That she wouldn't remember an event that occurred a mere few hours before. Or did they, as she hoped, think she was having some kind of breakdown?

'You couldn't find Kaya, so I looked for her myself.' The hint of triumph in her voice was clear for all to hear. She felt a weight settle onto the sofa beside her. Only then did she turn to meet the eyes of the police officer, pleased to see there was more sympathy in her eyes than there had been that morning. 'Isn't she beautiful?'

'She is,' PC O'Farrell agreed.

'She's back where she belongs.' Behind her, she heard Nick speaking softly to the other officer. The words weren't clear, but the anguish in his voice was. She felt a little guilty for this latest trick, but it wasn't as if she'd planned it, the idea coming to her in a flash when she'd seen the baby outside the shop. And it had worked. The light of suspicion in both officers' eyes had melted away. Now all she could see was the sympathy that was her due.

'Mrs Westfield... Sarah... that baby is beautiful but her name is Kayden, not Kaya. Nick told us about the sleepsuit you bought for your daughter, and I can see how you got confused. You got it on Etsy, didn't you?'

It seemed churlish not to reply when she was being so nice. 'Yes, I did.'

'So did Kayden's mum. She loves Kayden very much and is waiting downstairs in our car. Is it okay if I take Kayden to her?'

O'Farrell was good, Sarah had to give her that. Her repetition of the baby's name was designed to try to break through her belief it was Kaya. Had she been in any doubt, it might have given her pause for thought.

But she wasn't, and there was no need to prolong the act. 'I was so sure,' she said, shaking her head, trembling her lower lip, forcing a tear. 'When I saw her, that K, I was certain I'd found Kaya.' She twisted around and buried her face in a cushion. 'Tell the mother I'm sorry, so very sorry.'

She stayed as she was, listening to O'Farrell gently cooing as she lifted the baby from the cot, conversations between the officers and Nick, footsteps, doors opening and closing. All of it floated around her as she pressed into the sofa, trying not to think of what she'd done.

'Hey.' Nick's arm crept over her back and settled on her shoulder. She'd wanted the officers' sympathy; she didn't need his but accepted it from necessity. 'How about a hot cup of coffee and more of those biscuits you love, eh?'

Coffee and biscuits. The answer to every problem the world round. A friend had told her she drank far too much of the stuff. She did but this wasn't a time to stop. 'That'd be good.' Her voice was muffled by the cushion. She pushed upward and wiped her eyes with the back of her hand. 'That sounds good, Nick, thank you.'

She shut her eyes as he pottered about in the kitchen. It wasn't until he'd returned and they were sat like Tweedledum and Tweedledee that she asked the question that was itching the inside of her skull. 'Are they going to arrest me?'

Nick chewed and swallowed the biscuit he'd shoved whole into his mouth before answering. 'The police explained the circumstances to the child's mother. She asked that you get some help to deal with this terrible ordeal. I told the officers to tell her that we'd both go to someone. In fact,' he reached into his breast pocket and took out a business card, 'they gave me the contact details for a counsellor. I thought I'd give them a ring later.' He slipped the card back into his pocket. 'Whatever it takes to help you through this, Sarah.'

You? What happened to the 'we'? She'd liked to have asked, but then he'd have hurriedly backtracked and said that of course he'd meant 'we'. She wouldn't have believed him so there was no point in beginning that particular conversation.

This whole fiasco had achieved what she'd wanted to achieve – the officers no longer regarded her with suspicion.

That could only be a good thing.

29

Zoé-Lee knew they'd been very lucky. The manager of the convenience store had immediately checked the CCTV when the baby was reported missing. Thanks to the newspaper reports of Kaya's abduction accompanied by photographs of the grieving parents, he recognised the culprit straight away. It wasn't hard; Sarah Westfield had made no effort to disguise herself. He'd immediately contacted the station, the call transferred to the desk where Zoé-Lee and DS Lyn were trawling through the reports from all the people they'd contacted in the search for Kaya.

They were about to leave when the call came through from Nick Westfield.

They were even luckier that Kayden's mother, Daniella Curry, distraught and desperate to have her child returned, managed to listen to the extenuating circumstances behind the kidnap. 'Oh, the poor woman!' she'd said with quick sympathy.

'It's been over two weeks,' DS Lyn said. 'She's been keeping herself together up to now, but it looks as if it's all become too much for her.'

'God, yes, Kayden is only missing for an hour and I'm chewing my nails. You don't need to press charges, do you? If Kayden is returned to me safe, I don't see there's anything to gain by it. She needs to get help, though; she might do it again and the next mother mightn't be so nice about it.'

Mrs Curry agreed to stay in the car while the officers entered the apartment block, but when they returned a little over ten minutes later, with Kayden comfortably asleep in Zoé-Lee's arms, she was pacing up and down the pavement. She turned with a shriek when she saw them, racing towards them with her hands against her mouth as if afraid more screams would erupt to wake the child.

'Oh, my darling,' she said, taking the baby from Zoé-Lee. She pressed her lips to the baby's head then met the officer's eyes with a worried frown. 'Is she okay?'

Guessing she meant the woman they'd left sitting in the apartment, Zoé-Lee nodded, then raised her hand to touch the appliquéd K on the front of the child's sleepsuit. 'It was this that triggered everything. It seems she'd bought one exactly like it. When she saw your baby wearing it, I think she had a bit of a breakdown and thought she was Kaya.'

'Poor woman,' Daniella said, clutching her baby tighter. 'I hope you find her child.'

'We will,' Zoé-Lee said, with far more conviction than she felt. 'Right, let's get you home.'

* * *

Back at the station, the two officers sat at Kate Lyn's desk and mulled over the events of the morning. 'It throws a different light on the mother, doesn't it?' Kate said, tapping a pen on the scarred surface of the desk. 'Looks like I was right, and she'd been putting on a brave face. That façade was bound to crack after a while. All it needed was a trigger, and the K on the baby's sleepsuit was it.' She nodded as if, in her head, it was all sorted.

Zoé-Lee wasn't so sure. She couldn't rid herself of the notion that Sarah Westfield was, somehow, trying to pull the wool over their eyes. 'You don't think it's all a bit...' she shrugged, 'neat or something?'

'Neat? I don't follow.'

She smoothed a hand over her head. A thin strand of hair had escaped; she twirled it around her fingers for a few seconds then tucked it behind her ear. Perhaps she was being unreasonable. From the beginning, she'd judged Sarah harshly, condemned her for being a bad mother. Wasn't there a little bit of Zoé-Lee that was relieved to see a mother worse than she was? Because despite Tom being a wonderful father, Zoé-Lee struggled with guilt for leaving Raven every day. No, that wasn't quite right. It wasn't for leaving her, as such, but guilt for *wanting* to leave her to continue her career as a police officer. And no matter how she tried to convince herself that everything was working out for the best, she struggled with the feeling that she was failing at motherhood. Was her judgement of Sarah merely to make herself feel better? It was an unedifying thought.

'Oh don't mind me,' she said to DS Lyn. 'I'm just not keen on little packages tied up with bows.' This elicited a strange look from her Met colleague. 'You know,' she tried again, 'when things are too neat and tidy. Too convenient.'

'It wasn't very convenient for Mrs Curry.'

Zoé-Lee shook her head. Perhaps Sarah Westfield wasn't a bad mother, but there was still something off about her. It was impossible to explain a gut feeling. 'No, it wasn't. Mrs Curry is a nice lady, we were lucky she didn't create more of a fuss, but that isn't what I mean.' The tap tap tap of DS Lyn's pen was like a metronome; Zoé-Lee tried to tune into it and slow her thoughts down so they'd make sense. 'It's like, you know, first thing this morning, we were both suspicious of her, weren't we?'

'Yes,' Lyn agreed. 'Although you more than I. If you remember, I suggested she was putting on a brave face.'

What did she want? A pat on her bloody back? Zoé-Lee rolled her shoulders and forced herself to relax. There was no point in taking out her irritation on Lyn, who might very well be right. After all, everyone dealt with grief, loss, and other traumatic events in different ways.

'Let's read through some more of the statements before we call it a day,' she said, determinedly focusing on what they could do rather than on something as nebulous as her gut. It kept niggling her though, and twenty minutes later, she sat back. 'It's just...'

Lyn waited patiently.

'...didn't you get the feeling this morning, during our first meeting with her, that she was weighing us up?'

'No harm in that, we were doing the same, after all,' Lyn said reasonably.

'Yes.' Zoé-Lee was frustrated by her inability to translate her gut feeling into English. 'It's just...' she started again then raised her hands in surrender. 'I don't know. Something.'

Lyn frowned. 'You're thinking that she noticed we were suspicious and pulled the baby kidnap to get us on her side, is that it?'

'Exactly!' Zoé-Lee laughed and punched Lyn's arm. 'And it worked, didn't it? We're more sympathetic than we were earlier, aren't we? Before, we were wondering if she'd something to do with Kaya going missing; after, we were wondering if she'd snapped under the strain of it all.' She stood and paced the floor, one hand gripping the other. 'It was probably opportunistic rather than premeditated. Mrs Curry's young sister says she'd only taken her eyes off the buggy for a minute, but she was on her phone; it was likely to have been several. Along comes Sarah, peeps into the buggy, sees the baby wearing a sleepsuit with a K on it, and I bet it came to her right at that moment. Take the baby, make everyone think she's falling apart so they'll be more sympathetic—'

'And not suspicious.'

'And not suspicious,' Zoé-Lee agreed.

Lyn rocked her head side to side in a classic *I'm not sure* motion. 'It seems a little far-fetched though, doesn't it? We're supposed to be dealing with facts. Motive. And there isn't any.' She tapped the side of the computer screen. 'Every report indicates the Westfields were the perfect parents. She attended every pre-natal meeting, even gave up drinking during the pregnancy. It really all points to her having been a good mother. Unlike that TV programme we were talking about, if Kaya had died in some sort of accident, they'd have called an ambulance, or taken the child to hospital themselves. There was no reason for them to resort to such crazy subterfuge.'

There wasn't. And Lyn was correct. Every single report stated that Sarah and Nick Westfield were the ideal parents. 'Maybe I've been reading too many psychological thrillers,' she said with a forced chuckle. 'I let my imagination run away with me sometimes.' She pulled her chair closer to the desk. 'Come on, let's get this lot done. We should finish by tomorrow, then I can head home in the afternoon.' She couldn't see the point in going through every report with her Met counterpart, but she did what she was told even if it often didn't make sense.

Lyn suggested they go out for dinner when they'd finished. 'I know a good Italian.'

It had been a long day. A pizza and a glass or two of wine would be a good ending. 'You're on,' she said. Pointing towards the exit, she added, 'Give me a sec to ring Tom and Raven and I'm yours.' A minute later, she was on a WhatsApp video call, waving madly and making faces at her daughter who kindly gave a smile in response. 'You missing me?'

Like her, Tom watched far too many crime thrillers. 'Isn't that regarded as a leading question?' he asked, holding the phone so both he and Raven were in shot, jiggling the child on his knee.

'Is that a yes or a no?'

'Of course I miss you. We miss you. The house is way too quiet without your squawking.'

'Cheek!' She kissed her finger and put it on the screen, first on his face, then on Raven's.

'We're having to share one kiss.' He jiggled Raven harder. 'See that, she's rationing them now.'

'Go away, you lunatic,' she said. 'I should be home tomorrow afternoon, okay? Try to behave till then.'

'Love you,' he said.

'And crazy as you are, I love you too.'

'They're surviving without me,' she said to Lyn as they walked from the station. 'Why doesn't that please me more than it does?'

Lyn linked a hand through her arm. 'Cos we're contrary creatures. We're delighted that they're coping without us, but would prefer if they didn't cope quite so well.'

'That's the nail hit firmly on the head.'

They chatted about their respective partners and children for the rest of the evening. By the time she got back to her small hotel room,

Zoé-Lee was in a better frame of mind. Tomorrow, she'd finish what needed to be done here, then go home and Sarah Westfield could be Kate Lyn's problem from then on.

Home to Tom and Raven. Shouldn't Zoé-Lee be feeling more excited than she was, not swallowing a lump of regret that she was going to be missing out on what happened in London?

Did it make her a bad mother that she didn't want to rush home to her daughter?

She was a good police officer; she wanted to continue to be one. Couldn't she be a good mother too? Did it have to be one or the other?

That little voice in her head popped up. *If you had to choose – which would it be?*

30

Nick was hovering around Sarah, offering her fresh cups of coffee as soon as she'd drained the last drop of the previous one he'd made, one she'd only accepted to stop him staring at her as if expecting her to explode if he took his eyes away.

'Are you sure I shouldn't ring someone?' he asked, sitting beside her and taking her hand. 'Jade, maybe?'

'No,' she said, too bluntly. She gave him an apologetic smile. 'Sorry, I know you're trying to help, but honestly, all I need is some rest.' She felt his fingers tighten, his thumb brushing over the back of her hand. It took every inch of her resolve not to pull it away and scream at him to leave her alone.

It was the apartment. The walls were closing in on her. 'Maybe in a bit, we could go out for something to eat. An early dinner somewhere nice. It might encourage our appetites.' She used the opportunity to pull her hand away to pat her stomach. 'I've lost weight, and you're fading away, Nick. Maybe we could walk to that pub you like, The Three Johns, and have a pizza, what d'you think?'

'I think that's a great idea.' He reached for her hand again, this time taking it in both of his. 'I love you so much, so whatever makes you happy, that's good for me. You know I'd do anything for you, Sarah.' He brought her hand to his lips and kissed it. 'Why don't you lie down for a few hours first, try to get some sleep.'

Because that was going to make her world reset? 'I'll be fine here, honestly; I'll switch on the TV and maybe I'll nod off for a bit.'

She shut her eyes, hoping he'd take the hint and leave her be. His solicitous hovering was driving her crazy. If she wasn't careful, she'd spew out exactly what she was thinking, and that would be a disaster.

When he did move away, tiptoeing across the floor and out into the hall, she let herself relax, just a little. Despite everything, tiredness hit her, her eyelids became too heavy to open, she kept them shut and was drifting, drifting, drifting...

It was the sound of Nick's voice that dragged her back before she had as much as one wink of sleep. Who the hell was he ringing? An awful thought made her wake completely, if he was ringing his mother, if she appeared, Sarah wasn't sure she could control herself. She pressed a hand to her forehead. More and more these days, she felt herself falling apart.

She rested her head back and shut her eyes. If his blasted mother arrived, Sarah would simply lock herself into the bedroom till she was gone.

But it wasn't Nick's mother who arrived twenty minutes later, but Jade.

'Nick told me what happened,' she said, striding across the room, dropping to her knees, and folding Sarah into a tight hug. 'He thought you might like to talk about it so asked if I was free.' She released Sarah and sat back on her haunches. 'You look like shit, my friend.'

'And I feel exactly the same.' Sarah patted the sofa beside her. 'You'll give yourself dead legs if you stay like that.'

Jade got to her feet and sat beside Sarah, nudging her gently with her elbow. 'It must have been distressing, seeing a baby so like Kaya.'

'She was wearing the sleepsuit with the appliquéd K; remember I showed it to you?'

'Yes, I remember. When Kaya is home, she'll look so gorgeous in it.' Jade put a hand on Sarah's knee. 'You need to talk to someone. A professional. Before you go any further down that rabbit hole.'

'Kaya is missing, but I know she's okay. It's Nick. He hovers around me, pawing me, telling me how much he loves me. It's driving me crazy. I'm not sure a professional would be able to help with that.'

'I suppose he's trying to be there for you in the only way he knows.'

'Well, I wish he wouldn't!' Sarah turned to meet her friend's eyes. 'You were right, I can admit it now. It was rebound. Thinking I was in love with Nick. I don't love him; I'm not sure I even like him very much. One thing I do know is I want out.' It was a relief to finally say it, but she wasn't surprised to see a look of horror in Jade's eyes, nor was she surprised at her response.

'You can't leave him now. He's devastated about Kaya. Until she's found, you have to stay with him. You owe him that much.'

Sarah did. She reminded herself that he was a good man. That he didn't deserve her disloyalty. 'I know I do, but I'm not sure I can stay. I know I don't want to.'

Jade jumped to her feet, walked across the room to the window and stared out. Sarah watched her, wondering what she was thinking. Close as they were, her friend's cognitive processes were often... elusive or even completely out-there. Sarah considered herself a black or white character; Jade on the other hand, had always been forty shades of grey.

It was comforting to have her there, though. Sarah relaxed against the cushions behind and waited for her to speak, knowing whatever she said was bound to be sensible, if controversial.

She wasn't expecting Jade to turn around with an expression that Sarah had never seen before on her face and found hard to identify. Anger? Disappointment?

'You can say what you think.' Sarah tried a smile. 'You always do!' Her smile wasn't returned. Nor did Jade return to sit beside her.

Instead, she stayed by the window. The living room was west facing, the early-afternoon sun slanting into the room. A beam, breaking through the light cloud cover, illuminated the room and threw shade onto Jade's face. There was a darker side to her friend that showed itself now and then, but not usually to Sarah. She could see it there now, a hardness in her eyes, a tightness in her lips. She waited for her to speak and when the silence continued, whispered a puzzled, 'Jade?'

'You didn't want your daughter; now you don't want your husband.' Jade folded her arms across her chest. If her expression wasn't readable, her stance was making a clear statement – rigid and unbending. 'You are an incredibly self-centred woman who only cares for what you want, without any thought for the needs and wants of anyone else.' Unfolding her arms, she shoved her hands into the pockets of her jeans. 'You should be ashamed of yourself, but I doubt you have enough self-realisation, so will forever continue in your little world where only what you want matters. I suppose, as usual, you'll be looking for someone to sort this mess out for you. And that role, as usual, will fall to me, so I suppose I'll have to get rid of him for you.'

Without another glance in Sarah's direction, she walked, stiff-legged and jerky, from the room, the door slamming behind her to echo in the silence she left behind.

Sarah's mouth had fallen open in shock, remaining agape until a string of drool ran down her chin. She shut it with a snap and lifted a trembling hand to wipe away her shame. A cold numbness slipped over her despite the sunbeam that seemed to have pinned her to the chair. Jade was right. Of course she was. Sarah was a selfish, self-centred woman who only thought of herself. But she was so used to spilling her heart to her friend, so used to being listened to, and for Jade to offer advice that was almost always – or at least sometimes – taken, that this decimating analysis of her character was the more soul-destroying.

Selfish, self-centred, and now terribly alone.

31

I had to make sure my luck didn't run out. That it wasn't as I feared, too easy come, easy go.

It's impossible to describe the pleasure I got from seeing the woman I loved so desperately be so completely happy. The light had returned to her eyes, the bounce to her step, the glow to her skin. Her happiness in turn made my heart race, my eyes shine.

All was most definitely right in our world. And I had every intention of keeping it that way.

It was only a few days after Kaya came into our lives that the first niggles of worry developed, tendrils spreading, tightening, beginning to sting. And the more Meg's happiness shone, the tighter they got, until I wasn't sure I could bear it.

I knew the problem. As far as our world was concerned, Kaya was ours. I'd been promised all the necessary paperwork to prove it.

They'd promised. Of course, they had. But what if they changed their mind?

It would destroy Meg, and by association, me.

I couldn't let that happen. I had to make absolutely sure my happiness would last.

I'd already done so much; one more step and it would be finished.

32

Having resolved to put Sarah Westfield firmly out of her head, Zoé-Lee slept soundly all night. She woke with a yawn at six thirty and rolled over to grab her mobile from the bedside table, smiling as she checked the photographs Tom had uploaded of Raven having her dinner. As usual, she was wearing a good proportion of the food. He hadn't taken a photograph of himself, but she guessed he probably was too. She *was* looking forward to getting home to them both that evening. A good sleep had allowed her to rethink things. She didn't have to choose between being a good mother or a good police officer. It was possible to be both. She didn't have to wear her knickers over her uniform to be Superwoman.

After a good breakfast, she went to the station where she found DS Lyn already at her desk. 'Morning, early bird.'

Lyn smiled. 'Morning. You sleep okay?'

'I did. You can't beat a Premier Inn bed for comfort, plus I didn't have Tom's long legs kicking me during the night.'

Lyn nodded towards the computer screen. 'I got a start on the remaining reports. Nothing stands out to me.' She tapped on the keyboard. 'There's not many left to go through, if you want to get off home early, I'd say we'll be done by mid-morning.'

Just what Zoé-Lee had hoped. Slipping off her jacket, she hung it on the back of the chair before pulling it forward. 'Right, let's get with it then, shall we?'

They would have done, and she would have managed to slip away early if she'd ignored her mobile phone, but she didn't. 'D'you mind?' she said, taking it from her pocket. 'It might be Tom.'

But when she checked the screen, it was a number she didn't recognise. 'Hello, PC O'Farrell here.'

'Hi, it's PC Perrett from Minehead. Are you free to talk?'

'Sure.' Zoé-Lee raised an eyebrow at Lyn and mouthed *police* to let her know it wasn't a personal call. 'What can I do for you?'

'It might be nothing, but I thought I'd drop it in your basket anyway because you never know.'

'Right,' Zoé-Lee said, puzzled. 'Go on.'

'Something you'd said was niggling me. I wasn't sure what, then last night I was lying awake at two, trying to get to sleep, when I had a eureka moment.' A deep breath sounded like a hiss down the phone. 'It mightn't be anything important, but it was something I read in Sarah Westfield's statement. She said they'd gone to The Post Office pub because she wanted to bring her husband and child to places where she'd gone with her parents, yes?'

'That's right. Her parents loved the place. She said she wanted to revisit old haunts with a child of her own.'

'Well, that's the thing. She can't have gone there with her parents. The Post Office has only been a pub for a few years. Five at the very most. When she was a child, it would still have been a post office; she couldn't have gone there with her parents.'

Sarah Westfield had lied. Zoé-Lee wanted to punch the air in satisfaction. She'd been right all along. She knew there was something off about the woman. 'That's very interesting, thank you.'

'Will it help?'

Would it? Zoé-Lee had no idea, but people didn't lie for no reason. She just had to figure out what that reason was.

33

It was only a little lie, but it was enough to point the gnarly finger of suspicion right back at Sarah Westfield.

'What I don't understand,' Lyn said, 'is why she'd lie about something so stupid. She could have simply said she fancied going to that pub and left it at that.'

'She wanted to give us a good reason for going into that particular pub. Don't forget, they had to pass three others to get to it.'

There was a loud creak as Lyn rocked back in her chair. 'Okay, I'm getting confused in my head now. If the Westfields were acting alone, they could have gone to any pub, yes?'

Zoé-Lee frowned. 'Yes, I suppose.'

'So why did they want to go to that pub, and why lie about it?'

'Maybe the two women were involved somehow.'

Lyn rocked again, the chair's complaints a noisy squeal that she ignored. 'So even more premeditated than we'd been thinking. The two women we've been unable to identify went to that particular pub, to take that particular baby, a baby who may have been dead or alive.' She jumped up from the chair, sending it spinning behind her. 'Let's talk to DI Bilton. If anyone can make sense out of this mess, our Josephine can.'

Zoé-Lee would have preferred to get on the phone to DI Maxwell, but that decision was out of her hands. Silently, she followed her colleague down narrow corridors to DI Bilton's office. 'Here we go,' Lyn said, rapping on the door.

The 'come in' was almost immediate and the door was opened into a small, windowless office. The woman behind the desk looked up with an enquiring gaze and a pleasant expression which Zoé-Lee wasn't expecting. Her experience with senior officers – apart from Maxwell – had led her to believe most got more unfriendly as they climbed the ladder.

DI Bilton sat back in her chair and crossed her arms as if preparing to be entertained. 'Sit, tell me what's worrying you, DS Lyn.'

'This is PC O'Farrell from Devon and Cornwall, here to give me the lowdown on the Westfields at the NCA's request.'

'Nice to meet you, PC O'Farrell. I hope we've made you comfortable here.'

'DS Lyn has been very helpful, thank you, ma'am.'

'Good. Right, assuming this isn't a social visit, what can I do for you?'

Lyn shot Zoé-Lee a glance, then nodded and started to explain the situation. It was a rambling tale, Lyn hopping backwards and forwards so that even Zoé-Lee was confused by the time she was done. She looked at the DI, expecting her face to be creased in puzzlement, but instead she nodded as if it was all crystal clear.

'If I have this straight from that rambling, hoppity-skippity monologue, you have a suspicion that the Westfields may have had a hand in the disappearance of their child, am I right?'

'PC O'Farrell had her suspicions even before we learned that Sarah Westfield lied about the pub,' Lyn said.

'Really?' Bilton turned her head to look at O'Farrell. 'Tell me why.'

Subject to such intense scrutiny, Zoé-Lee felt colour rise in her cheeks. 'It's difficult to put it into words...'

'Try.'

Okay, this was her opportunity to prove she was a good officer. She held Bilton's gaze and spoke clearly. 'In the two weeks since Kaya was abducted, Nick Westfield has been visibly distraught each time I've seen him. He's lost weight, his cheeks are hollow and his eyes red-rimmed as if he was crying every minute we weren't with him. Sarah, on the other hand, has been composed and very detached. She strikes me as a cold woman.' Zoé-Lee took a deep breath. 'There's just something not right about her.'

'Gut instinct, eh?'

'You could call it that.' She lifted her chin. 'I think she took that child from outside the convenience store to try to throw us off the scent. Confuse us. Make us look at her more sympathetically.'

'And did you?'

Zoé-Lee shook her head. 'At first I did, sure, but something seemed off about that to me too. It was all too neat and tidy. Too convenient.'

Bilton rocked her chair side to side. 'Are you sure your gut feeling isn't being coloured by your obvious dislike of the woman?'

Was Zoé-Lee that easy to read, or had she made her feelings about the woman too clear? 'Yes, I'll admit, I don't like her. Some of that is me being a bit judgemental. I have a baby, just over a year old. At no time would I ever have handed her off to a stranger so I could have a peaceful dinner!' She imagined Raven's eyes filling with tears of disappointment if she had, her little baby brain trying to come to terms with abandonment. Or was Zoé-Lee reflecting her own feelings again? Sometimes, as a mother, it was hard to separate the two. Then a shocking thought crossed her mind. Was Raven feeling abandoned because Zoé-Lee had chosen her career over her? Truth was, she could have said no to Maxwell. Was she truly any different to Sarah? Forcing those disquieting thoughts from her head, she leaned forward. 'My dislike of Sarah Westfield is separate to a gut feeling that she's been trying to lead us astray from the get-go.'

Bilton's arms were still folded. The fingers of one hand, resting on the opposite upper arm, were tapping in succession as if playing the piano to an internal orchestra. Perhaps that's how her thoughts sounded. Zoé-Lee's were more a continuous, discordant clash. 'I think she took that baby because she could see we were suspicious.' She hoped to see an understanding light dawn in the detective inspector's eyes, but there was no change in her expression. She'd make a good poker player. Zoé-Lee tried, but generally her face was a clear map of her emotions. Was that what had made Sarah go to those extremes? Had she seen her obvious suspicion and decided to do something about it? 'It almost worked, too,' she said. She looked towards Lyn, who nodded. 'We were both feeling more sympathetic afterwards.'

'And then came the lie about the pub.' Bilton pursed her lips. 'One lie isn't much to go on. Neither, much as I give it great credibility, is gut feeling.' She looked from one officer to the other. 'I think it's time I met the Westfields. I spoke to the NCA this morning. None of the alerts have thrown up anything to add to the mix. I'm not saying they've lost interest, but with nothing to go on and too much on their plates, it's going to lose priority. But there's still a missing baby out there; I'm not willing to let this drift.' She tapped on her keyboard and frowned. 'Right,' she looked at DS Lyn, 'make an appointment to see the Westfields this afternoon. Late as possible. Let's give them time to worry.'

Late as possible. Zoé-Lee swallowed before raising a hand. Like a child. 'I was due to finish today.' *Forgive me, Tom, please forgive me, Raven, I do love you both but...* 'I'd really like to stay on, though. It's no harm, I think, for Sarah Westfield to be viewing me warily.'

Bilton nodded. 'I agree.' She looked back to Lyn. 'Make sure you tell them that it'll be me, you, and PC O'Farrell they'll be seeing. Let's see if that produces any result.' She waved them towards the door. 'Let me know when you have it organised.'

34

If I ever wavered, if I ever doubted my ability to do what needed to be done, all I had to do was to look at Meg as she sat with Kaya in her arms and breathe in the air of happiness that seem to float in a cloud around them. It was almost tangible, something I could suck in through my mouth and nose, absorb through my skin. Every cell, every atom of my body seemed to be infused with it. I felt lighter than air, filled with an effervescence I'd never known before and struggled to handle. It seemed impossible to love so much.

But to experience great love is also to experience great fear.

Coping with love at least brought pleasure. Coping with the fear, however, was different. As the days went by, as the love grew stronger and all encompassing, so too did the fear escalate until I could hardly breathe for the fingers of it that wrapped around me and squeezed.

I had no choice. That's what I kept telling myself. And it was true, I didn't. All it would take was for one cog in the wheel of our duplicity to break, and everything – all that we'd planned – would fall apart to send pieces of our life flying in all directions, before it all came to a shuddering halt.

Like most people, I would insist I wasn't capable of violence. But how do you know until you're faced with the choice? Would you kill if you had to? Inflict injury? As day followed day, I settled for the truth: I would do whatever was needed to protect my wife and my daughter.

Mine. I relished the possessiveness of the word. It inspired me. Made me believe it would all work out well in the end.

There was no point in delaying. In fact, the sooner I got it done, the safer we'd be.

Meg's laugh interrupted my musing. I crossed the room to join her, resting a hand on her shoulder as I leaned down to gaze at our daughter.

'She smiled,' Meg said. Then she laughed again. 'I know it's only wind, but still, she smiled and it was so lovely.'

And it was. And I'd do anything... everything... to keep it that way.

35

Sarah sat in shock for a long time after Jade stormed out. She was grateful Nick didn't appear to have heard; if he had, he'd have been in to comfort her. He'd never liked Jade; he'd probably have said *I told you so* and Sarah wouldn't have been able to hold back the tears.

She heard his mobile ring, as if at a distance. He used the spare bedroom as an office; he was probably sitting in there with the door shut. His voice came, intermittently, answering whoever had rung. It was probably his mother yet again. Sarah couldn't find the energy to care. She shut her eyes and tried to forget Jade's piercing condemnation. Was Sarah really that awful? Surely not. But if her best friend, the woman who knew her better than anyone, even Nick, thought so badly of her, perhaps she was.

It was a gut-wrenching, soul-destroying thought. She'd like to cry. To howl. To let every emotion that had been gathering layer upon layer over the last few weeks erupt in one enormous, tearful snotfest. But everything seemed frozen. Stuck in a lump in her throat. Perhaps she'd have been able to cough it up and start the howling process if the door hadn't opened and Nick's handsome face hadn't peered around the edge. He seemed surprised not to see Jade, indicating that he hadn't heard her storm off. 'She's gone already?'

With Jade's words still echoing painfully, Sarah pushed up her lips in a smile. 'Yes, she had to rush away, but thank you for calling her.' He'd meant well; he always did.

He came through, sat on the sofa and reached for her hand. 'I thought it would help you to talk with someone who was one step away from it all.'

It should have done. Over the years, Sarah had depended on Jade for her particular brand of common sense. Had she taken her for granted? Abused her kindness? She'd thought their support was mutual – hadn't Sarah listened when Jade's romantic liaisons had cracked, then fallen apart? Perhaps it was time to face the truth. Things hadn't been the same since that time following her split from Clem, when she'd wondered if their friendship, their relationship, wasn't drifting into something more intimate. A rocky time when she'd seriously considered whether Jade's love for her wouldn't be enough.

Perhaps she'd never forgiven Sarah for the choice she'd made.

'You look so sad,' Nick said, slipping an arm around her shoulder and pulling her closer. 'We'll soon have Kaya home, my love.'

Sarah drew a quick breath. Didn't it prove Jade was right? That Sarah was totally self-centred? Because, God forgive her, she hadn't thought about Kaya again since the police had taken that other baby away. But then, she didn't need to. Kaya may not be with her, but she knew she was all right. Being well looked after.

'We'll get through this,' Nick whispered in her ear, his warm breath tickling. 'The police will find Kaya, then we'll get our lives back on track and put this whole ordeal behind us.' He pulled her hand up and planted a wet kiss on the back of it. 'Us two against the world. D'you remember we used to say that when things seemed rough?'

She did, and they had, back when they'd been trying to buy an apartment and had trailed around one unsuitable, overpriced place after the other. That seemed a long time ago and now the words had a childish ring to them. Or was it simply that she didn't love him, and there was no *us two* any longer? She wished she could tell him. But not yet. A little more time was needed. She wasn't going to prove Jade right by only thinking of herself. 'I do,' she said, then with a sigh, shut her eyes. 'I might catch a few winks before we go out for dinner.'

'Actually,' Nick said apologetically, 'something has come up. Would you mind if we head off now? I'd like to be back here for six.'

She twisted to look up at him. 'Why?'

'Nothing to trouble you with. A Zoom meeting with some of my colleagues that I said I'd try to join.' He smiled down at her. 'Is that okay? I could give it a miss if you'd prefer.'

'No.' She shook her head. *See how accommodating I can be, Jade?* 'That's fine, I'll just go and freshen up and we can leave.' She pushed a hand through her hair. 'Maybe I should brush my hair too before I frighten the bar staff.' She smiled at him. 'Five minutes, no more, I promise.'

It made him laugh, as she knew it would. She was a ditherer, hopeless at getting ready at speed. But that was when she cared about things, about how she looked, what she wore. It had been a long time since either had bothered her. In their bedroom, she looked down at the wrinkled shirt she was wearing, almost decided it would do before yanking the buttons open with such force that one popped and skittered across the wooden floor. She left it there, opened her wardrobe, took out the first shirt her hand came to. She pulled it on and left it hanging loose over the chinos she was wearing. Make-up might have improved her ghostly pale face; she couldn't bring herself to care. She settled for splashing cold water on it and drying it roughly. When she pulled a brush through her hair, she winced when it caught in knots at the back. She dug the bristles in further, pulling it roughly till there were tears in her eyes and her hair was smooth and knot free.

'Ready,' she said returning to the living room.

'You look lovely,' Nick said, reaching for her hand.

She looked like she'd been embalmed, buried, and dug up again, but she appreciated the lie. At least she should have done. She was second guessing every thought now thanks to Jade.

They peered through the main door of the apartment block before opening it. The first couple of days, there had been reporters outside desperate for a sound bite or a photograph of the grieving parents. The occasional one still turned up, but not that afternoon. Something more exciting or newsworthy had obviously taken them elsewhere.

It was a twenty-minute walk to the pub, the route taking them along Islington High Street. It was a nice afternoon for it: the blue sky was brushed with wisps of white, the sun making everything seem brighter, cleaner. Nick insisted on holding her hand, gripping it tighter as they stopped to cross the street. 'We should walk to the lights,' Sarah said, as she did every time, hating to rush across the street in the hope that some maniac driver didn't decide to rev up and run them down.

Nick laughed at her, as he always did. Some things never seemed to change. 'White Lion Street is right there,' he said pointing to the road directly opposite. 'I can almost see the pub. Why would you want to walk all the way down to the lights when we can be across in seconds?'

'Because it's safer.' She didn't know why she bothered because he never listened.

'Now,' he said and she felt the tug on her hand as he took a step forward. She hadn't bothered looking, stupidly trusting in his ability to spot a gap in the flowing traffic, so when she heard the accelerating roar of an engine, she thought it was unconnected to their journey. That it was coming from somewhere else. Until the car hit them, sending them both flying, her hand still bizarrely clasped in his until they were pulled asunder by the weight of their bodies. Lighter, she wasn't flung as far, and was in luck, landing on refuse bags awaiting collection. The bags split on impact and, later, when she relived the accident again and again, the stink of their contents was associated in her head with excruciating pain.

Nick wasn't so lucky. His flying body was hit mid-air by a van, it ricocheted and bounced off the bonnet of another car before coming to its final resting place in the middle of the road.

Sarah was conscious. There was an eerie silence as if the world had stopped turning, and everyone was holding their breath to see what happened next. And then, as the pain exploded, so did the noise, the screams, shrieks, shouts. Not from her, although she thought she might have moaned. Then there were faces, and hands, mouths opening and closing. She shut her eyes on the intense pain and let it carry her away.

Someone's voice made her stir. A firm voice reassuring her, repeating consoling words. 'You're going to be okay. We'll look after you now; you just hang in there.'

Everything was going to be okay? She wanted to laugh. This, she wanted to tell them, was the last fucking straw. But of course, she didn't. She didn't say a word, and whatever they did for her, whatever they gave her, it worked and she felt herself floating above it all and for the first time, in a long, long time, she felt at peace.

36

It was DS Lyn who drove to the apartment for their 6 p.m. appointment with Sarah and Nick Westfield. DI Bilton took the passenger seat, leaving Zoé-Lee to sit in the back. There was no conversation during the drive, so she was able to relax back and stare out the window. London wasn't a city she knew but all she was seeing was high-rise buildings, lots of traffic and grim-faced pedestrians. Did people look equally grim in Devon? Perhaps they did, she wasn't sure. She'd have to investigate when she got home, although she wasn't sure when that was going to be.

Tom would understand, even support her decision to stay a little longer. She was lucky to have him. He wasn't perfect, not Superman, and despite what she'd thought earlier, she wasn't Superwoman, but between the two of them, they seemed to be muddling through. It wasn't perfect, but it was pretty damn close. When that annoying little voice told her that something had to give, that she wasn't Superwoman and she couldn't have it all, she had to remember that pretty damn close was pretty damn good. She was so lost in her thoughts that she wasn't listening to the conversation between Bilton and Lyn, nor did she hear Bilton's mobile ringing, and the tense conversation that followed. It was only when the car swerved dramatically, throwing her against the door and dragging an *oof* from her, that she realised something was up.

Straining against the seat belt, she leaned forward. 'Have I missed something?'

'The Westfields,' Bilton said as if that explained everything.

'What about them?'

'They've been in an accident. They're in hospital.'

'An accident?'

'A hit-and-run on Islington High Street. It's not looking good.'

Zoé-Lee sat back. She'd been a police officer for long enough that little shocked or surprised her any more. But oddly, she was both shocked and surprised at this. A hit-and-run. It wasn't unusual, of course. Despite the best efforts of the police, there were an awful lot of lunatic drivers on the roads.

A few minutes later, they were pulling into the car park of St Bartholomew's Hospital.

The Westfields were still being treated in the accident and emergency department, and it would be several minutes before they could speak to the consultant in charge.

They found a quiet space to stand and wait.

Zoé-Lee's thoughts were spinning as she tried to decide if the hit-and-run was another piece of the same puzzle. She couldn't see where it might fit, but that didn't mean it didn't belong.

'I can almost see your brain wrestling with this, PC O'Farrell,' DI Bilton said quietly. 'You don't believe in coincidences, no?'

'They happen, of course, but...' Zoé-Lee shrugged, unhappy to be put on the spot. 'I don't know. I suppose it's because I've been suspicious of Sarah Westfield almost from the beginning, and now when we've caught her out in a lie and were on our way to confront her with it, she's involved in a hit-and-run. It just strikes me as odd.'

'What? You think she walked in front of a car to get out of answering sticky questions?' DS Lyn raised an eyebrow. 'Seems a bit far-fetched.'

'A bit dramatic and certainly risky,' Bilton said. 'You're expecting them to walk out with a few scrapes, are you?'

Zoé-Lee was almost embarrassed to admit she was. She was betting the couple would have a few bruises. They'd be shaken but not broken. Sufficiently shook up to make the police back off from asking any questions until they'd recovered. And in a day or two, when they had, and when the police asked their questions, they could cite this latest trauma as the reason their answers were slow to come. Although no matter how much time she had, Sarah was going to find it difficult to explain visiting a pub for old times' sake that hadn't existed in those old times.

'Looks like we'll have to wait and see what the consultant says about their injuries, won't we?' Bilton pulled out her mobile, nodded towards the exit, and walked off.

It was another twenty minutes before a scrub-suited man pushed through double doors from the inner sanctum and looked around, his gaze flicking around the busy area before settling on the two officers, Zoé-Lee's uniform marking them as who they were.

'Looks like the big chief,' Lyn said. 'I'll run and grab the DI.'

The scrub-suited man crossed to Zoé-Lee. 'You waiting for news about the Westfields?'

She nodded, then looked towards the exit, relieved to see Bilton and Lyn hurrying through the door.

'Detective Inspector Bilton, Metropolitan Police,' Bilton said, showing her identification, then with a tilt of her head towards the other officers, added, 'DS Lyn and PC O'Farrell.'

'I'm Dr Winslett, the consultant on duty. I've been involved with both Sarah and Nick Westfield's care since they arrived by ambulance earlier.' He spoke slowly, enunciating each word slowly and carefully as if afraid he'd be misunderstood.

'When can we get to speak to them?' Bilton asked.

He narrowed his eyes as if assessing how much to tell her, before looking back to the doors he'd just come through. Perhaps wishing he'd stayed the other side rather than be the giver of bad news.

Because it was bad news; Zoé-Lee could tell from his expression. It was one she'd worn herself too many times. That careful attempt to be sympathetic yet professional. She was never quite sure she'd aced it. She *was* sure he hadn't. 'They're dead?' Blunt, but she never saw the point of gentle euphemisms: *they've passed away* or *didn't make it*, or worst of all, *they've gone to a better place*.

He didn't appear offended. 'You're half right.' Before he could elaborate, the door he'd come through opened and a young, scrub-suited female waved frantically. Without an explanation he probably thought redundant, he vanished.

'Half-right?' Bilton stared after him. 'What the hell is that supposed to mean?'

'That they're half-dead, maybe, by which I suppose he means badly injured.'

They weren't left guessing for long, the consultant reappearing almost as fast as he'd gone. He didn't apologise. 'The Westfields. Yes,' he said as if pulling their file from his head. 'As I said, you were half-right, officer,' he nodded in Zoé-Lee's direction. 'Nick Westfield's injuries were too severe and despite our every effort, I'm afraid he didn't make it. Sarah Westfield was luckier. Some rubbish bags seemingly broke her fall, so apart from bruising sustained from the collision with the car, a broken wrist from the impact on landing, and a minor concussion, she's okay. We'll keep her in overnight to be sure but I'm envisaging her well enough to be discharged in the morning.'

'Can we speak to her?' Bilton asked.

He looked saddened by the request. 'Is that necessary? I recognise their name so I know their child is still missing, and now she's lost her husband. She's understandably distraught. Her parents are on their way. I think any questioning about the hit-and-run could wait till the morning. She has, in any case, little to no recollection of what occurred. Your time would possibly be better spent interviewing eyewitnesses to the event.'

Zoé-Lee wasn't sure how the DI would take being told how to do her job by the consultant. She shot DS Lyn a surreptitious glance, relaxing when she got a wink in reply.

It seemed Bilton was slow to take offence. She merely nodded, handed the consultant her card, and said they'd return in the morning and would appreciate it if Sarah Westfield wasn't discharged until they saw her. They exchanged smiles, each happy with the compromise.

As they walked in a single line through the crowded entrance and back to the car, Zoé-Lee was still trying to untangle her thoughts, her suspicions having turned out to be just as crazy as DS Lyn had thought.

She'd stupidly, and unprofessionally, allowed her dislike of Sarah Westfield to cloud her judgement.

She was still castigating herself when she sat into the back seat of the car, wrenching the seat belt around her roughly.

'Well, it seems you were right to be suspicious of the hit-and-run,' Bilton said, twisting around to look at her. 'Just not for the right reason.'

Sometimes it was better to say nothing. Especially when Zoé-Lee couldn't think of a word to say anyway that wasn't scatological.

'I spoke to the officers who responded to the hit-and-run. They've taken witness statements from nearby pedestrians and a couple of drivers. As per usual, some didn't see what was going on, but three, a driver and two pedestrians, said it looked as if the car deliberately swerved to hit the Westfields.'

Zoé-Lee felt her jaw drop open. This, she hadn't expected. 'Someone tried to kill them?'

'It very much looks that way. They've started to check CCTV to ascertain where the car came from, and where it went.' She gave DS Lyn a nod. 'Let's get back to the station, see if they've located it.'

As their car sped through London traffic, Zoé-Lee stared through the window, trying to think of a possible connection between the missing Kaya and the attempt on the Westfields' lives. It sounded too bizarre for there to be one but she knew there had to be.

She might very well be overly suspicious, might be allowing her dislike of Sarah Westfield to affect her judgement, but she knew she was right about this.

37

Sarah was being moved again. It didn't matter because she couldn't feel a thing. She'd have smiled if she'd been able, would have asked them to keep her this way for a long, long time. Consciousness came and went, glimpses of light, fragments of words, little made sense.

She'd no idea how much time had passed when she opened her eyes, but a quick look around told her that she was in a ward. There were three other beds. Three female occupants. She wondered where Nick was and hoped they were looking after him. He wasn't a good patient. The merest sniffle and he was convinced he had pneumonia.

How badly was she injured? Her left arm was in a plaster cast. What else had she damaged? She shifted her bottom slightly in the bed, then moved her toes, scratching one with the nail of the other. It was a relief to feel, to know there was no paralysis. Everything else seemed to be in working order. She'd been hooked up to a monitor; lifting her head slightly, she was able to see the readings. All looked to be okay so she relaxed back and shut her eyes.

When she opened them again, it was brighter, the ward noisier. The woman in the next bed had a radio tuned to a news station. Sarah turned her head slightly, trying to hear. Perhaps while she lay there incapacitated, they'd found Kaya.

A young woman in an unflattering orange pantsuit came in pushing a trolley that rattled as she moved through the ward. She went from bedside to bedside, lifting the used jugs and glasses and replacing them with fresh ones, chattering to each patient as she went. She'd reached Sarah's bed when the nine o'clock news came on the radio.

'Can you turn that up so I can hear it?' the woman on the far side of the small ward asked the radio owner.

Her request was immediately granted and the sombre voice of the newsreader drowned out the other sounds.

Politics, politics, and more politics. Sarah was almost lulled back to sleep by the droning voice when it said they were moving to local news. If they'd found Kaya, she guessed it would have been the lead story, but maybe not; it was worth listening for a bit longer.

'Police are appealing for witnesses to a hit-and-run on Islington High Street yesterday evening where a man was killed and a woman seriously injured. Names have been withheld until relatives have been informed.'

Nick! Pushing the sheet back, Sarah tried to get up. She pulled off the leads attaching her to the monitor sending it caterwauling. The other women started shouting at her not to get out of bed, at the ward attendant to get help. It didn't matter; Sarah was too weak, too drugged to manage more than slide one leg from the bed before she flopped back.

'All right now,' a voice said gently as Sarah's leg was lifted back into the bed, the sheet pulled over her, and the monitor leads reattached. There was a loud swish as curtains were pulled around the bed and the scrape of a chair on the floor as it was pulled closer. 'My name is Caroline Ness; I'm the charge nurse. Before we talk, do you need something for the pain?'

Guessing that the nurse was referring to physical aches, and not the searing agony that seemed to have cut her heart in two, Sarah gave a slight shake of her head. Every part of her body hurt, but her life had changed from the few minutes before when she'd have happily remained slightly out of it. She needed a clear head to absorb it all. Nick was dead. She hadn't loved him, but her heartache was genuine. He'd been a good man. The father of her child. He didn't deserve to die in such a stupid accident.

The charge nurse was still speaking; Sarah tried to concentrate.

'...they did everything they could, but he'd sustained such serious injuries that it was hopeless.' Caroline settled the pillow back under Sarah's broken wrist, then stood and did the same with the one behind her head. 'Your parents have been notified,' she said, looking down at her with kind eyes. 'They're on their way. I'll leave the curtains pulled to give you some privacy, okay?'

She didn't seem to expect an answer which was just as well because Sarah couldn't think of one word to say. She shut her eyes. The curtains swished as the nurse left, then Sarah was alone.

Childless, husbandless.

Exactly the way she'd wanted her life to be.

38

It didn't take the police long to get a clear idea of what had occurred on Islington High Street. Between CCTV and ANPR cameras, they traced the Westfields' journey from their apartment and onto the High Street and followed the dark-grey Ford Escort that trailed them. It pulled into the kerb now and then to allow the couple to remain ahead.

They knew from DS Lyn's call to Nick Westfield to set up their 6 p.m. appointment that they were heading out for something to eat. It didn't take much deduction to guess they'd stopped to cross the road where they did in order to walk up White Lion Street to The Three Johns, a popular pub and eatery. It was poor luck that the point where they stopped was midway between two CCTV cameras, but good luck that dashboard cameras from three different vehicles had enabled them to get a clear idea of what had occurred. And there was absolutely no doubt: the grey Escort had swerved to hit the couple dead-on.

They managed to track the car further until it vanished into a maze of apartment blocks where the car parks had CCTV but none of the many exits had. They weren't surprised when a call came in from a concerned member of the public to report a car alight on a small side road nearby. There was also no surprise when they ran the car's fire-charred number plates to discover it had been stolen only a few hours before.

'Why on earth would anyone want to murder the Westfields?' DS Lyn twirled a pen between her fingers. 'There was nothing dodgy about them, was there?'

Zoé-Lee shook her head. 'We did a full check on both. She's a well-regarded and popular general practitioner; he was in finance. They have a mortgage, but they're not in over their heads. Good social network with both sets of parents close by. We dug deep but found nothing untoward.'

'Yet, you still have your doubts about her,' Bilton said.

'Yes.' Even now, with her theory about the hit-and-run blown to pieces, Zoé-Lee still had her doubts. She clasped her hands behind her head. 'I keep going back to her handing Kaya over to strangers. I have a little girl and couldn't imagine ever, no matter the circumstance, doing such a thing.'

'Even if it was to save her life?'

Zoé-Lee gave a disbelieving laugh. 'You mean some form of blackmail or something? "Give us your baby or we'll kill her, you, or someone you love." Isn't that drifting into the realms of fiction? What would their motive be? The Westfields aren't well off, so it wouldn't be money.'

'I'm simply throwing it out there,' Bilton said reasonably. Snapping the pen from DS Lyn's hand, she tossed it onto the desk, sat back and folded her arms. 'All we know for a fact is that Kaya is still missing, someone tried to kill both Westfields and did kill Nick.'

Zoé-Lee frowned. 'Maybe one crime is linked to the other. Someone took little Kaya, right?' She didn't wait for the nod of acknowledgement, running on with the thoughts in her head. 'Perhaps the Westfields inadvertently spoke to the wrong person. They might not even have realised it, but it might have put the frighteners on whoever took Kaya and they decided they had only one option. To get rid of both parents.' She waited for Bilton to raise her eyes to the ceiling at this admittedly off-the-wall idea.

Bilton didn't, but she did shake her head slowly. 'If I wanted to murder someone, I'm not sure I'd depend on running them down. There's a risk it wouldn't achieve the aim.'

'It would have done, I think, if Sarah hadn't landed on those rubbish bags.'

'Perhaps.' Bilton wasn't convinced. She glanced at her watch. 'Right, it's almost midnight, there's nothing more we can do tonight. Let's get some sleep and meet back at the hospital at eight, okay?'

'It's okay if I stay on here, isn't it?' Zoé-Lee wasn't sure if she wanted the answer to be yes or no. She desperately wanted to get home. She missed Tom, missed her daughter, but she couldn't leave till she knew what was going on here. Preferably not till they'd found Kaya, or at least discover what happened to her. They were close. She knew they were.

Bilton was already on her way out the door; she stopped with her hand on the handle. 'I've already told DI Maxwell we need you for a bit longer. He said we could hang on to you for as long as necessary.' She waited a beat before asking, 'That's not going to be a problem, is it?'

Of course it wasn't. Tom was looking after Raven. They wouldn't miss her.

Not even a little bit.

Guilt was a bitch.

39

Back at the hotel, Zoé-Lee sat with her mobile and watched the WhatsApp videos Tom had sent her of Raven smiling and eating. Dressed first in a multi-coloured T-shirt and leggings, then a bright-yellow pyjama suit. There were none of her crying. Because she hadn't, or because her amazing husband had wanted to spare her those shots? She touched a finger to her child's face. A happy, loved little girl who was lucky to have two parents who adored her.

She tapped a message for Tom.

> You're such a good dad. And the best husband. It's got more complicated here. I'll be home in a couple of days. Love you.

She wasn't surprised to see an answer appearing almost immediately. He'd have been waiting, half-asleep, to hear from her.

> Stay safe. Love you too. So does Raven.

It was almost enough to put her mind at ease. Hearing his voice would make it complete.

'Hi,' she said when the call was answered.

His voice was gruff with sleep. 'Hey.'

'Sorry, for ringing; it's been a long day and I just needed to hear your voice.' She resisted the temptation to tell him the latest news. Time enough when she got home. 'Go back to sleep. Kiss Raven for me in the morning.'

'Okay. Sleep. Love you.'

And that was all she needed. Following a quick shower to wash away the dirt of the day, she climbed naked between the sheets and shut her eyes. They flicked open almost immediately. She was lucky. A good husband. A beautiful daughter. Sarah Westfield had had both. Now she had neither.

For the first time, Zoé-Lee felt genuine sympathy for the woman.

Unfortunately, not enough to wipe away her continued suspicion. Tomorrow, maybe they'd get some answers.

* * *

It was impossible to know when or if she'd get something else to eat that day so Zoé-Lee made good use of the hotel breakfast buffet again. She took a couple of photographs of her laden plate to send Tom and added a message she knew would make him smile.

> Don't you wish you were here?

She ate with one hand, continuing to message him with the other until she was finished.

> Got to go. Have a good day, give Raven a kiss from her ma.

A few minutes later, with her uniform hat under her arm, she stepped outside the hotel. Lyn's car was parked in a space that was marked no parking. Zoé-Lee pulled the passenger door open and slid inside. 'I'm sorry, have I kept you waiting?'

'I'm always early, don't worry.' Lyn started the engine, indicated, and pulled out into the flowing traffic. 'D'you sleep okay?'

'Yes, I generally do regardless of what's going on. What about you?'

'Took me a while to switch off.'

Zoé-Lee stared out at the traffic and the pedestrian-clogged footpaths. 'It's a long way from Devon,' she said, as if to herself, then turned towards her colleague. 'DI Bilton seems sound.'

'She is. Best DI I've ever worked with. Fair. Gives credit where it's due, doesn't climb over bodies on a race to the top like some.'

'My DI, Andrew Maxwell, is the same. We're lucky; I've heard some awful stories.'

Lyn indicated and changed lanes. 'I've probably been in some of them. I think I've had some of the worst.'

Swapping gossip, they were laughing as they pulled into the car park of the hospital a short while later. St Bartholomew's looked busier, more imposing in daylight. They parked, legally this time, and walked together to the main entrance. 'There she is,' Lyn said. 'I swear, no matter how early I am, she's always there before me.'

'Morning, ma'am,' they said in unison as they joined DI Bilton at the entrance.

'Morning.' She waved towards the interior. 'Right, let's see what Sarah Westfield has to say for herself.'

Not a lot as it turned out. She'd been transferred to a bed in a medical ward and was lying under the covers, bruises on her face standing out in contrast to the sickly pallor of her skin.

'Please be gentle with her,' the nurse said as she pointed her out. 'She's barely spoken since she heard her husband was killed. Not even when her parents came in a couple of hours ago. They've left but are coming back in a bit. The doctors think Mrs Westfield might be in shock. She was due to be discharged but they've decided to keep her for another day, maybe two.' She shoved her hands into the pockets of her tunic top. 'We had the curtains pulled around the bed to give her privacy but she asked for them to be pulled back.'

Bilton stared through the window into the ward and nodded as if coming to a decision. Turning to DS Lyn, she said, 'You stay here. Three of us would be too intimidating.' She didn't explain her decision to take

Zoé-Lee instead, walking away with her on her tail as they entered the unit and stood at the end of Sarah's bed.

Her right arm was in plaster and elevated on a pillow. From where she stood, Zoé-Lee couldn't see an inch of skin that wasn't marred by bruises or scrapes. She wondered how much pain she was in, if she'd been given analgesia and if so, how reliable answers to their questions would be. But it wasn't for her to decide. She stayed at the foot of the bed while DI Bilton sidled up towards the head.

'Mrs Westfield?' Bilton waited for a response and when it didn't come, tried again. 'Mrs Westfield, it's Detective Inspector Bilton, Metropolitan Police, and PC O'Farrell from Devon and Cornwall whom you've met before. We have a couple of questions to ask you if you think you can manage to answer.'

They waited patiently until finally they saw Sarah's eyelashes flicker. She opened her eyes and stared blankly ahead for several seconds before drawing a shuddering breath and focusing on Bilton.

'We're sorry for your loss, Mrs Westfield,' Bilton said. 'We're also sorry to intrude on your grief but we want to find who did this to you and bring them to justice.'

When Sarah smacked her lips together, it was Zoé-Lee who correctly interpreted the sign. She crossed behind the detective inspector, picked up a glass half-filled with water and held it out to Sarah. When she made no move to take it, Zoé-Lee held it to her mouth, as if she was a child, tilting it slowly as Sarah began to drink.

'Thank you,' she said, her voice husky.

'More?'

'No, I'm good.'

Zoé-Lee put the glass down and returned to her position at the foot of the bed. She felt Sarah's eyes following her, the dislike in them almost palpable. Was it because Zoé-Lee had made it clear how she felt about a mother handing her child to a stranger, or something more?

Bilton pulled up a chair and sat. 'Can you tell us what you remember?'

'We were going for something to eat. We should have crossed at the lights. I didn't see the car coming, just heard the roar of an engine, then we went flying.' It was all said in a slow, dull monotone. Numb, disbelieving words of grief and shock. 'Nick always held my hand when we crossed together. As if I'd be safer that way. It all happened so quickly but I remember distinctly the feel of his hand being pulled from mine as we were thrown in different directions.'

'Did you see the car?'

'No.'

'Mrs Westfield, I don't want to distress you, but do you know of anyone who would wish you or your husband harm?'

Sarah had been staring into space but this question made her turn her head to look at Bilton. Too quickly, the action caused her to wince and press her lips together.

'Are you all right? Would you like me to fetch a nurse?'

'No, just give me a sec.' She shut her eyes, opening them a moment later to turn slowly and meet the detective's gaze. 'I don't understand your question. Harm us? The car hitting us was an accident, wasn't it?'

'I'm afraid not. We've watched dashcam footage of the crash and listened to witness statements. It appears that you were deliberately targeted. It was only your luck in landing where you did that prevented you from sustaining more serious injury.'

Sarah grunted, her mouth twisting into a smile. 'They told me I'd been thrown onto bags of rubbish. Some people,' she looked directly at Zoé-Lee, 'would say I'd landed where I belonged.'

Zoé-Lee kept her gaze steady, refusing to look away even as she felt a blush colouring her cheeks. It wasn't the time for apologies, for making excuses, for admitting that she'd got it wrong. She was relieved when Bilton spoke and drew Sarah's attention.

'Can you think of anyone—'

'Who'd want to harm us?' Sarah interrupted her. 'No, of course not! We were ordinary people living an ordinary life till Kaya was kidnapped, not the kind of people who make enemies – or at least not the kind who'd want to kill you.'

Bilton sat forward suddenly. 'But enemies, yes?'

Sarah lifted a hand in a weary motion. 'Poor choice of words. I'm a GP. There have been patients, there'll always be patients, who were, are, or will be unhappy with their care. And in life, there will always be people you fall out with: noisy neighbours, family, friends.'

'But is there anybody who stands out?' Bilton persisted.

'No.' The word was followed by a tired sigh. 'Is that all?'

Bilton sat back. 'For the moment. There may be more questions at a later date, but meanwhile, if you think of anything, ring me any time.' She took a business card from her jacket pocket and waved it. 'I'll leave it on the locker beside you.'

Sarah shut her eyes. Whether in response, or because she was weary, Zoé-Lee wasn't sure. The pointed remark about the rubbish told her that Sarah was aware of her antagonism. It would have been nice to have dropped the lie about The Post Office pub into the conversation to see how she managed to scramble out of it. She was good at that. Zoé-Lee didn't know if DI Bilton had noticed, but from her position at the foot of the bed, it was obvious. When Bilton had asked Sarah if there was anybody who stood out, there was a definite hesitation before she'd answered 'no'.

If she had her suspicions, if there was someone she thought might be responsible for the hit-and-run, why wouldn't she tell them? Was she shielding someone? And what, if anything, did it have to do with her missing daughter?

Zoé-Lee clenched her hands into tight fists. She could feel it. They were close.

40

Is there anybody who stands out? What Sarah was thinking wasn't possible, was it?

She shut her eyes and hoped the two police officers would get the message and leave her in peace, but they didn't move. She could feel them there, staring at her. Despite their perfunctory words of sympathy, there hadn't been a shred of it in their expressions, only judgement. It was more than clear what that officer from Devon thought of her. It was in every twist of her mean mouth and dart of her nasty, sharp eyes. Sarah could feel them on her, burning into her already bruised and battered flesh. Every part of her ached. She could ask for something to take the pain away, but whatever they gave her would only remove the physical pain; it would do nothing to lessen the mental agony.

With her eyes shut, she would swear she felt Nick's hand wrapped around hers. It was there now. She wanted to look, to check it was her imagination, but the officers were still there, waiting for her to fall apart. What did they want? For Sarah to confess to unimaginable crimes?

What if she told them that she knew Kaya was safe? Would that help?

A rustling, the scrape of a chair, the low, indecipherable murmur of voices, footsteps moving slowly away, fading until all that was left was the raspy breathing of the woman in the bed opposite and the background hum of the ward. Sarah opened her eyes and looked down at her hand.

Of course Nick wasn't holding it. Not in this life and she'd no belief in the next.

Nick. Such a good man. She should have loved him; never really understood why she hadn't. He'd certainly loved her, told her again and again. Hadn't she loved that in those heady first few weeks together when she couldn't believe she'd finally met a man so willing to commit, so happy to say *I love you*, so eager to take her hand in his, to show the world they were together? She wasn't sure when that changed, when she began to find him too clingy, too affectionate, too everything. Before they were married? Shortly after?

He'd deserved better. It was a consolation that he had never known she hadn't loved him; that she'd never told him she'd planned to leave him. That to the end, he'd believed in their happy family unit. Believed they'd have Kaya back and live happily ever after. Luckily, he'd never known the truth.

Is there anybody who stands out? The officer's question dragged her thoughts away from Nick. What she was thinking was crazy, wasn't it? Maybe even the product of a disturbed mind. The concussion. That was it. It had to be.

'How're you feeling?'

Sarah opened her eyes slowly. It was almost a relief to have her tangled thoughts interrupted even by such an irritating question. She swallowed the first retort, the *how the fuck do you think I feel*, when she saw the pleasant smiling face of the unsuspecting nurse. 'A bit sore,' she said.

'Right, let's see if I can get you something to help with that.'

'Nothing too strong,' Sarah said quickly. 'I don't want to be woozy.'

'Pain relief with no wooziness side-effects coming right up.' With a nod, she was gone, returning minutes later with a small container. 'Here you go.' She filled a glass from the carafe of water on the bedside locker. 'Two pills guaranteed to take the edge off that pain.' She waited till Sarah had swallowed the proffered pills, then handed her the water, waiting till a few sips were swallowed before taking it away. 'You refused breakfast but you really should try to eat something.'

Why? To keep her strong so she wouldn't break when more crap was flung in her direction? But the nurse was being kind; it wasn't her fault that Sarah's life had become a very unfunny joke. 'Maybe later, thank you.'

'Now that you're feeling more like talking, there are counsellors available. I could give them a shout, ask them to come to see you. It might help. You've been through a terrible ordeal.'

Had the nurse not read her notes? She should be saying *ordeals*. Plural. Didn't she know that Sarah was the woman who'd handed her three-week-old baby over to a stranger? A woman who had a husband she didn't deserve. 'I'm not sure talking to anyone is going to help.' How pathetic she sounded. 'Not yet anyway but thank you.'

'Okay.' The nurse filled up her glass, pulled over a bed table and left the drink within reach. 'If you need anything, just press your bell. I'll come back in a bit, see how you're doing.' And with that, she was gone.

If Sarah thought she'd be left in peace, she was soon enlightened. First, her parents returned. They'd come, hours before, but she'd been too out of it, too shocked and stunned to speak to them.

'My precious girl,' her mother said, collapsing onto the chair and burying her head in the blanket tucked around Sarah. Her father, afraid to touch her bruised body, kissed the air above her cheek and muttered something she couldn't make out. He stood back then, as if he'd done his bit, and with his usual lack of common sense, told anyone who came within his orbit that it was a sad state of affairs when you couldn't go out for a walk without someone trying to run you down.

Sarah tried to tell him it hadn't happened like that. That a random car hadn't mounted the pavement and knocked them down. She wanted to tell him that Nick had been murdered, and that she owed her life to bags of rubbish. That made her laugh, drawing both parents' eyes in her direction, mouths agape as if she'd committed some terrible solecism. Or maybe they thought she was going to fall apart and they'd have to deal with the outcome. Maybe have her stay with them. They'd hate that, as would she.

She lifted a hand in apology. 'I'm all over the place.'

'There's a photo of you and Nick in the local paper,' her mother said. 'On the front page too. Maybe the news of his death will stir the conscience of whoever took Kaya and they'll bring her back.'

If it had simply been the hit-and-run, it probably wouldn't have warranted as much as a paragraph in the newspapers, but it was more than that. Not only was she the woman whose child had been abducted; she was also the woman whose husband had been killed by a maniac. There'd be speculation. Would any of it come near to the horrendous truth of it all?

Unlikely.

Her parents, though, needed to hear the truth. Or at least some of it. As briefly as she could, she told them that the hit-and-run hadn't been an accident, that someone had tried to kill them both. They were understandably horrified. Her father wanted to march off to the police station to ask what they were doing to find the culprit. Her mother struggled to control her tears.

Good people, good parents, they stayed a while longer, words of love and reassurance tripping off their tongues. 'We've brought you clothes for whenever they let you leave,' her mother said. 'I've put them in here.' Her hand tapped the bedside locker. 'We can pick you up, and you can come to stay with us for a few days, okay?'

'Thanks, Mum,' Sarah said. She wouldn't, they'd drive her crazy, and she them, but she was grateful for the offer.

They left then, with more assurances of their love, more promises to take care of her.

And then Sarah was alone, and she'd no choice but to face the horrendous, unbelievable idea that had popped unbidden into her head during her conversation with the police detective.

Is there anybody who stands out?

One person did.

Jade.

41

The following day when she was deemed well enough to be discharged, Sarah pulled on the jeans and baggy T-shirt her mother had brought in for her and rang her parents with the good news.

'We'll come and pick you up,' her mother said.

The words were in the no-nonsense tone Sarah remembered from her childhood. It was tempting to give in. They'd grate on each other after a while, but it would be nice to be looked after until she was feeling less shaken. If she didn't have plans, she might have been swayed. 'You're so good. Thanks, Mum, but it's okay. Jade is here; she's going to come home with me and stay for a few days. So you don't have to worry.'

'If you're sure?' Her mother sounded both sad and relieved. 'You know I'm here for you if you need me.'

'I know, Mum,' Sarah said with genuine affection. 'I'll call over to see you as soon as I'm feeling a bit stronger, okay?'

She put the mobile into her back pocket and picked up the sad plastic bag holding her few possessions. 'It's Caroline, isn't it?' she said to the nurse who came to check her out. Sarah thought it was a good sign that she remembered her name. 'You've been very kind; thank you for looking after me so well.'

'You take care of yourself.' The nurse handed her a neatly folded piece of paper. 'This is a prescription for pain relief. You can get it filled in the pharmacy downstairs before you leave, if that'd help.' She looked around, puzzled. 'Is there nobody to take you home?'

'My parents are waiting outside in the car park.' Sarah had no idea if there were rules and regulations about leaving the hospital unattended, but it seemed best to lie. There were no parents waiting, no Jade to see her home.

Sarah had things to do, and it was better to do them alone.

Her mother had brought in the hooded sweatshirt Sarah had asked for. It was one of Nick's. Perhaps her mother had thought she'd wanted to wear it for sentimental reasons. She never asked so Sarah didn't enlighten her, didn't tell her she wanted it for far more pedantic, practical reasons. It would be easy to pull over the cast on her arm, and would provide a handy disguise. She swung the long straps of her handbag over her head so the bag was sitting over her stomach. With the large sweatshirt pulled on over it, her body shape and size were altered, and with the hood pulled up over her hair, not even her mother would recognise her.

It wasn't her mother she was worried about. It was the reporters who might be lurking around the exit, anticipating her discharge. They'd be desperate to get a shot of the tragic, newly widowed, childless woman.

If they were there, they'd expect her to be accompanied by someone. They wouldn't look at her in the sweatshirt, the cast on her arm tucked away in its generous folds, a scruffy plastic bag swinging casually from her other hand.

She didn't know if they were there or not, she kept her head down, her eyes on the ground in front of her and walked with purpose from the hospital. The taxi she'd ordered from the main reception minutes before was already waiting on the road as she'd requested. She climbed in and looked directly ahead, focusing on the back of the driver's head rather than looking out the window, afraid the nausea that had never gone away despite what she'd told the doctor that morning, would be exacerbated by the blurring lines of buildings and passing traffic as the taxi made its way to her destination.

The nausea wasn't due to any lingering ill-effect of the concussion. It had coincided with the awful suspicion that had hit her as she'd spoken to the police the previous morning. She wasn't sure how she'd managed to keep it hidden from the detective inspector, or to keep her expression from twisting in horror. She wasn't sure she had been so successful with the Devon police officer. O'Farrell had kept her beady eyes on Sarah the whole time. She'd seen them narrow and was surprised no pointed comment had been forthcoming. Maybe the detective inspector, whose name escaped her, was a dragon and didn't appreciate input from junior officers.

'Here we are.' The driver twisted in his seat to look at her. 'Miss? We're here.'

She returned his gaze, puzzled for a moment before realising that the rocking, jolting movement of the taxi had stopped and they had, as the driver pointed out, reached their destination. Another wave of nausea swelled; she sagged against the seat under the weight of it.

'You sure you're okay?' The face that was staring at her was kind, the voice genuinely concerned. 'You look awfully pale, miss.'

She felt pale. As if every drop of blood in her body had rushed to shore up her ailing heart. It would be better to go home. She felt in her pocket for the card the detective had left for her. If she went home, she could ring her, explain, let her deal with it, then she could climb under the duvet and hide away until this nightmare was over. Home – without Nick, that wonderful, kind, generous man she'd married who'd adored her and who'd deserved better than marriage to a woman who didn't love him back.

Ignoring the driver, she stared through the window at the house. If she was right, the person who'd murdered Nick was inside.

And if she was right, Sarah knew it was all her fault.

She paid the fare and stepped from the taxi. It was time to face whatever lay ahead.

42

It was a Saturday. Sarah knew the doorbell would be answered eventually. She pressed it twice to be sure, and when it wasn't answered, pressed it again, for longer. Until her finger was sore.

When she heard the rattle of the safety chain being withdrawn, she stopped and rubbed the bell-shaped indent on the pad of her finger with her thumb. Every sound she heard through the door was magnified: the clunk of a key being turned, the clink of the snip on the Yale lock. She swallowed frantically as nausea once more rolled.

As the door was pulled open, she took one step back and reached a hand out for the porch wall to steady herself.

'Sarah! You're out!' Jade pulled the door further open, took a step towards her friend and enveloped her in a hug. 'Goodness, in the few days since I've seen you, you've lost even more weight.' She frowned with concern as she stepped back to look at her friend. Puzzled, she looked over her shoulder to the road. 'How did you get here? Where are your parents?'

'I got a taxi.'

'On your own! Why didn't you ring me? I'd have come for you. Honestly, the hospital should be ashamed of themselves allowing you to leave like that.' Keeping an arm around Sarah, she bustled her into the house. 'You look like you need a nice cup of tea.'

The back of Jade's terraced house had been extended to provide an open-plan space that incorporated kitchen, living and dining. Sarah was guided to one of two small sofas.

'Here, let me help you off with that ginormous sweatshirt first.'

Sarah dropped the plastic bag on the floor at her feet and allowed Jade to help her off with the sweatshirt. It was draped on the back of the sofa, her handbag dropped on top of the plastic one.

'Now sit,' Jade said, watching with narrowed eyes as Sarah lowered herself to the sofa. A plump cushion was placed under her broken wrist before Jade stepped away. 'Right, you rest up and I'll go and make you something to eat.'

She spoke as if she hadn't torn Sarah to shreds a mere three days before. She held up a hand to stop her. 'Just tea, please, I really don't want anything to eat.' Now that she was there, the words of accusation wouldn't come. The idea that had struck her the previous day had been a crazy, far-fetched one. She'd had concussion, she'd been delusional. That's all it was. And that was the reason for her nausea too. Nothing to do with Jade and those silly words she'd said as she'd ranted at Sarah. *I suppose I'll have to get rid of him for you.* They'd merely been words. Like the oft said but never meant *I'd kill for...*

What would Sarah kill for? The ability to go back in time? Perhaps to the minute Kaya was taken, when she'd thank the women but refuse to hand over her child; or to the minute before the car hit them so she could insist she and Nick walk to the lights? Or maybe to that moment when he'd asked her to marry him, and this time, she'd shake her head and say 'no thanks'?

All the things she'd kill for. Her eyes stung. From tiredness, from the sudden hot tears that threatened to overspill and run down her face. She'd pulled up the bottom of her T-shirt to wipe them away when she heard the patter of Jade's bare feet on the tiled floor.

'Here you go. A nice mug of tea. I wish you'd try something to eat, though.' Jade moved a small table near to Sarah's right side, placed the mug on top, then flopped down on the other sofa with a sigh.

It was set at an angle to the one where Sarah sat. When she turned to look at her, Jade was staring at the unlit wood-burning stove and only her profile was visible. It didn't matter; it wasn't necessary to see her expression to know that Sarah had been stupidly delusional when she'd suspected her of having anything to do with the hit-and-run. Her friend might have her dark side, but there wasn't an ounce of malice in her.

Sarah picked up her tea and had a sip. How foolish she'd been. She, of all people, should have known better; she was a doctor, she knew the consequences of head injuries. She took another sip of the tea. Cupping her hands around it, she gently swirled the contents. 'They want me to do another TV appeal. The police,' she added as if there was any doubt who *they* were. There had been a message earlier from that detective inspector; she hadn't replied.

It ended Jade's fascination with the unlit stove. She turned to stare at Sarah in surprise. 'Really? Are you going to do it?'

Was she? She'd done several over the first couple of weeks, each of them an ordeal. But then she'd had Nick to cling to. Now, she was on her own. 'I think they're hoping that another appeal, with me dressed in widow's weeds, might be effective.'

'Shit.' Jade ran a hand over her mouth. 'Sad to say, but they might have a point.'

'Poor widow has lost her husband, so give her back her baby, eh?' Sarah waited for a response, surprised to see her friend's attention reverting to the damn stove. It was time to go home, put this nonsense behind her. She'd finish her tea, order an Uber, and go back to her apartment.

'Poor widow!' Jade's laugh was a harsh, forced cackle that continued for several seconds before stopping abruptly as she got to her feet.

Sarah, taken aback, watched as she crossed to the wall opposite and flicked a switch. The stove burst into life with make-believe flames.

An electric stove. Why had Sarah never realised it was a fake woodburner? The same way she'd never realised how angry Jade could get until recently. Maybe she only ever saw what she wanted to. She was trying to think of something to say when Jade turned and walked to the other side of the room, her arms folded and head bent. For one awful moment, it looked as if she wasn't going to stop and her head would smash into the window, sending glass flying in all directions.

What had Sarah said to cause such a dramatic reaction? Had she sounded too self-pitying, too self-centred? She felt a lump in her throat, another swell of nausea, the few sips of tea she'd taken gushing into her mouth. She clamped a hand over it and swallowed frantically, all the while keeping an eye on Jade, who had stopped centimetres from the glass.

'Poor widow.' Jade turned, rested back against the window and stared across the room, pinning Sarah to the sofa with her eyes. 'You didn't love Nick. You were going to leave him. You'd have already left him if you hadn't misplaced your child.'

In her confusion, it was the word *misplaced* that stuck in Sarah's head. Misplaced! Like a set of house keys. Or a book she'd been reading. A casual *oh I've put it down somewhere and can't for the life of me find it*. A word that made light of her loss. Was it her fault? Had she made her lack of love for Kaya so apparent to all? She wanted to scream at Jade, to say she *had* loved, *did* love her daughter, that she'd been confused. But the face was still twisted in anger. There didn't seem to be any point in arguing. 'I think I'd better be going,' Sarah said, putting the mug down.

'Why, because the truth is too hard to hear?' Jade pushed away from the window and returned to the sofa, flopping down on it with a loud hiss. 'Shit, you're a nightmare, you know that? You moaned about how unhappy you were being a mother, moaned even more about being trapped with a man you didn't love. And here you are, no child, no husband, and you're still complaining.'

There was something wrong with that thinking, but Sarah was so stunned that she couldn't find the words to argue her case. The pain relief she'd taken earlier that morning was wearing off and everything was beginning to hurt. Physical pain, mental confusion. 'I...' she started only to stop when she heard Jade laugh.

'Oh yes, start with that, that's classic you, isn't it? Everything's about you. I, I, bloody I.'

Sarah took a couple of deep breaths, willing the latest wave of nausea to subside along with the desire to cry big, fat tears. It was all so unfair.

'And after all I've done for you too. I'm so sick of you.'

Ignoring the rolling nausea, Sarah stared. Her crazy idea – had she been right? She glanced towards the door. Her mobile was flat. She had lied to the hospital staff about where she was going, used the phone at reception to ring for a taxi, and had asked the driver to wait for her out on the street rather than the car park. Nobody knew where she was.

It was, as the saying goes, the straw that broke the camel's back, and Sarah felt herself fall apart. What did it matter what happened next? 'All you've done for me!' Her voice came out louder than she'd intended. She saw the look of surprise on Jade's face with satisfaction. Time to fight back. Maybe her ridiculous, crazy idea hit the damn nail right on the bloody head. 'That's what this is all about, isn't it? Get Nick out of the picture, be there for me, and this time, maybe I'll fall into your ever-willing arms.'

'What?'

'You heard me. The hit-and-run. The police said it wasn't an accident. I think you got rid of Nick.'

This time, Jade's burst of laughter wasn't cruel or sarcastic; it was genuinely amused. 'Seriously!' She wiped a tear from her eye. 'You think I killed Nick? I'm not sure why I'm laughing really; it's not in the slightest bit funny that my oldest friend would believe I'm that much of a monster.' She got to her feet again and without another word, crossed to a cabinet, opened a door, and bent to take out a bottle and two glasses. 'If ever there was a time for a drink, this is it.' She sat and poured a generous amount into each glass. 'Here,' she said, putting one on the table beside the mug.

It wasn't a good idea to mix alcohol with pain medication, Sarah knew that, but it didn't stop her from picking up the drink and sniffing it. It was whisky. Not a drink she liked. She downed it in one and held out her glass.

'Glad to see some things don't change,' Jade said, knocking back her own drink and refilling both glasses. 'Now can you please tell me what fucking maggot has got into your head to say such a ridiculous thing?'

43

Sarah took the second whisky and stared into it. Had she been wrong? She had been before, so many damn times. The alcohol was easing the pain or numbing the pain receptors anyway. 'The press hasn't picked the story up as yet, but they will. It wasn't a random hit-and-run. The police said the car deliberately swerved to hit us.' She looked across the room. Met Jade's eyes and tried to read what they said. Maybe she could have done if it hadn't been for the residual effects of being thrown through the air, the concussion, painkillers, the alcohol, the wrenching loss.

Jade gave a slight smile. There was a sadness to the twist. 'And you thought I'd have done such a thing?'

Sarah rubbed a hand over her forehead. Her head was aching, her hand trembling and the nausea was still bothering her. She shouldn't be drinking alcohol. She lifted the glass and swallowed half. 'The last time we met, I told you I wanted out of my marriage to Nick, but I couldn't leave until Kaya was found. I remember you saying that my life was a mess and it would be up to you as usual to sort it out for me.'

Jade looked as if she couldn't believe what she was hearing. 'I meant by listening to you going on and bloody on as you always do. I meant by offering advice, by being there for you when you made whatever decision you finally made. What I didn't mean was that I was going to kill that poor fool, Nick, to release you from a marriage you should never have gone into in the first place. I've never said I told you so, but I'm saying it now: I bloody told you at the time that marrying him was a bad idea.' She slouched back after her rant, lifted her glass, and took a mouthful. A thought struck her and jolted her forward again. 'You were hit too, not just Nick. Why would I have tried to kill you, for goodness' sake? You know how I feel about you.'

Sarah did. She'd taken enough advantage of her friend's romantic feelings for her over the years. Had milked it for her own ends. Was that it? Had she been looking at the hit-and-run from the wrong angle? 'Yes, I do know.' She frowned as she tried to unravel this new, worrying thought. 'Was that it, Jade? If you couldn't make me happy, nobody was going to, and poor Nick was simply in the way.' Even as the sentence hung in the air between them, she realised how crazy she sounded.

So did Jade, who shook her head. 'Would you listen to yourself! What a ridiculously over-inflated ego you have!'

Sarah put the glass down and rested her hand on her forehead. 'Would it be possible to have another cup of tea, or even a glass of water. Please,' she added, seeing Jade's frown.

Her request was met with a heavy sigh as Jade's anger faded. 'You look wretched; are you sure you should be out of hospital?'

Wretched was an understatement. The aches and pains seemed to be multiplying, the nausea getting worse, not better. She shouldn't have had the whisky. Proof that she shouldn't have done came in one dramatic gush from her stomach before she could stop it or turn her head away. The deluge covered her chest and the pillow Jade had put under her broken arm. It was a mess. She was a mess. Finally, she did what she hadn't done after Kaya was taken, or Nick was killed: she cried, loud sobs from her broken heart.

44

Sarah must have passed out because when she opened her eyes, she was lying full-length on the sofa in Jade's living room. There was a soft pillow under her head, a cushion under her arm, the vomit-stained T-shirt she'd been wearing was gone and a blanket had been draped over her. Everything still ached but the awful nausea had subsided. Hopefully permanently.

A small lamp had been left on but otherwise the room was in darkness. She'd obviously been there for hours. The house was quiet, only the soft hum of the fridge in the kitchen breaking the silence. She could get up and go home or stay and face Jade in the morning.

Perhaps the nausea had affected her mind because with it gone, her thoughts were making more sense. The idea that Jade had tried to murder her, and had murdered Nick, was beyond nonsensical. Her friend might have her dark side, but she'd never shown any tendency towards violence. All she'd ever been was kind and generous with her time and care. And Sarah had repaid her with suspicion and mistrust.

She was still wondering what to do when she heard a slight squeak as the door to the hallway was opened a crack, a light behind illuminating Jade in the gap. 'I'm not asleep,' she said.

'I don't think you fell asleep,' Jade said, coming into the room. 'I think you fell unconscious.' She slid her hand along the wall for the light switch and pressed it, blinking as her eyes readjusted.

Sarah shuffled into a seating position and stared at her. The faded, cotton pyjamas with a rip at the knee made her look younger, more vulnerable than her usual weekend jeans and navy T-shirt combination. Her hair was mussed as if she'd spent hours lying in her bed tossing and turning. She looked as bad as Sarah felt.

'This is the best I could find,' Jade said, handing her a T-shirt. She didn't offer to help her to dress.

Sarah watched as Jade filled the kettle and switched it on before moving around the kitchen in silence, opening and shutting cupboard doors. She ached for the time when conversation would have flowed easily between them, and if they weren't speaking, the silence would have been comfortable... not this tense void waiting to be filled.

She pulled the worn, cotton T-shirt over her head and manoeuvred the cast carefully through the armhole. Every movement hurt. Resting her head back, she shut her eyes, taking a deep breath when Kaya's face papered the inside of her eyelids, the image dissolving and reforming into Nick's face. He smiled sadly as if he was aware of his demise.

'Come to the table and have something to eat.'

Sarah reluctantly opened her eyes. It sounded more like an order than a request but she wasn't going to argue. After her ludicrous and cruel accusation, she was grateful Jade was still speaking to her.

Moving was difficult when everything hurt. She held her cast close to her chest, shuffled to the edge of the sofa. Every movement made her wince. Had she been alone, she'd have groaned. Conscious of Jade's eyes on her, she bit down on her lip and pushed to her feet.

Jade had poured tea into a mug for her. She'd also buttered a slice of toast and cut it diagonally into quarters. Sarah picked up the mug and took a sip. 'Thank you.'

'It's only tea and toast.'

'I meant for not throwing me out. I'm not sure I'd have been so kind, so understanding.'

Jade looked at her for a long moment, as if weighing up what she'd said. Slowly, she shook her head. 'No, you wouldn't have been.'

Sarah waited for her to add that she was joking but she didn't.

Jade must have realised her comment needed elaboration. 'Just because I love you, it doesn't make me unaware of your shortcomings.'

Sarah was in no position to take offence. She had, after all, accused her friend of murdering Nick. How could she have been so stupid? 'My shortcomings,' she said. 'You're referring to my total self-centredness?'

'That, and your inability to see the big picture, to face up to your mistakes and make difficult decisions.' Jade licked toast crumbs from her fingers before reaching for a second slice and buttering it with a total lack of concern. When she was finished, she took a huge bite, chewed slowly, and swallowed before speaking again. 'But you're fun to be with, you have a way of looking at life that amuses me, and despite being totally selfish, you are kind and generous, and a dedicated doctor who truly cares for the patients in her care, which, these days, is very admirable.'

Sarah didn't know whether to laugh or cry. 'Thanks, I think.' She picked up a triangle of toast and nibbled the pointed end. 'Can you forgive me for being so stupid?'

'For thinking that I was so besotted with you that I'd rather see you dead than not have you, you mean?'

Sarah cringed. Was that really what she'd said? Yesterday was all a bit of a blur. Or maybe it was simply easier to forget rather than having to face up to what she'd done. *Her inability to face up to her mistakes.* Just as Jade had said. 'When the detective asked if there was anyone who wanted to harm us—'

'You thought of me!'

'Not immediately.' As if that made it easier. She dropped the piece of toast on the plate. 'You have to remember that my head was all over the place. I had concussion. Nick was dead, Kaya still missing.' *Poor me.* She shook her head. 'God, you are right, I'm such a pathetic piece of work.' She picked up her tea. 'I'm sorry. I really am. Sorry for being a lousy friend, for being stupid, for arriving here uninvited, for puking over your sofa. For every fucking thing.'

Jade sat back in her chair and folded her arms. 'What about sorry for giving Kaya away? Or doesn't that count?'

45

Sarah wasn't sure she'd heard right.

But it seemed Jade was going to make sure her words weren't misinterpreted. 'Don't look so surprised. I know you better than anyone and know exactly how your brain ticks. You didn't love Kaya and thought she'd be better off with someone who would love her as she deserved.'

'That's even more ridiculous than me accusing you of trying to kill me and Nick! If I'd been that desperate to get rid of Kaya, I could have put her up for adoption.'

Jade shook her head. 'No, Nick adored her, he'd never have agreed.'

'So what, you think I set the abduction up? Don't be so bloody ridiculous! Where would I find someone to take Kaya, no questions asked?' She looked around for her bag. 'I need to take something for the pain.'

Jade got to her feet, returning a moment later with the handbag in one hand, a mobile in the other. 'I put your phone on to charge last night.'

Sarah popped two pills into her mouth. It would be a while before they'd take the edge off the pain. It didn't matter; it was keeping her alert. 'You really thought I'd arranged for someone to take Kaya?' When Jade nodded, she barked a laugh. 'Bloody hell, we both read too many psychological thrillers. It's no wonder we're friends; we have the same far-fetched way of thinking.'

Jade didn't appear convinced. 'You promise you'd nothing to do with it?'

'Of course I didn't!' Sarah almost shrieked the words.

'Then why—' Jade stopped, held a hand up and shrugged. 'It doesn't matter.'

'No, come on, out with it. Let's clear all the damn tables while we're at it!'

'Right, I will if you drink your tea and eat your toast.'

Sarah glared at her. 'Fuck's sake!' But she drank the tea, ate most of the toast, and accepted another cup of tea when Jade held the teapot out. 'Right, get on with it.'

'Why did you never seem particularly bothered that Kaya was missing?'

Sarah froze.

'Nick always looked distraught, and he'd lost so much weight. His grief was obvious, whereas you...' She shrugged again as if that said it all.

Jade was right. Compared to Nick, Sarah had appeared unaffected by the kidnapping of their child. 'Nick fell apart; one of us had to stay strong, deal with the police, do those ghastly TV appeals.'

'But there was more to it than that?'

It was the worst thing about having a friend who knew you almost better than you knew yourself. 'I was the one who'd handed Kaya over to that woman; there were plenty of people who were happy to lay the blame right at my feet. One of the police officers couldn't keep the judgement from her eyes.' She picked up the mug, cradled it, then put it down without drinking. 'Worst of all was the guilt. I blamed Kaya, even before she was born, for keeping me in a marriage I no longer wanted to be in. Blamed her for being a baby, for needing me to be there. My feelings for her were so tangled up in my desire to be out of the marriage and away from Nick's smothering possessiveness that I didn't realise how much I loved her until she was gone.'

'Sounds like you'd nothing to do with her abduction, but...' Jade stopped again. 'I heard you say that you knew she was safe. It's one of the things that made me suspicious.'

'I think it made the police suspicious too.' Sarah sighed. 'It was why I took that poor baby, Kayden, from outside the convenience store.'

Jade's eyes widened. 'Ah, yes, I did wonder.'

'I wanted them to see me as the victim, not the perpetrator, because if they were focusing on me, they weren't looking for whoever took Kaya.' Sarah placed her hand over her heart and tapped. 'I can feel it here that Kaya is safe. That might sound incredibly stupid and out there, but I can't help that. In my heart, I know she's safe somewhere.'

Sarah wanted to see even a glimmer of understanding cross Jade's face. If she couldn't convince this woman who knew her so well that she wasn't involved in Kaya's abduction, how could she convince anyone else?

46

Everything was the way it was supposed to be. I never got tired of sitting and staring at Meg, a bottle in her hand, our baby curled up in her arm.

Her happiness was my happiness.

Our love was complete. Kaya had made it so.

There was only one small problem.

One last thing I needed to sort out.

Only then would we be safe.

47

Sarah left Jade's house once the pain relief had kicked in. The last few minutes were spent in uneasy silence as they tried to come to terms with the suspicions they'd had of each other. Their friendship, the years they'd know each other, they suddenly seemed to count for nothing. Maybe some friendships had an inbuilt use-by date.

In the taxi, she checked her mobile and quickly answered messages from friends. Her parents had rung several times. 'Sorry,' she said, when her mother picked up on the first ring. 'I fell asleep as soon as I got home. It did me good; I feel much stronger this morning.' Some truth was mixed in with the lies. She did feel stronger, physically. It was only inside her head that the weakness lingered.

When the taxi pulled up at her address, she climbed out awkwardly and stood looking up to the window of the apartment. *All hers now.* It was ironic. All those months wanting to be free of their marriage, of Nick, and here she was, with exactly what she wanted, only to find it wasn't. At least, not like this.

She turned back to the taxi, half-thinking about returning to Jade's and begging to be allowed to stay, but she was too late; it had already eased away from the kerb. If she wasn't such a pathetic wreck, she might have run after it. Maybe waved her broken arm for good measure. Her eyes following the taxi, caught movement on the opposite side of the street. A figure who ducked around the corner out of sight as Sarah tried to get a better look. But they hadn't moved away. She could see their arm lying along the edge of the building and as she stood staring, she saw a face peer around, then quickly withdraw.

So many emotions rushed through Sarah that she staggered under the weight of them and cried out, a sound that was half fear, half disbelieving laugh as she teetered on the edge of hysteria. She slapped a hand over her mouth, took a deep breath through her nose and let it out slowly, her eyes never leaving the corner of the building.

It's difficult to walk backwards when your body aches all over, and you're afraid to take your eyes from one distant point, but Sarah managed it, backing up till she felt the door behind her. Keeping watch for her peeping-Tom, she shoved a hand into her bag to search for the keys. Everything was more difficult one-handed and it took her a few minutes to locate them among the rubbish that had accumulated at the bottom. Finally pulling them out, she opened the main door, and with one last glance at the corner of the building opposite, hurried inside and slammed the door behind her.

Breathless, she rested against the wall. It had been her imagination, that's all. Or rather her disturbed thought processes. Unsurprising given everything that had occurred, the painkillers she was popping. Her imagination. There was nobody out there.

Pushing away from the wall, she crossed to the lift. It was then she heard it – Nick's laughter. Coming to her as if he was there, right beside her. Then his voice, telling her to hurry up, that he'd race her to the fourth floor.

She used to wait till he'd run ahead before hammering on the lift button, laughing as she did so. Bouncing out on the fourth floor, sometimes before him, she'd greet him with a laugh and a kiss. Sometimes, when the lift was slow, he'd be there before her, looking back down the stairwell as if wondering where she was. She'd jump on him, startling him, then they'd both laugh and fall into the apartment together.

There had been happy times. In the early days. Sometimes, she forgot that.

She took the lift and at the top, when the door opened, hurried through the echoes of laughter from days gone by, the keys in her hand, struggling to see through her tears to fit the correct one into the lock.

Inside, the echoes of laughter died away, replaced with an uncomfortable silence. She'd been in the apartment alone before, but always with the anticipation of Nick's arrival. Now, this was it. No husband, no child.

The last time she'd been home, she'd been a wife; now she was a widow. She walked from room to room, picking up and dropping things belonging to Nick. A jumper he'd taken off and left draped across the back of a chair. A book he'd started and would never finish, a supermarket receipt marking where he'd left off. A glass, the edge smeared with the lip salve he favoured. She thought about pressing her lips to it, but even on her own as she was, she didn't want to be such a hypocrite.

She hadn't loved him, but oddly, she missed him.

Dropping her bag on the sofa, and the plastic bag on the floor, she looked around the apartment. They had insurance. It would pay off the mortgage. The apartment would be hers; she could sell up, pay Nick's parents back the money they'd borrowed and move on. Maybe she'd follow her dream and find a GP position somewhere rural.

Without her daughter?

There was no way to explain the feeling she had. The one that told her Kaya was safe and being well looked after. *Wishful thinking.* That's what Jade's eyes had said. Perhaps. Sarah couldn't explain it. Or she didn't want to. What was it her friend had said – that she was always reluctant to face up to the truth?

Perhaps it was true but she knew she was stronger with that knowledge to cling to.

Crossing to the unit in the corner, she bent to open the cupboard and removed the toys she'd shoved inside what seemed a lifetime ago. She put them on the sofa and sat beside them.

And there she was, with exactly the life she'd wanted. Husband free, child free.

She picked up one of Kaya's toys and held it to her face.

Plush bears, it appeared, were the perfect repository for tears.

48

A combination of exhaustion and painkillers ensured Sarah slept all night. A restless sleep, she tossed and turned in the clutches of nightmares and woke in the morning unrefreshed. The sheets were twisted, the duvet had slipped to the floor and somewhere during the night, Nick's pillow had gone flying across the room. It sat in a corner looking abandoned.

It was hard to drag her gaze from it, so she lay there, eyes wide and staring. It would have been nice to have gone into work, to feel needed and useful, but she guessed that wasn't an option. With no baby to feed or change, no husband to pander to, there was no reason to get up. She was back in the single, childless life she'd wanted.

Poor widow. Jade's words taunted her and forced her from the bed. Anyway, there were things to do. A funeral to arrange. That damn TV appeal to prepare for. Widow's weeds to find.

She might not have loved Nick, but he had been her husband, he deserved respect, and if dressing like a grieving widow was what she needed to do, then so be it.

Everything was rendered more awkward by the cast on her arm. She used a large plastic bin liner to protect it while she had a shower and washed her hair. It took time and every swear word she knew to get it done.

She'd have liked to tie her hair back but one-handed, it was an impossible task so she left it loose and tucked behind her ears. Widow's weeds weren't as difficult to find in her wardrobe as she'd thought. Black jeans and T-shirt would do for that day, and smarter black trousers and a wide-sleeved shirt for the TV appeal whenever the police had it organised. The same outfit would be perfect for Nick's funeral.

Nick's funeral. She needed to ring his parents. She'd spoken to them briefly while she lay in the hospital bed but had no memory of what had been said. All she remembered was their red eyes and devastated expressions.

Black clothes and no make-up, she hoped she looked suitably funereal as she video-called her parents-in-law on WhatsApp. 'Hi,' she said when it was answered, angling the phone so they had a clear view of her.

She was instantly sorry she hadn't simply rung them. Faced with their honest grief, she felt like an imposter. She *was* an imposter. It made it worse when their first words to her weren't about their loss but concern for her.

'We were speaking to your mother; she told us you were home and your friend was staying with you. We're pleased you have someone to help you through these difficult days.'

Sarah shut her eyes on the lie that had been passed from her parents to Nick's. 'Thank you.' Their sorrow was almost palpable and she searched for something comforting to say. There were probably appropriate words, suitable clichés or aphorisms, but not one came to mind so she settled for a version of the truth. 'It's strange being here without Nick. He filled the apartment, you know, with his laughter and his love.'

'He was a good boy.' Mrs Westfield dabbed at her eyes with a handkerchief. 'I hate to ask, but I assume there's no word about Kaya?'

'No.' She told them about the new TV appeal. 'I don't know when it will be. Soon, I'd imagine.' To make the most of her grieving widow status.

Mrs Westfield wasn't a stupid woman; she understood why the police had suggested another appeal. 'Your grief might stir the conscience of whoever took her. Nick's death might achieve something good.'

Your grief. Sarah wanted to cry for all the pretence. For the loss she didn't feel and for the one she did.

Mr Westfield stared at her from the phone. His face was pale and he appeared to have shrunk in on himself, his shoulders slouched, cheeks hollowed. Even his voice had taken on a quavering quality as if the loss of his only child had sucked the heart from him. 'We'll help with the funeral of course; with anything you'd like us to do.'

She wanted to cry in the face of his misery, stupidly grateful that there were people who had sincerely loved Nick and would mourn his loss. 'Thank you. It won't be for a few weeks yet.'

'A burial, not a cremation. Of course, you'd know he hated the thought of a cremation.'

She didn't. It wasn't something they'd ever discussed. Why would they have done? They had their whole lives ahead of them.

'You'll give a eulogy, won't you?' Mrs Westfield said. 'I know Nick would like that.'

A eulogy. A paean for a man she didn't love. Wasn't it the least she could do? 'Of course I will.'

'We'd been so worried about him before he met you. He'd had one failed romance after the other and he was a man who desperately wanted someone to love. Then you came along like an angel from heaven and made him so happy.'

Sarah kept her smile in place with difficulty. *One failed romance after the other?* It was the first time she'd heard this. She and Nick had never discussed their previous partners apart from a laughing mention that they'd both had histories. Maybe those old girlfriends had quickly tired of his neediness, his possessiveness too. Only stupid Sarah, herself on the rebound from a failed relationship, had hung on for too long.

Thankful that Nick's parents would never know the truth, she said, 'He was a lovely man, and he made me happy too.' It was partially the truth. Nick had been a lovely man, and there were moments when they were happy together, just not enough. The conversation with his parents faltered and sputtered until there was nothing left to say. 'I'll ring again in a day or two when I have dates for the funeral,' Sarah said.

'Thank you. Take good care of yourself.'

The poor widow. Of course she would. Hanging up, she dropped her head onto her hand. One phone call and she was spent. *Or just feeling sorry for herself.* She forced herself to keep going, to make the necessary phone calls to her parents, her friends, Nick's employer, mutual friends. One after the other, mostly the same words to each, accepting commiserations, promising to keep in touch, to let them know the funeral arrangements.

She found an undertaker by doing an internet search for the nearest one. Expecting to have to do a lot herself, she was relieved to find they did a comprehensive service to include announcements and all the other minutiae that would probably take them seconds and her hours. The most difficult task, since they were going with a burial rather than a cremation, was to choose a coffin and she was staggered by the choice. She knew from the hospital that an open casket was out of the question thanks to Nick's injuries, but apart from that, the choice was still immense. There were cardboard coffins, personalised ones, wool ones. 'Unbelievable!' she muttered, flicking through them before deciding on a traditional solid oak coffin to please Nick's conservative parents.

It took only five minutes to give the undertaker sufficient information to book the funeral service on a date almost three weeks away. She paid for it in full and that was one huge job out of the way. It wasn't until it was all done that she realised she'd been crying the whole time. She hadn't loved Nick, he'd driven her crazy at times, but she'd have given anything to see him walk through the door.

Wiping tears from her eyes, she stood and crossed to the window. The clear view of the wide street below was one of the reasons they'd fallen in love with the apartment. It gave a feeling of space and light.

Sometimes, she'd look down on the little people passing below and invent magic lives for them. Not that day, her mind too occupied with what on earth she was going to say at Nick's funeral. Maybe words would have come to her if her gaze hadn't drifted and stopped on someone who was looking up.

She pulled back in alarm, then laughed uncertainly. She was being silly. Nobody standing below could possibly see into the fourth-floor apartment, nor could they see her. With false bravado, she moved back to the window and stared out again, prepared to laugh at her foolishness. Instead, she gasped. They may not be able to see her, but there was definitely someone down there staring intently at her window.

She hadn't imagined that feeling earlier either, had she?

Someone had followed her and now someone was watching her.

She'd been so obsessed with the crazy, warped idea that Jade had been responsible for the hit-and-run, and so relieved to be proven wrong, that she hadn't given any consideration to who the guilty party might be. It might be that the police were wrong, and Sarah and Nick had simply been victims of a random act of violence. Perhaps some idiot had seen two bigger idiots crossing the road where they shouldn't, and had decided to teach them a lesson.

But if the police were right, and it wasn't random?

She had told them that she and Nick were ordinary people who had been living an ordinary life till Kaya was abducted. It had been the truth, more or less. It wasn't necessary to explain that she'd wanted a divorce. There was nothing extraordinary about a marriage falling apart. But since the abduction, everything had changed. Nick was dead, and Sarah was being followed and watched. Nick was dead... she was still alive. If they had been targeted, if someone had deliberately set out to try to kill them, maybe there was someone out there who wasn't happy with a job half done.

49

Sarah should ring the police. Luckily, she hadn't told them her crazy idea about Jade, so she wouldn't lose all credibility when she told them her latest concerns, her belief that she was being followed and watched. She tried to calm down and think logically. It might have nothing to do with the hit-and-run; she may have simply picked up a stalker. Her face had been in the papers and on the news often enough recently to have drawn the wrong kind of attention.

She'd have suspected a reporter from one of the tackier tabloids had they been more in her face, but members of the press didn't tend to hide behind buildings, nor would they be staring up at her apartment window without a hope of getting a photograph.

A band of tension wrapped itself around her head and squeezed painfully, mangling her already tangled thoughts. Perhaps the concussion had been more serious than the doctors in the hospital had realised. It would be far better to believe that instead of the alternative, that everything, all that had happened in the last few weeks, had driven her over the edge. Far better to believe either option than to consider that there was someone out there wanting to do her harm.

She took a deep breath. No, she might be close to that edge, but she wasn't over it. She was tired, stressed, all perfectly acceptable in the face of what she'd been through. *Poor widow*. She slapped the thought away. Under the circumstances, she'd every right to be feeling sorry for herself. No, she wasn't over the edge but her scrambled brain was definitely playing tricks on her. After all, she'd imagined she'd heard Nick's laughter, hadn't she?

Nick's laughter, Kaya's happy gurgle. If she listened hard, she could still hear them. The faintest echoes as if drifting from an alternative universe. It didn't mean they were both dead. Nor did it mean she was going crazy.

Wiping tears from her eyes, she edged slowly back to the window. There was no point in being stupid; if there was someone down there, staring at her window, she would ring the police and let them deal with it. If there wasn't, it was proof she'd imagined it, and she'd forget about it.

Her shoulders slumped in relief and the band of tension around her head eased when there was nobody suspicious below. She stood a long time, peering up and down the street, checking every one of the innocent people who were going about their daily business, their faces a tiny blur, none showing the slightest interest in the sad, pathetic woman four floors above.

Turning from the window, she stared around the apartment. There was no echo of laughter any more, no baby's gurgle. It was all so very, very quiet. And suddenly small. The walls were closing in on her making it hard to breathe, harder to think. She needed to be outside, be among people, feel the sun on her face.

She brushed aside her earlier fears, grabbed her bag, and left the apartment. If there was someone watching or following her, she didn't notice and no longer cared. All she wanted to do was keep walking, one foot in front of the other, eyes fixed on the pavement ahead, veering around oncoming pedestrians without ever looking up to see their faces.

It wasn't until she reached her destination, a park she'd frequented several times in the last few weeks of her pregnancy, that she looked up. It was a pretty park with neat, colourful flowerbeds and a well-designed children's area. A couple of mothers were standing chatting as their offspring played. There was nobody else in sight.

She sat on the same bench she'd used every time, lifted her face to the sun and shut her eyes. It was a warm day, but the heat wasn't penetrating to the cold that had settled around her heart. Laughter drifted across from the women. Were they friends or had they bonded over stories of their children? It was a club Sarah had sniffed at; now she'd give anything to belong. To be able to stand with them and exchange funny stories of motherhood. She'd stand with one hand on the handle of Kaya's buggy because she was a good mother; she'd never take her eyes off her child.

Sarah kept her head back and her eyes shut, letting the women's laughter swell and fade, swell and fade. It had been maybe a month since her last visit. She'd been as big as a house and had struggled to sit on the rather low bench, leaning a hand on the back of it and lowering herself slowly onto the seat. It had been raining earlier that day and the playground was empty. Rainwater from the wet bench had wicked up her maternity trousers and she hadn't been able to bring herself to care. Not even when she'd felt a chill seep into her knickers.

Only a month ago. She'd been wallowing in self-pity. Married to a man she didn't love, having a child she thought she didn't want.

And now, look at her. Widowed and childless. Definitely a case of be careful what you wish for. If someone had told her back then that she'd lose both, would she have cheered? No, of course not, she'd been miserable, she hadn't been – wasn't – a monster.

She'd never have wished harm on Nick. He'd been a good man. He'd deserved better. The conversation she'd had with his mother earlier came back to her, making her frown. Sarah hadn't known that Nick had had *one failed romance after the other*. He'd never discussed his relationship history, neither had she, although she had told him when they'd met that she'd recently split with an ex after a three-year relationship. She'd told him it hadn't ended well. It had been the perfect opportunity for him to have offered stories of his own failed romances. He hadn't. On the contrary, he'd indicated that he'd been the one to end previous relationships and said he hadn't met anyone he truly loved, till he'd met her. Now it looked as though he'd lied to her. Perhaps she hadn't known him as well as she'd thought.

It didn't matter; he'd loved her, and she hadn't wished him harm. Nor, despite her confused feelings about her pregnancy, had she wished for Kaya to be taken from her.

A month ago, she'd been in turmoil, unhappy in her marriage, blaming her pregnancy for being unable to escape. Only when she'd separated her feelings for Nick from her feelings for Kaya was she able to see the truth. She loved her daughter and wanted her back. When she was returned, *when* not *if*, Sarah would spend the rest of her life proving her love.

For almost an hour, she sat there, watching children play, soaking up the sun. Trying to get rid of the chill that lingered inside her. The feeling that Kaya was safe was still with her. Safe, but with someone else, she needed her daughter home.

Sitting for so long had been a bad idea and she groaned as she tried to stand, needing to wait as a sharp pain eased before trying again. She held on to the back of the bench as she stretched her muscles, only then attempting to walk away with jerky steps that made her feel one hundred years old. They had eased by the time she reached the exit.

There was a café on the way. It was busy, bustling, lively. She didn't hesitate. It was putting off the inevitable return to the empty flat, but another hour, some food, and a decent cup of coffee might make that return easier.

She ordered at the counter and took her tray, balancing it in one hand, as she crossed to an empty table in the corner. Despite the bruises that marked her face and arms, nobody gave her a second glance; everyone was too consumed by their own lives. And in the ordinariness of it, the notion that someone was stalking her suddenly seemed nonsensical.

The coffee was excellent, the sandwich very tasty. And she'd been right, it was doing her good. And still she was reluctant to finish and go home, lingering over the last drops of coffee until there was nothing but froth left in the bottom of the cup.

Regardless of her insistence that the earlier worry about stalkers was nonsense, she couldn't help darting a look up and down the street as she exited the café and started the journey home.

When she arrived at the apartment building, she saw that someone had left the main door ajar. It wasn't an unusual occurrence; the door was heavy and if left to swing shut, the lock frequently didn't catch. Normally, she'd be irritated by the lapse. That day, she was worried. She peered through the glass. There didn't appear to be anyone on the other side waiting to pounce on her.

She made sure the door was shut tight behind her. Later, she'd email the management company and ask them to remind all residents to ensure the door was shut after them. It wouldn't make much of a difference. The residents who would read it were those who were already conscientious. But Sarah would feel better for having done something.

The lift door opened immediately when she called it, opening on the fourth floor a short time later. Sarah was thinking about the eulogy she'd promised to write. Lost in her thoughts, she stepped out and walked the short distance to her apartment door.

It was open. She been so desperate to escape the increasing claustrophobia of the apartment, had she been stupidly careless and not shut it properly behind her? Surely not. The lift door swishing shut behind her startled her. She yelped, twisting to look behind her, the movement too quick for her damaged body and drawing a further groan of pain.

It was tempting to call the lift again and return to the ground floor. She could ring the police. But what if she had simply left her apartment door open? There was only one way to find out. There seemed no point in delaying and before her nerves took control, she crossed and put her hand on the door. It seemed sensible to be wary, so she stood a moment listening for sounds from within. When none came, she pushed the door open so hard, it hit the wall behind with a loud clunk. As she stepped over the threshold, the silence was broken by her heavy breathing and the thump of her heart. The small entrance hall was as she'd left it. An umbrella was propped by the side of the hall table, the ceramic elephant still on top of it where it should be, its trunk still raised.

She'd left the damn door open, hadn't she? What a fool she was!

She was still castigating herself as she crossed to the living-room door. Having convinced herself that all was okay, when she opened the door and saw the mess, the shock made her stagger.

'Shit!' She put a hand out for the doorframe to stop herself falling as she stared at the chaos. In the couple of hours she'd been gone, someone had wreaked havoc in the room. Drawers had been pulled out; the contents emptied onto the floor. Cupboard doors hung open. In the kitchen, dried pasta and rice spilled from burst packets that had been swept from the shelves. Turning away from the scene of destruction, with a hand on the wall to support her as she walked, she made her way to the bedrooms. It was the same in both. The drawers of the bedside tables in the main room had been pulled out and upturned onto the bed. Wardrobe doors stood open, some of the clothes pulled from the hangers. Every drawer in the chest of drawers had been yanked out, the contents in a heap on the floor.

It was the same in the spare bedroom, the one Nick had used as an office. It was as if they'd opened every drawer of the filing cabinet, pulled files out and thrown them into the air to land willy-nilly. The only things that hadn't been touched were Kaya's. The flat-pack crib was still balanced against the chest of drawers holding her clothes, the Moses basket still sat on top where Nick had put it on their return from Devon.

He'd put all her toys neatly inside. Sarah reached for a plush, pink bear and held it close as she walked from room to room. There was nothing of value kept in the apartment. Her handbag, with her purse and mobile phone, had been with her. This, all of this, was simple, mindless destruction.

She couldn't handle this alone. The detective's card was still in the pocket of her jeans. She pulled it out and rang the number.

'DI Bilton.'

'It's Sarah Westfield. I went out. Just for a couple of hours. I'm back now. In the apartment. I've been burgled.' Her usual fluency seemed to have deserted her. She sagged against the wall. 'It's a mess.'

'You're sure the perpetrator isn't still on the premises, Mrs Westfield?'

Sarah wasn't sure of anything. Could someone be hiding in the apartment? She hadn't yet checked the bathroom. 'I don't know.' How pathetic she sounded. How pathetic she was. She swallowed the lump in her throat, but there were tears in her voice when she spoke again. 'I don't think so.'

'I'll send officers around. Go to a neighbour's, stay there till they arrive, okay?'

'Yes, okay.' She wouldn't. She didn't have more than a nodding acquaintance with any of the neighbours, and she didn't want the prurient curiosity of strangers to deal with on top of everything else. Instead, she yelled out, 'The police are on their way!' But if there was someone hiding in the bathroom, they were staying quiet. She edged along the wall to the door, shoved it open with a quick movement and stepped back. It was a small space, there was nobody hiding inside. Back in the living room, she stood at the window with her back to the mess and stared down at the street until she saw a squad car pull up below.

She hurried to press the main door release to allow them in and waited at the apartment door till they arrived. Minutes later, the lift opened and two uniformed officers she'd never met before stepped out. They seemed surprised to see her. 'We were told you'd be with a neighbour,' one said when she introduced herself.

She didn't bother to explain, standing back to wave them inside after they showed her their warrant cards. In her anxiety, they could have been showing her supermarket reward cards for all she knew. Her brain simply wasn't able to process any more information that day. They looked like police officers; that would be enough.

She stayed in the hallway as they went from room to room, assessing the damage.

'It's a mess, all right,' one said when they had finished. 'Can you tell if anything is missing?'

'Nothing obvious. We don't keep anything valuable here anyway.' Sarah lifted her hand to show her wedding and engagement ring. 'I'm not a jewellery lover and this is about it, apart from a few costume pieces which they didn't bother to take.'

'No expensive watches or things like that?'

'No.'

The other officer was examining the front door. 'Just a simple Yale lock; any self-respecting burglar would be able to open it in seconds.' He tapped the mortice lock further down the door. 'This wasn't engaged?'

'No, we rarely used it.' Or rather *she* rarely did. Nick had been more security conscious.

'And you say you found the main front door open?'

'Yes.' She shrugged. 'Unfortunately, it's an ongoing issue; people come through, let the door swing behind them and the lock doesn't always engage.'

'Right, well, it looks as if some git took advantage.'

His expression said more than words did. That people like her who didn't bother to lock up properly were always going to be taken advantage of. She wanted to grab him. To mention her earlier fears that she was being watched, maybe even stalked. She wanted to argue about the coincidence of she and Nick being the victim of a hit-and-run and now being the victim of a burglary. Wasn't it one coincidence too many on top of the abduction of their child? She wanted to ask just how much more she had to take before she fell apart. She wished DI Bilton had come. She might have been able to speak to her and talk about her growing worry that the trashing of her apartment was some kind of warning. These two weary police officers were sympathetic but ultimately uninterested in what they seemed to have decided was an opportunistic crime.

They took details and advised her once again to increase her security. 'If you intend to file an insurance claim for anything lost or damaged, you'll be able to say a report has been made. If you ring the station later, they'll give you a number to quote.'

As if that was the whole reason for their attendance. Perhaps it was. After all, they made no assurances the burglar would be caught.

When they'd gone, Sarah did what she should have done earlier: she inserted the key in the mortice lock and turned it.

50

Zoé-Lee and DS Lyn were in DI Bilton's office discussing their lack of progress. They were no closer to finding little Kaya, no closer to finding the driver involved in the hit-and-run that had killed Nick Westfield. It was time for Zoé-Lee to get back home where she belonged. Back to Tom and Raven. The thought of her husband and daughter would have made her smile if DI Bilton hadn't answered the phone and immediately held up a hand to catch their attention.

'You're sure the perpetrator isn't still on the premises, Mrs Westfield?'

Zoé-Lee exchanged a quick glance with DS Lyn and sat forward, suddenly alert and back in full police mode.

'I'll send officers around,' Bilton said. 'Go to a neighbour's, stay there till they arrive. Okay?' She cut the connection and redialled to organise the attendance of the nearest squad car. When she was done, she drummed the fingers of one hand on her desk, a frown carving her forehead neatly in half. 'Sarah Westfield's been burgled.'

Zoé-Lee sniffed. 'Another attempt to claim victim status?'

'Harsh,' Bilton said with the slightest of smiles. 'You've been against her from the beginning; you don't think she deserves a little sympathy?'

'If she was really burgled, yes, but I doubt she was. I bet we'll hear that there were a few drawers and cupboards opened and that was it. The kind of fake scene you could learn from watching any crime drama. There's probably a bloody YouTube video on how to make it look as if you've been burgled.'

'Yes, but you thought the hit-and-run was a set up too, didn't you? And it certainly wasn't. So how about you put your dislike of the woman to one side, eh?'

Zoé-Lee felt colour washing her cheeks. It was a gentle slap on her wrists, but it was a reprimand all the same. Worse, she knew she deserved it.

'I've asked them to let us know as soon as someone attends the scene,' Bilton said. 'Meanwhile, I want to go through everything we know about the abduction again. There has to be something we're missing. Somebody knows where Kaya is.'

They'd been through it all already. Several times. But none of them discounted the process as futile. Sometimes, simply looking at information from a different angle was enough to identify a crack that could burst a case wide open. But not this time. At the end of almost an hour, they were no wiser.

The ringing of the phone was a welcome interruption.

Bilton answered. Her end of the conversation, consisting of 'mmm' or 'mmhh' didn't enlighten Zoé-Lee or DS Lyn, who sat expectantly until the call finished.

'That was one of the officers who responded to the call to Sarah Westfield's,' Bilton said. 'The apartment had been trashed. Drawers emptied, contents of cupboards pulled out.'

'Ha!' Zoé-Lee couldn't resist the triumphant cry. 'I was right this time. I bet there was nothing taken, and no damage.'

'They said it was a mess, but there was no obvious damage.'

'What about the front door?'

Bilton shook her head. 'No evidence of tampering or of force, but there was only a Yale lock and we know how easy they are to open. The mortice lock hadn't been used and there isn't an alarm. On the ground floor, the main entrance door had been left open. According to Mrs Westfield, that's a frequent occurrence.'

'It's just all too pat, isn't it?' Zoé-Lee said.

'Leave aside your antipathy for the woman for a minute,' Bilton said, her voice sharp. 'If the main door was, as Westfield suggested, left open, maybe some opportunistic scrag-end decided to see if he could use it for his own ends.'

'Her apartment is on the fourth floor.'

'Apartments on the ground and first floor are more likely to have increased security because of the accessibility. Any scrote of even modicum intelligence would have headed to the third floor. Maybe he tried a few there, couldn't get access because the residents there did use their mortice locks. Perhaps the Westfields' apartment was the first he found that he was able to access.'

'Perhaps.' Zoé-Lee wasn't convinced. 'I know I sound as if my dislike of her is colouring my judgement but there's something odd about all of this.' She got to her feet, her tangled thoughts making her restless. 'Her child is kidnapped. Then she's involved in a hit-and-run where her husband is killed. And now she's been burgled.' She took her seat again, a curious expression on her face. 'I wonder if...' She stopped with a shake of her head.

'Go on,' Bilton said in the voice of someone who was never surprised at the weird or wonderful theories thrown in her direction.

Zoé-Lee sat forward. 'What if the burglary and the hit-and-run are connected? It's back to my original idea that maybe Sarah or Nick spoke to the wrong person and made whoever took Kaya nervous. They didn't have a lot of choice and decided to get rid of them. The hit-and-run was partially successful. Perhaps they'd hoped to find Sarah at home to finish off what they'd started, and trashed the place because they were pissed she wasn't there.'

Bilton sat back in her chair, rocking gently to and fro as she digested this. 'I'm always loath to quote Sherlock Holmes but as that great detective said, "once you eliminate the impossible, whatever remains, no matter how improbable, must be the truth."' She stopped the rocking motion. 'Perhaps whoever has Kaya thinks that getting rid of the biological parents will make them safe.'

'They're probably right,' Lyn said. 'If both Westfields were dead, and with no new leads, we wouldn't give up, but the investigation would eventually slide down the list of importance and drift into cold-case territory.'

They all knew the reality. Other cases would come to claim their attention and regardless of their desire to find Kaya, without the parents shouting to keep it alive, it would drift inexorably downward.

'If this crazy idea is right, doesn't it mean Sarah Westfield is in danger?' Zoé-Lee mightn't like the woman; it didn't mean she wished her harm.

'Yes, it does.' Bilton began to rock again, her hands on the desk, fingers playing a dull tune, the tempo increasing as she thought. 'But the chances of my being allowed to sanction overtime based on this are non-existent.' She looked from Lyn to Zoé-Lee. 'Which leaves you two.' She laughed at their look of dismay. 'Relax, I don't mean forever, just for today and tonight. I'll work on the powers that be meanwhile. Make your presence visible; it might be enough to frighten whoever it is away.' She nodded at Zoé-Lee. 'You head there now. DS Lyn will take over at midnight.'

'Right,' Zoé-Lee said. It had been her crazy idea; she could hardly complain.

'Find out if Sarah has noticed anyone hanging around recently, okay?'

'Will do.' She got to her feet. 'I'd better get going then.'

'Keep your eyes open. We've no idea how close we are to the truth here, so expect anything, suspect everything, and don't let your guard down.'

Thirty minutes later, having walked from the station to the apartment, Zoé-Lee rang Sarah Westfield's doorbell and waited to be let in.

51

When the police officers had left, Sarah took one look around the devastation and wanted to cry, weep, wail and bury herself under the duvet. It was tempting to ring her parents to ask for help, but if she did, she'd have to explain why she was in the apartment alone. There were a few friends she could ring, but she'd told them all the same story, that Jade was staying with her. If she told them all the truth now, that she'd lied about Jade staying, that moreover she'd accused her of being involved with Nick's death, and in turn that Jade had been suspicious of Sarah, what a great big can of wriggling worms she'd open.

No, she'd have to cope. She took two painkillers, supported her broken wrist in a scarf tied around her neck, and got on with the clean-up. She hauled the vacuum cleaner from the hall cupboard and pulled it into the kitchen where rice and pasta from the burst bags had spilled onto the counters and the floor. Pasta crunched underfoot as she stepped forward with the nozzle. It was strangely satisfying to see it all soon sucked up. Within minutes, the kitchen looked as it always did.

The living room was next. It might have made sense to go through everything and throw stuff out while she was at it, but that was for another day when she had two working hands. For now, she desperately wanted to have some semblance of normality restored so she picked up the drawers. Empty, they were easy to lift with one hand and slide back where they belonged. Without any consideration as to what went where, she picked up the items that had been dumped on the floor and dropped them back inside, shutting each drawer as it was filled. The books were soon back on the shelves. Old DVDs and CDs, most of which could be given to charity shops or simply dumped, she piled back into the cupboard. The sofa seats were more difficult, each heavy and awkward to lift with one hand. She was sweating and swearing by the time she had them slotted back in place. The cushions were easier and were soon propped where they should be. Her only plant, one her mother had bought them as a housewarming gift, was picked up and replaced on the mantelpiece, the loose soil and broken leaves on the floor sucked up with the vacuum cleaner.

It had taken almost an hour. If she didn't open the cupboards or the drawers, it all looked as it usually did. One down, two to go. Dragging the vacuum behind her like a naughty dog, she headed for her bedroom. If she stopped to think, she'd give up, so she didn't stop, didn't think, working on autopilot to shove everything back into the wardrobes and drawers willy-nilly. She'd have liked a fresh duvet cover but one-handed, it would be an exhausting task so she settled on clean sheets.

Only the room Nick used as an office was left. It was tempting to leave it for another day but she remembered the eulogy she'd promised to give. She didn't want it hanging over her, like a chore. In the room he used to laughingly refer to as his man-cave, amongst his things, she hoped she might find inspiration.

The spare room was a good size for a second bedroom in a not-so-big apartment. It was certainly big enough for Nick's desk, and the tall, metal filing cabinet he'd picked up in a charity shop for a fiver. She ran a hand over it, remembering how they'd carried it home between them.

The drawers had been yanked open, the files pulled out, their contents tossed onto the floor. A mini mountain of documents. All work related: they would make little sense to her. She sat on the floor beside them and shoved several papers inside each cardboard file. When she was done, she stood and put them back in the filing cabinet.

The desk, a solid wood piece that had been expensive, was a traditional design with three drawers on each side of the footwell. Most were sitting open, some but not all of the contents strewn about. It looked as if her burglar was running out of time, or perhaps frustrated at finding nothing of value. She had read of people who left money clearly visible in case someone broke in, in the hopes they would take the money and leave. She'd also read of homes that had been completely trashed, paint thrown around, urine and faecal matter stomped into the carpet. At least she'd been spared that.

She looked to the corner where Kaya's belonging sat, untouched. That too she was grateful for.

Nick was... had been... incredibly untidy. He'd used a desktop computer with a large monitor, the edges of which were covered in Post-its with dates or phone numbers scribbled on them in his neat writing. The monitor had been knocked over but didn't appear to have been damaged. She straightened it and smiled at the Post-its before pulling the chair closer to sit.

The old, leather Chesterfield chair had been another charity-shop find. Ten pounds to purchase, it had cost him a fortune to have re-covered. She smiled as she rocked back and forth on it. It gave her an idea for the eulogy. The joy Nick found in things. His love of charity-shop finds. His constant enthusiasm. Yes, that would be something to say.

The surface of the desk was strewn with a mixture of stuff he'd usually kept there, and what looked like the contents of one of the drawers: packets of rubber bands, a couple of boxes of corkboard pins for a corkboard he didn't possess, and bizarrely, a knife from the kitchen. Any thought that it might have been brought there by the burglar was swiftly discounted. There was a knife block in the kitchen holding bigger, sharper knives had they wanted to arm themselves. It must have been left there by Nick, when he was having lunch on one of those days he worked from home.

Putting the knife to one side, she scooped everything into the open top drawer. What seemed like hundreds of pens, pencils and packets of paperclips went into the second.

Keeping busy was proving therapeutic. It kept her mind from

drifting back to her fear that this had been more than an opportunistic burglary. That her earlier fears were valid. She didn't want to go there, didn't want to consider that she'd become a statistic – yet another woman who'd attracted a stalker simply for daring to stand out. Had the more sympathetic DI Bilton come, rather than those two rather dismissive police officers, she might have mentioned her fears to her.

Shutting the second drawer, she was surprised and relieved to see one underneath still shut. The burglar had obviously become bored with his search through work-related rubbish. She pulled the handle, surprised when it didn't open. Leaning over the edge of the chair, she tried again, grunting in frustration when it didn't budge.

Everything was harder with one hand. Pushing back from the chair, she got down on her knees. Only then did she realise the drawer wasn't jammed; it was locked. And it looked as if the burglar had discovered this too. Suddenly, the knife she'd found made sense, the edge of the drawer chipped and dented where an attempt had been made to force it open. It had failed because the desk hadn't been a cheap charity-shop find; it would take more than a kitchen knife to force the locked drawer.

It made Sarah pause. Perhaps, after all, the burglary had been simply opportunistic and not a professional burglar who'd surely have come equipped with tools to open locked drawers like this one.

She sat back on her haunches. Why had Nick found it necessary to lock it? Some confidential work-related files, perhaps. Getting to her feet, she had a rummage through the mess on the surface of the desk before giving up. Had there been a key, the intruder would have found and used it and not wasted time trying to force the drawer.

Where would Nick have kept a key? On the same bunch as his house keys? Possibly. The hospital had passed his few personal belongings on to his parents when they'd gone to identify his body. His mother had cried when she'd passed the wallet, watch and bunch of keys over to Sarah as she lay in her hospital bed. They'd sat beside her in the bed for hours until she asked a nurse to put them in the drawer of the bedside cabinet. When she'd been discharged, they'd been put into the same blue plastic bag as her few items. The bag she'd dropped on the living-room floor when she came home.

Back in the living room, she opened the cabinet door, some of the items she'd shoved so untidily inside earlier tumbling out. More fell when Sarah grasped the edge of blue plastic and pulled gently until it was free.

She took it back to the desk to open. Ignoring her belongings, she took out Nick's, put the wallet and watch aside, and jiggled the bunch of keys. The house keys were easily recognisable, they were the same as her own, but the small, brass key was different.

Leaning down, she slotted it into the lock. It turned smoothly. She left it in the lock, the bunch jangling as she slid the drawer open, her breath held behind tightly pressed lips. What had her easy-going, open husband needed to hide?

52

There was only one item inside the drawer. A file marked simply, *Kaya*.

Sarah cleared a space on the desk in front of her and took it out. She ran a finger over the handwritten letters of her daughter's name before opening the cover and pressing it flat. 'Oh wow!' The exclamation was dragged from her when she flicked through the contents. This was what Nick had kept locked away; this is what was most important to him? She picked up the first item, a copy of her initial pre-natal scan. She remembered he'd stared at it in awe, whereas she'd regarded this evidence of the life growing inside her with something akin to dismay. Who'd have thought Nick would want to keep such a thing?

She lifted the next paper. Another scan, the one where they'd found out they were going to have a girl. Nick had wanted to come home and paint the spare room pink in anticipation until she'd reminded him it would be his office for another year at least. Refusing to be done out of celebrating, he'd insisted on going to a shopping centre and buying a ridiculous amount of pink baby clothes.

'Crazy man.' She smiled sadly at the memory and put the scan down to pick up the next item. Anticipating some other Kaya-related document, she didn't understand what she was seeing at first. Realisation came quickly and furrowed her brow. It was a printout of someone's medical notes. Her eyes swept over it. Not just any patient. One of Sarah's. What on earth was it doing in a file in Nick's desk? Perhaps he'd found it lying about and put it away for safety, meaning to tell her, then forgetting.

Sarah frequently took work home, often spending hours updating her notes. Had she been careless? She remembered Nick pointing out, more than once, that she'd left a file open on her laptop. It was foolish of her. The clinic was strict about confidentiality and misplacing patients' notes would have meant serious trouble for her.

Odd though. Why had she needed to print out this patient's notes? She read through the first page, trying, and failing to place the woman mentioned, one whose IVF had failed and who'd been advised not to try again. She'd been suffering from depression as a result and had come to Sarah for help. When she turned to the second page, a memory flickered of a woman whose lank, unwashed hair had obscured most of her face, and who had been unable to meet Sarah's gaze. As she read through the notes, she nodded in agreement with herself. She'd done the right thing and had suggested the woman go for counselling.

That was it. She hadn't returned, and Sarah had no idea whether or not she'd followed her advice. She remembered she'd been so struck by the woman's air of sadness that it had remained on her mind for a few days. Hadn't she even told Jade about it over a few drinks? Probably. Jade would have listened sympathetically. Nick, on the other hand, was rarely interested in hearing about her patients, finding their ailments, as he used to phrase it, 'icky'. Had she told him about this woman? She couldn't remember if she had, or why she'd needed to print out the notes.

And with Nick gone, the puzzle as to why it ended up in such a strange place would remain a mystery. She put it to one side and continued to look through the file. A photo of Kaya was next, blown up to A4 size. It made Sarah smile.

The next item didn't. She picked up the red book, the personal child health record she'd been given in the hospital. It contained all the details of Kaya's birth: date, time, weight, and size. All her vaccinations would be documented in it, every health visit. What was it doing here?

She vaguely remembered shoving it into the top drawer of the dresser in their bedroom where she kept anything important. It should be there alongside her passport and driver's licence. She remembered returning those to the drawer not an hour before; hadn't the red book been there too? She shook her head at the thought. It can't have been, because here it was. It couldn't be in two places.

Nick had obviously taken it. Why would he have done such a thing? Without asking, or at least telling her.

Another puzzle that would remain unsolved. She rocked in the Chesterfield chair as she looked at the final few items in the file. Photographs of Kaya, from seconds after her birth, before she'd even been cleaned up, to photographs taken in the days before they'd gone to Devon. Sarah had never seen most of them before.

She looked at each item as she slipped it back between the covers of the file. Nick had always taken security more seriously than she had. Was that what this was about? Keeping his precious daughter's paperwork safe? He hadn't told Sarah he'd taken the red book because he'd have known she'd be annoyed that he'd gone through her stuff to find it. 'What a crazy man,' she mumbled, picking up the red book and placing it on top of the rest.

When she had Kaya back, she'd need to make an appointment to register her birth. She'd need to bring the red book to do that; at least she knew where it was.

She'd put the final photograph of Kaya on top, had closed the cover of the file before something struck her and she opened it again. It hadn't been the photograph of Kaya's cherubic face. Sarah slid that to one side, picked up the red book and opened it.

It was wrong.

No, not wrong. It was the correct book. Official.

She'd only flicked through it before; now she looked at page after page. Most was exactly as it had been, but where the details of Sarah and Nick's names and their address should have been – where they *had* been – was now blank. She held the book up to the light, checked carefully. Their names hadn't been removed; they'd never been there. This wasn't the original red book that had been altered; it was a duplicate.

A growing disquiet made her jump to her feet, sending the wheeled chair crashing into the wall behind. If this was a duplicate, she should still have the original. She hurried into their bedroom and yanked the drawer open. She'd tossed everything back inside earlier, so it was a mess. But the red book should have stood out. It didn't, and increasingly frantic, she rummaged through the contents. Her passport and driver's licence were there. There was some paperwork related to savings accounts she had. More to do with a credit card she'd thought about taking out but hadn't. Other bits and pieces. But not Kaya's red book.

Back in the spare room, she sat, picked up the duplicate again and flicked through it, wanting to believe that perhaps she'd been mistaken. Imagining things. Maybe even a little paranoid. Was that it? She'd imagined people following her, being watched, now this.

One final look through the book and she knew there was no doubt.

There was something terribly wrong here. Something unbelievably, earth-shatteringly wrong. The sound of her heart thumping seemed to fill the room. Maybe she was having a heart attack. Perhaps hearts did break. Her hand trembled as she put the book down and reached for the patient notes she'd read earlier.

Maybe it wasn't a case of Nick being a crazy man; maybe he'd simply been crazy. Or she was. Because what she was thinking was beyond bizarre, wasn't it? The notes trembled in her hand as she looked at them. No, she wasn't crazy. This was why they were in the same folder as the red book, with the copies of the scans, and the photographs of Kaya. Sarah thought she understood everything at last. She read the notes again, the patient's name standing out this time... taunting her.

Megan Cotterell... Megan... Meg.

53

Sarah looked at each piece of evidence for a second time – and that was how she was looking at it now: as evidence. Then, leaving the file on the desk with the contents strewn over the surface, she went back to the living room and stared out the window. There was nothing suspicious out there but she was suddenly unsure of everything.

Had she totally lost the plot? Because what she was thinking was so far beyond belief that it sent darts of pain through her head. Maybe that was it? The concussion had affected her reasoning ability. It made sense. There had been numerous studies on the lasting effects of head injuries.

Jade would have listened, laughed, and told her to get a grip, but that relationship was damaged. Possibly beyond repair. There were other friends. She imagined the conversation, their sympathetic voices. Imagined them turning to their partners with sad eyes to tell them Sarah wasn't coping. That she was having some kind of breakdown. It might even be true.

She turned, her eyes darting around the room. Was that it? She'd had a breakdown and to cope with it all, she was inventing a storyline to account for the loss of Kaya. They were still learning so much about the brain, what it could do, how it could cope and adapt to circumstances.

Was that it?

Was she so consumed with guilt for having handed Kaya over to that bloody woman that it was easier for her brain to cope by shifting blame elsewhere?

The name on those notes was a coincidence, that's all. Meg wasn't necessarily short for Megan. And there could be any number of reasons for Nick to have that red book in his possession. For their personal details to have been erased somehow.

Name one.

Her inner voice was irritating, but also right; she couldn't name one.

The intercom buzzed, startling her, her yelp loud enough to make her laugh hysterically. She clamped a hand over her mouth and stared at the intercom as if whoever was waiting for a reply four floors below might hear. They could wait. There was nobody she wanted to see, nobody she wanted to speak to. She wanted to be left alone to fall apart in the privacy of her home. Because that's what was happening. She could feel all the nuts and bolts that held her together loosening, coming undone.

But it seemed not even that was left to her. They'd taken Kaya, Nick; now they wanted the rest of her.

She didn't care. Couldn't care about anything. She was floating on a sea of pain, of sheer unadulterated panic and confusion, where she wasn't sure what was real, or what was being conjured up by her warped and possibly damaged brain.

The intercom buzzed again, for longer. It dragged her back. Whoever it was, was determined to get her attention. They might have phoned but she'd switched her mobile to silent.

With the way her life was going, whoever it was might call the police, break into her apartment. Shock the neighbours. Damage her damn door. Better to answer. Staccato thoughts were all she seemed able to manage. She jabbed the button on the intercom. 'What?' It wasn't her normal response to someone calling but she was all out of social niceties.

'Mrs Westfield?'

Sarah took a deep breath and let it out slowly. It helped calm her enough to answer politely. 'Yes, who is this?'

'It's PC O'Farrell. May I come up?'

Because the day hadn't been bad enough already? Sarah wanted to say no. Actually, she wanted to tell the snotty faced, judgemental cow to fuck right the hell off. Hadn't she had enough? *Poor widow.* Jade's mean, cruel words jabbed painfully.

'Right, as long as it's quick.' Sarah pressed the button to let the officer enter then opened the apartment door. Leaving it ajar, she returned to the window she'd spent so much of that day simply staring through, as if the answer to all her dilemmas was written along the length of the road below.

'Mrs Westfield.'

'I'm kind of busy, so just spit out whatever it is you want to say, then leave please.' So much politer than the words she wanted to use.

'I'm afraid it's not that simple.'

Sarah almost laughed. Of course it wasn't going to be simple. Her life was a train wreck.

'Is it okay if we sit and talk?'

Sitting and talking to the police officer who'd looked at her so disparagingly was near the top of a list of things Sarah didn't want to do ever again; it was below having her child abducted, her husband being knocked down and killed, breaking her wrist and being burgled, but it was there. 'You can sit; I'm okay as I am.' If she sounded childish, petulant even, she didn't care. She could see O'Farrell's reflection in the window and watched as she hesitated before crossing to the sofa where she sat, awkwardly, on the edge, as if afraid Sarah was going to turn and pounce on her. Maybe bash her over the head with her plaster cast. It would serve the sanctimonious cow right if she did.

'Following your burglary, we had a meeting to discuss your case and have come up with a disturbing theory.'

Sarah was struggling to accommodate what she'd discovered in Nick's office, but she heard something different in the officer's voice. Perhaps even a little sympathy. Enough to make her turn to face her. 'What kind of disturbing theory?'

'Please.' O'Farrell waved to the seat opposite. 'This is going to be hard.'

For whom? Sarah wasn't keen on being directed what to do in her apartment. She crossed to the kitchen, opened a cupboard for a glass, and a drawer to take out the painkillers she'd stuffed in the corner of it when she'd tidied up earlier. Her movements were slow, measured, giving her time to calm her rattled brain as she filled the glass with water and swallowed the tablets, one at a time.

'Right,' she said, taking a seat to the side, forcing the officer to twist to look at her. 'If I could have a précis, please, this has been a hell of a day as I'm sure you can appreciate.'

O'Farrell shifted in her seat and rested an elbow on the arm of the chair. 'A précis. Right. Okay.' Her eyes flicked around the room, then back to Sarah. 'The officers who came earlier told us nothing had been taken, and there didn't appear to be any damage.' She looked around the room with a raised eyebrow as if to prove her point. 'You restored order so quickly that I think we're right. We don't think it was a burglary; we think someone wanted to finish what they'd attempted to do with the hit-and-run.' She waited for a second, as if allowing that to sink in before she continued. 'We think it has something to do with Kaya's abduction.'

Sarah stared, then blinked rapidly, opened her mouth then shut it again. 'I thought I was being watched; thought I'd seen someone staring at the apartment from the street. I was afraid I was going crazy with all that has happened.'

'I'm not surprised; you've been through nightmare after nightmare.'

Sarah felt her eyes filling. This time, she hadn't imagined it; there was genuine sympathy in the officer's voice. 'I was convinced you all thought I had something to do with Kaya's abduction.'

'Is that why you took the baby from outside the supermarket?'

There didn't seem to be any point in lying. 'You were treating me as the guilty party. I knew I wasn't and was afraid you were wasting your time looking at me instead of searching for her. I thought taking the baby would make you look at me more sympathetically.' She gave a defeated grimace. 'It didn't work, did it?'

'Not really, I'm afraid. In fact, it had the reverse effect.'

Sarah nodded. She'd made the mistake of underestimating the

police. She probably wasn't the first to do so. 'What made you change your mind?'

'I have a daughter. Raven. She's fourteen months. I hate leaving her but I love my job and I'm lucky; my husband works from home so he looks after her. When I heard you had handed your daughter over to a stranger just so you could have a peaceful dinner, I judged you and that coloured the way I looked at everything for a while.' She shuffled in her seat as if trying to get more comfortable. 'One of my colleagues asked me if I minded leaving Raven for so long. It was when I heard the judgement in her voice that I realised how unfair I'd been. We all make decisions that might be seen as wrong by someone else.'

'Those two women played me so well. Two of the most ordinary people you could meet.' Sarah shook the memory away. 'Your daughter's name, Raven, it's unusual.'

O'Farrell gave a quick smile that immediately softened her face. 'She was born with a shock of inky black hair. I wanted her to grow up strong. Tom wanted her to be unique. Raven seemed the perfect choice.'

'I like it. We wanted to give Kaya a unique name too. Nick's maternal grandmother was Dutch so that's where it comes from. It means pure.'

'Nice.'

Sarah found herself relaxing in this new-found rapport. It was good to have someone to talk to, to be able to share her own crazy theories. 'I don't think you're right, though.' She smiled at the look of surprise that flitted across O'Farrell's face before it returned to a neutral, professional one. 'I had thought there was nothing missing but while I was tidying up, I discovered a few things.' She struggled to her feet; the pain relief had taken the edge of the aches but not removed them entirely. 'I'm getting something to drink; would you like something?'

'No, I'm good, maybe later.'

This made Sarah stop and turn back. 'Later? Ah, okay, so this isn't a flying visit; you're here to provide protection, are you?'

'Until we can figure out what's going on, DI Bilton thought it was essential.'

Even with their new-found friendlier relationship, Sarah wasn't sure she wanted an officer to be foisted on her. Even if it was supposedly for her own good. Anyway, she thought they had it wrong.

Returning with a glass of water, she sat, sipped it slowly, then told O'Farrell about what she'd discovered that afternoon.

'Okay,' the officer said when she'd finished. 'You're sure this red book that you found in the locked desk drawer isn't the one you were given in the hospital.'

'I thought it was, at first, but then I saw that our details, mine and Nick's, were missing. And I remembered that I'd stuck a photograph of Kaya inside the front cover. Just to make it more personal. Everything else was the same as the original.'

'So whoever broke in took the red book from your bedroom dresser.'

'Yes. I think that's why they broke in. The rest,' she waved a hand around the room, 'the mess was a means to hide what they'd taken. If I hadn't found the red book in Nick's drawer, I'd never have noticed. It's not something I'd have looked for until I needed it.'

'You hadn't registered Kaya's birth?'

'No, we hadn't. It was something we'd planned to do in a couple of weeks. We were going to make a day of it, have lunch, celebrate.' They had six weeks to register the birth. She'd wanted to do it immediately. It had been Nick's idea to put it off, to make more of an occasion of it. She guessed she knew why now.

O'Farrell was frowning. With a grunt, she got to her feet and stretched, lifting both arms over her head. 'Sorry, knots,' she said, then moved to take a different seat, one where she wasn't twisting to look at Sarah. 'It looks like whoever took Kaya came for the one document they'd need to register her birth.'

'Yes, but...' Sarah swirled the water around in the glass, the motion soothing, allowing her thoughts to form an orderly queue. 'I don't think it was the one they came for. I think they were looking for the one Nick had locked away. They'd tried to open the drawer; they'd taken a knife from the kitchen. But it's a big, solid desk, not easy to get into. The key to it was with Nick's house keys, in a plastic bag on the floor. They missed it.'

O'Farrell was struggling to make sense of what Sarah had said, her face screwed up in thought. 'Your husband had made a copy?'

Sarah nodded, then placed the glass on the table beside her and got to her feet. 'Hang on, there's something else.' She returned a moment later and handed over the patient notes she'd found earlier. 'This was in the same file. If you look at the top, you'll see it's from the clinic where I work. I thought at first I'd mislaid it and Nick had picked it up and locked it away to keep it safe. It puzzled me, though. I rarely need to print out notes; everything is done online these days.'

She sat back in her seat, keeping her eyes fixed on O'Farrell's expression, waiting to see if she'd come to the same conclusion as Sarah had done. Not one to jump too quickly to conclusions, she read it through, then turned back to the front, started to read again.

Sarah was amused to see her lips move when she read the second time, as if to ensure each word was clearly imprinted on her brain.

'Shit!' O'Farrell looked up from the document, mouth and eyes wide in disbelief. 'Megan... Meg!'

'Indeed.' Sarah smiled, relieved to see she hadn't jumped to a ridiculous conclusion.

54

Zoé-Lee read the details through for a third time. 'This Megan Cotterell had tried and failed to have a child of her own. You couldn't do anything more for her but send her for counselling?' She saw Sarah rear back, offended. 'Sorry,' she held up an apologetic hand. 'That didn't come out the way I meant. What I was trying to say was there nothing else you could do for her?'

'It was all I could do. I mentioned adopting, but I remember she freaked out on me and said it wasn't an option, so I didn't push it. Adoption isn't for everyone, and she was so adamant that there didn't seem any point. I gave her the details of a number of groups who offer support to childless women and the name of a sympathetic counsellor. And that was the last I heard from her. She never returned to the clinic.'

Zoé-Lee waved the notes. 'Over a year ago, yet you remember her.'

'I didn't remember her name or her face. You must understand, I see so many people and I only saw her that once, a time when she was depressed and turned in on herself. But I remember the details of the case; there are always some that stick in your mind. It must be the same for you. I remember her being so terribly sad. Grieving really, I suppose. I remember talking to my friend Jade about her later over a drink. Just in general terms – there was no breach of confidentiality.'

But there had been somewhere. Zoé-Lee was holding the proof in her hand. 'Did you mention it to your husband?'

'To be honest, I don't know. Nick was never particularly interested in hearing about the nitty-gritty of my job, insisting it grossed him out. But...'

Zoé-Lee watched as guilt and grief took turns flickering across Sarah's face. Finally, before she spoke, her face had settled into grim acceptance. 'If I was working from home, which I frequently did, I'd set my laptop up there.' She nodded towards the table behind the sofa. 'I'd often leave it open while I went to do other things: make a coffee, have a shower, even pop out to the shops for something I'd forgotten. I never thought about it. Kaya was too young to go near it. I thought I could trust my husband.'

'Mrs Westfield—'

'Oh for goodness' sake, call me Sarah, will you?'

Zoé-Lee easily forgave the growl of anger. It very much looked as if Nick Westfield was responsible for Kaya's abduction. She wasn't surprised when Sarah's next words were the same three she heard on the lips of so many victims.

'I don't understand.'

Zoé-Lee wasn't sure she did either. Nick had seemed the perfect picture of a grieving father. 'Had your husband ever given any indication he disliked Kaya? Perhaps mistreated her in some way or yelled at her if she cried?'

'No, no!' Tears trickled from the corner of Sarah's eyes. She wiped them away with an impatient slap of her hand. 'He absolutely adored her; it was me who had the problem with Kaya.'

'You?' Now it was Zoé-Lee's turn to say, 'I don't understand.'

Sarah got to her feet again, walked to the kitchen and opened the fridge. She returned with a bottle of wine and two glasses. 'Are you allowed? No? Well, you'll have to watch me then because I need a drink.' She sat, poured a glass, and took a tiny sip. It seemed enough to give her courage to speak.

'I'd been in a relationship for three years with a guy I was crazy about, but who was reluctant to commit and who dumped me when I said I needed more. I suppose I was on the rebound when I met Nick only a few weeks later. He swept me off my feet, told me he loved me, spoiled me with crazy romantic gestures, so even though I thought it was too soon, when he proposed only a couple of months later, I said yes. We were married six months after we first met.' She snorted. 'You know that old saying about marrying in haste, etc.? Well, that was me. Within a few weeks of marrying, I knew I'd made a mistake.

'Nick was lovely but he smothered me, always pawing me, telling me how much he loved me, adored me, would do anything for me, yadda yadda yadda, until I wanted to scream. He was possessive too, jealous of any man who looked at me, resentful of my male friends.' She picked up her glass, took another sip and shook her head. 'I think he was even resentful of my career. I love being a GP, but even I will admit that it sucks up a lot of my time and emotions. Emotions I think Nick wanted to be concentrated on him.'

Zoé-Lee thought she knew where the story was going. 'Then you got pregnant. I assume that was a mistake?'

'You'd think.' Sarah swirled the wine. 'I'm not a stupid woman, so I don't know why I acted so stupidly.'

Zoé-Lee waited, hoping the conversation would start to make sense because so far, it wasn't.

'I was getting older. Maybe I was still hurting from that three-year relationship that had gone nowhere. I suppose I really wanted our marriage to work, long after I knew it wasn't going to. It was Nick who brought up the idea of having a baby. I was stunned at first, but then thought maybe it would be exactly what we needed.'

'You got pregnant in the hope it would help your marriage?'

Sarah nodded. 'That and, well I suppose I listened to that tick-tocking biological clock too. I told you it was stupid. As soon as I told Nick I was pregnant, he became more clingy, more adoring, more possessive. It didn't help that it was a difficult pregnancy. I had hyperemesis gravidarum; d'you know what that is?'

'Bad morning sickness.'

'As good an explanation as any.' Sarah took another tiny sip of wine and sighed heavily. 'I firmly believe in the right to choose, but I have a personal objection to abortion so I was stuck. I tried, believe me, I really tried to reconcile myself to the pregnancy, to my marriage, but sometimes I could see Nick looking at me strangely. In the end, I couldn't hide how unhappy I was. Poor Nick, it just made him try even harder, promising again and again that he'd do anything for me.'

Zoé-Lee had had morning sickness early in her pregnancy and remembered how awful she'd felt. But it had lasted only a couple of weeks. She'd read about hyperemesis gravidarum. It was hard to miss all the articles about it when someone as well-known as Kate Middleton had suffered with it. Referring to it as bad morning sickness wasn't doing justice to the condition. Sarah, stuck in an unhappy marriage, with mixed feelings about her pregnancy, must have had an absolutely miserable time of it. 'I'd imagine that it became a cycle of torture: the worse you felt, the more he tried, the worse you felt.'

'Yes, that's it,' Sarah said. 'And I felt so guilty. I believed he was a good man, that the fault lay with me. I'd tell him it was my hormones to blame. A bad idea because he thought once Kaya was born then everything would be better, but it wasn't. I felt even more trapped and I blamed her for it. I did what was necessary for her, but it was Nick who showered her with love. That's why I simply don't understand how or why he could be involved in anything like this.'

Zoé-Lee, who'd been involved in sufficient domestic abuse cases over the years, thought she understood. 'Nick may have loved Kaya, but I think he loved you more. Perhaps he'd seen your change of heart and blamed the child for it. He may have thought if she was out of the way, your feelings for him would revert to the way they were.' There was no reason to point out how lucky Sarah had been. Nick had loved the child too much to do her any harm. It looks as if he'd simply decided to find her a different home. To rehome her, like an unwanted cat or dog. She dampened down the sudden flare of anger and tuned back into what Sarah was saying.

'I learned something from Nick's mother recently that I hadn't known before. She said that he'd had several relationships before me that had ended in disaster. He'd never mentioned previous girlfriends;

we just admitted that we'd both had a past and left it at that. Now I'm wondering if there had been issues.'

'More than likely. Leopards and their spots. It sounds to me that his love for women quickly crossed the line into obsession which made most, sensibly, run for the hills. Because you were, as you say, on the rebound, you were more vulnerable.' Zoé-Lee thought she understood why he looked so wretched after Kaya had been abducted. It hadn't been grief; it had been desperation that his plan hadn't worked.

There was silence as both women considered all that had been said. Suddenly, Sarah jumped to her feet.

Startled, Zoé-Lee followed suit, swinging around as if an intruder had been the cause of Sarah's abrupt movement. But the room was empty. 'You okay?'

'Yes, more than okay. I know where Kaya is. Megan's address is on the notes. I'm going to go and get my baby.' She pulled out her phone, used her thumb to tap out a message and put it away. 'An Uber is on the way.'

'You can't go in, all guns blazing, Sarah! I'll ring the station; we can organise a team.'

'You do that, I'll see you there.' She grabbed her bag and was heading out the door at speed, leaving Zoé-Lee behind.

'Shit!' If she didn't follow, if Sarah went on her own, who knows what might happen. She pulled out her radio as she raced after her, speaking into it as she reached the ground floor, letting DI Bilton know there was a situation that was quickly blowing out of her control.

'Go with her, try to stop her. We'll be there as soon as we can.'

How she was supposed to stop a woman who was racing to the rescue of her child, Zoé-Lee had no idea. She gave Bilton the address she'd memorised and rushed through the main door in time to see Sarah getting into a taxi.

55

Sarah jumped into the Uber when it pulled up moments later, grateful when O'Farrell slid in beside her. She wasn't sure what to expect when she got to Megan Cotterell's address and it would be good to have someone on her side. Soon, she'd have Kaya back. And she'd spend the rest of her life making up for the first weeks of neglect.

'Thanks for coming with me,' she said, turning to look at the officer. 'What's your name, anyway? I can't keep calling you PC O'Farrell; it's a bit of a mouthful.'

'It's Zoé-Lee.'

Sarah smiled. 'Never just Zoé?'

'Nope.' Then her rather severe features melted into an echoing smile. 'Tom calls me Zee sometimes.'

Zee, a sharp, spikey name; it suited her better. 'You'll be glad to be finished with all this madness and get home, I'm betting.'

'I will. I hadn't expected to be away so long, really. But Tom's a good man. He wants the best for me and my career. He's really good with Raven too.' She shook her head, her smile fading. 'Better than me if I'm honest. He has a routine. I think he finds when I'm home, I upset it.'

'A good man. That's what I thought Nick was. God, I was such a fool.' Sarah sat back. She was grateful the officer didn't try to placate her with useless words, sitting silently beside her, her presence alone enough support.

It was a few minutes before Zoé-Lee spoke again. 'Can I ask you something?'

Sarah had been staring out the window, lost in her thoughts, planning what to say and do when they arrived. She turned to look at the officer. 'Why not? Although I would have thought you knew all about me at this stage.'

'You lied about the pub in Lynton. The Post Office. You can't have gone there with your parents when you were younger. It's only been a pub for a few years.'

It was so unexpected a question that Sarah laughed. 'Someone didn't do their research fully.' She lifted her free hand and see-sawed it. 'It wasn't precisely a lie and I wasn't deliberately trying to mislead you; I simply didn't think an explanation was necessary.'

'And that is?'

'When I was a child, the pub that is now The Post Office was indeed a regular post office. The building next to it, which is now a charity shop, used to be a pub. It was called The Post Office Pub because it was next door to the post office.' She almost laughed as Zoé-Lee tried to get her head around the explanation. 'You can see now why I didn't bother telling you that on the night of the abduction. I hadn't been to Lynton in years so I did an internet search to make sure the pub was still open. But it wasn't till we arrived that night that I realised what had happened.'

'You'd told Nick where you were going.'

'Yes, I'd mentioned we'd be going to The Post Office Pub. He obviously had set it up for the abduction to happen there.' She turned away, muttering, 'The bastard.'

It was several more minutes before the Uber negotiated the traffic and pulled up outside a pretty, detached house. 'Here we are,' Sarah said, pushing open the door. She climbed out and looked up at the house. Lights were on at the windows. They were home. Her baby was inside.

'We should wait,' O'Farrell said, looking at her watch. 'They'll be here soon.'

Sarah was still staring at the house. Normal, unthreatening. Inside, her baby was probably sleeping. 'A horde of police on her doorstep might frighten Megan into doing something stupid.'

'It's not just Megan though, remember; there's another woman. They took your child; we have no idea what more they're capable of.'

'They didn't take Kaya; Nick gave her to them.' The bastard had manipulated her. If he weren't already dead, she'd kill him. He'd wanted to be buried. Fuck that; she'd have him cremated and flush his ashes down the toilet.

'They might have been involved somehow in the hit-and-run too; you have to keep that in mind. They might have killed Nick.'

Sarah turned to her. 'Or they were manipulated and used by Nick, as I was. Who's the guilty party and who's the victim here, Zee? Because I'm not sure; are you?' She didn't wait for an answer, pushing open the wooden gate and walking up the short driveway to the front door. This was it. She pressed the doorbell, heard it chime within, and took a step back to wait. Excitement was fizzing through her. She was going to see Kaya, going to hold her, breathe in her delicious baby smell. Her daughter.

She recognised the young woman who opened the front door as the woman who'd sat beside Nick in the pub. The woman Sarah had handed Kaya to. The recognition was mutual. Megan attempted to shut the door, jumping back in alarm when Sarah pushed past her, using the cast on her broken wrist as a battering ram.

'No, you can't!' Megan pulled at Sarah's T-shirt. 'Andrea, help!'

Sarah swiped at her again with the cast, feeling the solid connection with immense satisfaction and a dart of pain that didn't slow her down. She looked to the end of the hall where light was pouring through a partially open door. That's where Kaya would be. Hearing steps on the stairway, she ignored the shouts behind her, O'Farrell's voice among them trying to get control of the situation, and Sarah ran, bursting through the door.

She found herself in a perfect, open-plan room, similar in layout to her apartment, but three, maybe four times the size. It was a family space and at any other time, she'd have admired the proportions, the décor and furnishing. But the only thing she cared about was the bassinet set in a corner of the room. Tuning out the raised voices, she hurried across to it. Her breath, stuck in her chest, came out in a soft hiss when she looked down at the picture of gorgeousness inside. Sleeping through the fuss, Kaya's little fists rested on either side of her head, lips pursing now and then as if in memory of the last drink.

'Hello, my little darling.' Sarah bent over the bassinet and touched Kaya's cheek softly feeling the love for her child swell. She'd have liked to have picked her up and held her tight but the angry, raised voices were coming closer.

'Get away from her!'

Sarah turned. O'Farrell was acting like a cork in the doorway to keep the two women in the hallway, but there was more strength in their desperation and she was pushed back. She stumbled, crashed hard into the cupboards behind before falling to the floor, her hat skittering across the tiles. Down but not out, Sarah could hear her speaking into her radio, calling for immediate assistance.

It would come, but not fast enough. Megan and Andrea were bearing down on her, their expressions saying they were going to do whatever it took. She moved in front of the bassinet and spoke loudly. 'Kaya is my daughter.'

Andrea's face twisted in anger, her words coming out in a snarl. 'You didn't want her!'

'That's not true!' How could she explain how her feelings for Kaya had become entangled with her feelings for Nick? The overriding guilt she'd felt for her treatment of both?

'He said you'd been miserable during the pregnancy and even more so since the birth.' Megan's voice was gentle, her eyes filled with tears. 'He said you'd be happier without her, that if we took Kaya, you'd be able to return to the way things used to be.'

The way things used to be! None so blind as those who don't want to see – and Nick hadn't wanted to see the truth. Perhaps if she'd known about his string of previous failed relationships, she might have seen his neediness in a different light. Perhaps he'd felt abandoned by those women and was determined to do anything to prevent it happening again. Classic borderline personality disorder. A useless diagnosis after the event, nor was it going to help in her current predicament. 'Nick was wrong. I love Kaya.' She was so intent on watching Megan, so determined to make her understand, that she hadn't seen Andrea move into the kitchen, wasn't aware of her closing in on her from the other side until she felt a sharp pain in her upper arm and looked down to see a bead of blood.

'Move,' Andrea said, jabbing the point of a large knife again, harder, the point slicing deeper.

Sarah didn't react until the third jab went deeper again. It seemed she was out of options. She took one reluctant step away from the bassinet, twisting to take another glance at her daughter. She'd found her; she couldn't lose her again. 'More police are on their way.'

Andrea jabbed again. 'Over there.' She waved the knife to the other side of the room. 'Megan, run upstairs, throw a few things into a bag. Quick as you can; we only have a few minutes.'

Sarah had no choice and moved where she was directed. She'd wondered why Zoé-Lee had been quiet since her radioed request for help. Now she knew. The officer was still on the floor, a ring of blood around her head. 'Zee!' Ignoring Andrea's shout, she dropped to the floor beside the fallen officer. She was on her side, her breathing regular. Sarah placed two fingers on her neck. There was a pulse but it was faint.

'Get up!' Andrea shouted.

'Just a second.' Sarah eased the eyelids open, one, then the other. 'Oh, Zee,' she said, when she saw what she dreaded. One of her pupils was huge, one tiny. A quick look at the wall of cupboards she'd fallen against told her what had happened. She'd hit her head against one of the metal handles. Sarah looked up at Andrea, who was waving the knife too close for comfort. 'She has a head injury; she needs to get to hospital.'

'If the police are on their way; they can look after her. Now get up.'

'No, please, we can't just leave her like this. She could die.' And Raven would lose her mother. 'We have to do something.'

'The only person I care about is upstairs, understand. I don't care about you.' She pointed the knife at O'Farrell. 'I don't care about her either.' She jabbed the sharp point into Sarah's shoulder. 'If you'd been killed at the same time as that stupid husband of yours, we wouldn't be in this predicament.'

'You were the driver who ran us down?'

'Give the woman a medal.' A loud gasp made her turn. Megan stood in the doorway. The bags she was holding hit the ground with a thump.

While Andrea was distracted, Sarah took a final look at Zoé-Lee and struggled to her feet. There had to be something she could do, something she could say to stop them getting away with Kaya. A dart of pain in her broken wrist momentarily distracted her. Using it as a battering ram must have unset the break. Her fingers were starting to swell. That arm would be useless in any attempt. Any attempt? What did she think she could do? She'd already proved she wasn't Superwoman. She should have listened to the officer who was lying badly injured at her feet; they should have waited. All she could do now was to try to delay their getaway. The police had to be there soon.

Andrea and Megan were locked in some unspoken battle. Sarah wasn't sure what was going on but the tension was palpable. It was all she had; she had to use it. 'You broke into my apartment too, didn't you? And trashed it.' When both faces turned her way, Sarah knew two things. Megan wasn't aware of all that had gone on, and Andrea was beginning to fall apart.

It was Andrea who spoke, jabbing the knife into the air with every word. 'That bastard, Nick, he promised me all the paperwork I'd need to register Kaya's birth but he kept making excuses.' Her face twisted in anger as she took a few steps closer to Sarah. 'The last couple of times we spoke, I could hear it in his voice; he was beginning to have regrets. That's when I knew I had to get rid of him. Of you both.' She waved the knife inches from Sarah's face. 'You should have died, you stupid woman.'

There was a fanatical look in the woman's eyes. Sarah eyed the knife and took a step backwards, hitting the cupboard behind. Where the hell were the police? 'The police know who you are now. Wherever you go, they'll be right behind you. How long do you think it'll be before they catch you?'

'You don't think I've made contingency plans?' Andrea sneered. 'As soon as I saw your idiot husband start to wobble, I knew this day might come. So don't you worry, we'll get far enough.'

'You won't be able to register Kaya's birth with the red book you stole. It has our names in it.'

Andrea took a step closer, placing the point of the knife in the V of Sarah's T-shirt. 'It doesn't matter. I'll find someone who can doctor it so that it'll pass. As you should have learned by now, I'll do anything that's necessary. So don't you worry.'

Megan was still standing in the doorway, a stricken expression on her face.

Andrea shot her a glance. 'Grab the bassinet, Meg. We have to get going.' She pressed the point of the knife into Sarah's skin, drawing a bead of blood that immediately soaked into the fabric of the T-shirt. 'You, pick up the bags, and don't do anything stupid. I haven't decided yet whether it's better to take you with us or kill you, so don't give me a reason to make a choice that won't be in your favour.'

Megan hadn't moved. 'You killed Nick? When we read about it in the newspaper, you said it had been an accident that had been lucky for us.'

'She lied,' Sarah said. 'The same way as Nick lied when he told you I didn't love Kaya.'

'Why would he do such a thing?' The young woman sounded dazed, her eyes flitting between Andrea and Sarah as if trying to understand what was going on and failing dismally.

Megan was definitely the weak link in Andrea's plan. Sarah had to keep pressing. 'He thought I didn't love her; truth is, I didn't love him. He couldn't handle that. He thought if she wasn't in our lives that I'd love him again.'

'But you wouldn't?'

Sarah shook her head. 'He used to tell me he loved me so much that he'd do anything for me.' She looked pointedly at the knife-wielding woman who was continuing to press the blade into her skin. The pain was becoming almost unbearable. Her only hope was Megan. 'I'm guessing that Andrea has said the same to you. People like her, like Nick, think that they love, but they don't, not really. They obsess; it's different.'

'Ignore her, Meg; she doesn't know what the fuck she's talking about. Grab the bassinet; we don't have much time.'

Sarah heard the sound she'd been waiting for. Sirens, faint but growing louder. Another couple of minutes, that was all she needed.

Megan cocked her head, listening to the same sound. She moved then, crossed to the bassinet, and picked it up.

'Good girl,' Andrea said with a smirk of satisfaction as she pressed the knife harder.

The pain was intense. Sarah rode with it, refusing to let it overpower her. She was so close; she wasn't going to lose Kaya again. She had to hold out for an opportunity to try something, anything, to stop them getting away with her baby.

The sirens were getting louder. 'Right,' Andrea said, 'you're going to move to the back door. Try anything and you'll be sorry.' Taking the knife away, she pointed towards the exit. It didn't look as if Sarah had any choice and with a final look to where Megan was standing with the cot hanging heavily from one hand, she took a step forward, moving as slowly as she could.

Andrea pulled the door open and pushed Sarah through. 'Move!'

Sarah half-expected another jab of the knife and turned in surprise when she heard Andrea yell.

'Megan! What're you doing?'

Andrea raced back into the house, but she wasn't in time to stop Megan opening the front door, the bassinet bumping against the wall as she hurried out just as police cars pulled up outside.

Sarah wanted to scream in satisfaction. Instead, she took the opportunity that was offered her, slammed the back door shut and leaned her full weight against it to keep Andrea inside. She wouldn't have managed to keep her position for long, but she didn't have to. Seconds later, a police officer rounded the corner of the house, took one look at her and indicated that she step away. It was an order she was happy to take. She moved into the garden and sank onto the grass. It was over.

Kaya was safe. She'd soon be home with Sarah where she belonged.

56

Sarah placed Kaya back into her cot and tucked the pink blanket around her. The sight of her daughter sleeping peacefully was one she'd never tire of. The thought of how close she'd come to losing her was one she'd never manage to put completely from her head.

Kaya would sleep now for a few hours. A happy routine they'd settled into over the three days since her return. It would give Sarah a chance to ring the hospital. She'd used her connections to find out that Zoé-Lee would make a full recovery, but Sarah still checked, every day. She planned to visit as soon as she was allowed.

While Kaya slept, it also gave Sarah the opportunity to pack all Nick's belongings away. His clothes had already gone to a charity shop. Tomorrow, someone from his office was coming to pick up the work files he'd kept in the spare bedroom. When that was all done, the apartment would go on the market and Sarah and Kaya would start afresh.

The filing cabinet was almost empty. One remaining drawer to unpack and that was it. She'd pulled it open and had lifted out the first handful when the doorbell rang. For the first couple of days, she'd been pestered with reporters wanting the nitty-gritty details of her story. She'd refused to speak to anyone. Luckily, the intercom system allowed her to be selective. Only faces she recognised gained access to the apartment. Family, friends, and DI Bilton.

Yesterday, to Sarah's relief, the doorbell hadn't rung even once. A good first step towards returning to normality. Putting the files into the waiting box, she returned to the living room and looked at the intercom screen. *Jade.* Her friend had rung a couple of times over the last few days, but Sarah had put off a visit. It looks like she'd decided to present her with a fait accompli.

She could ignore it. Jade would think she'd gone out, or away. Or she might guess that Sarah didn't want to see her. But if their relationship was ever going to return to the mutually beneficial, friendly one it had been, Sarah had to make a choice. She missed her friend. They'd had good times; they'd have them again. She pushed the release button. 'Come on up, Jade.'

She waited by the door, smiling more broadly when her friend stepped out of the lift with the biggest bunch of sunflowers she'd ever seen. 'Oh wow,' she said when they were pressed into her hand. 'They're simply beautiful.' Her eyes, as they were doing a lot recently, filled with tears. She buried her face in the bright-yellow faces of the flowers.

'Don't cry, you idiot,' Jade said, wrapping an arm around her shoulder. 'Come on, I've brought a bottle as well.' In the kitchen, she shook her head at the cast on Sarah's arm and reached to take the flowers back. 'Let me put them in a vase for you.'

'I can manage,' Sarah said, then grinned and handed the bunch over. 'But very awkwardly.' She opened a cupboard and took out a vase. 'Here you go.'

'Right, go, take the wine over, sit. I'll just be a sec.'

Sarah picked up the bottle of red wine. 'Thank goodness for screw tops. I can definitely manage to open this.' Leaving Jade to sort the flowers, she brought the bottle and two glasses over to the living room, set them on the low table beside the sofa and sat to wait for her friend to finish.

'Here you go,' Jade said, placing the vase in the middle of the table. 'Open that wine while I have a look at Kaya.' She crossed to peer into the cot at the sleeping child. 'Hello, gorgeous,' she said, before turning. 'They said she was okay, didn't they?'

'Yes, they said she'd been well looked after. Megan obviously adored her.'

'She'll go to prison though, won't she?'

Sarah poured wine into the two glasses, picked up one and sat back. 'Her defence team will no doubt argue she was being controlled and manipulated by Andrea, so she might get off with time served. DI Bilton said it was a possibility.'

'It sounds wrong, though.'

'I don't know. I saw Megan's horrified expression when Andrea said she'd killed Nick and would kill me too if I didn't do what she wanted. I don't think she'd any idea what the woman was capable of.' Sarah stood and crossed to check on her daughter, as if the memory made it necessary. Returning to her seat, she sighed. 'I check her so much, I'm in danger of becoming obsessive.'

'I think you're allowed to be a bit overprotective for a while.'

'Just for a bit,' Sarah said, with a smile that quickly faded. 'I hope they do go easy on her; after all, it was thanks to her it ended the way it did.'

'No brownie points for Andrea though, eh?'

Sarah's hand automatically went to the scar on her chest. The surgeon's best embroidery notwithstanding, she was going to be left with a permanent reminder of the most frightening hours of her life. 'She tried to backtrack later, swore she'd no part in the hit-and-run and only said she had to scare me.'

'Ha, I bet the police weren't swallowing that.'

'No, but if she sticks to this new version of events, it will mean I'll be called as a witness when it goes to court.' She put the glass down and relaxed back against the cushions. It was good to have Jade there. The way it used to be. When she felt the hand curl around hers, she smiled. 'I'm glad you called around.'

'You know I'll always be here for you, Sarah. Hell, you know I'd do anything for you.'

Sarah almost winced at the words; they were ones Nick had used so often. She didn't want to hear the same words from Jade. She tried to ease her hand away but the fingers tightened on it immediately.

'You know how I feel about you, Sarah,' Jade said, sitting forward and twisting to look at her. 'We could be good together. You, me, and Kaya. Before Nick, I know you were ready. Now he's gone, and it's back to you and me, with Kaya a wonderful addition.' She squeezed the hand she held. 'We'll be a family.'

If there was one thing Sarah had learned from all this mess, it was that you can't force yourself to love someone. It hadn't worked with Nick; it wouldn't with Jade. 'I'm sorry. Really sorry if I led you to believe I was interested in more than a friendship. You're a good friend, I do love you, but not in that way.'

'But you could.' Jade raised Sarah's hand to her lips and kissed it.

'No.' Sarah pulled her hand away, pushed her friend back and struggled to her feet. 'I just don't see you that way.'

'But I love you.'

The cry seemed to come from Jade's heart and it made Sarah's ache. 'I'm sorry.'

'Sorry!' Jade picked up her glass and downed the contents in two gulps. 'After all I've done for you.' She refilled her glass and took another mouthful.

'You've been very supportive, and I do appreciate it.' Sarah wished her friend would stop drinking. A bad drunk, she became quickly obstreperous. 'How about some coffee?'

Ignoring the question, Jade knocked back the remainder of wine in her glass and reached for the bottle again. This time, she filled her glass to the brim, ignoring the wine that slopped over the sides onto her lap. 'All I've fucking done for you,' she said slurping half the glass down. 'If it hadn't been for me, you'd still be married to that rebound idiot.'

'If it hadn't been for you?' Sarah was suddenly sorry she'd answered her doorbell. 'I don't understand.'

'I told you, didn't I?' Jade looked up at her with a strange smile. 'I'd do anything for you.'

As Sarah looked down at her friend, she wondered if, finally, she was going crazy because the horrendous thought that was fighting for place in her head couldn't be true.

Andrea had killed Nick. She'd admitted as much, even if she was now desperately trying to backtrack.

But when Sarah met Jade's eyes and saw that odd smile again, she knew that Andrea had lied.

57

Sarah couldn't move. She'd been through so much in the last few weeks, but this might be more than she could weather; this might be the final horror to tip her over the edge. *Jade, her best friend.* She wiped a hand over her forehead. Perhaps none of this was real. Yes, that had to be it. She was lying unconscious in the hospital bed and having a nightmare. It took Jade standing up and swaying slightly inches away from Sarah's face to make her face reality. 'The hit-and-run. That *was* you.'

'You sound surprised, but you had guessed, don't forget. Luckily, you've always been so easy to manipulate and it was simple to convince you I had nothing to do with it.'

'I don't understand.' She seemed to be saying that a lot recently. 'You killed Nick. For God's sake, why?'

Jade lifted her hand, pointed her index finger, and jabbed Sarah in the chest. 'You should be grateful. I released you from a marriage you didn't want to be in. You were too weak to get out of it yourself; I could see you fading bit by bit, every day.' She collapsed back on the sofa and picked up her wine glass. 'Someone had to do something.'

'But...' Sarah felt weak, nauseous. 'I don't understand. You didn't just run Nick down; you ran me down too. You tried to kill me.'

'No!' Jade jumped to her feet again. The movement sent a stream of wine flying from her glass to hit the wall behind. It trickled down it like blood. 'I swerved to make sure I didn't hit you full on.'

Sarah remembered the stink of the rubbish bags that had burst open on impact. She'd broken her arm; she might have broken her neck. Jade was looking at her as if begging to be believed. Was she trying to convince herself or Sarah? If Jade had wanted to get rid of Nick, she could have chosen a time when he was alone. No, the truth was in the eyes that couldn't quite meet hers. Jade hadn't swerved to miss. It was pure luck that the rubbish had broken Sarah's fall. Jade had been willing to kill rather than continue to suffer from unrequited love. It was beginning to look as if her love for Sarah was even more twisted than Nick's.

'We could be good together,' Jade insisted. 'You're selling this place; I could sell mine. We could get a bigger place. Maybe one with a fab open-plan layout like in the Cotterells' house.'

Sarah's throat was dry. She reached for her wine glass and took a sip, keeping her eyes on it as she did so, afraid Jade would see the fear in them. Fear for herself, for her daughter. Because suddenly, she knew this friend, this woman she'd known for so many years, was capable of anything. When had Jade's love turn to an obsession that had warped her mind?

How do you know what the Cotterells' house is like? The question had formed in her head but remained unsaid. It had puzzled Sarah how Nick had known about Megan. She knew she'd never told him and had assumed he'd searched through her computer and had got lucky. Now she understood. Sarah had mentioned Megan to her best friend, Jade; she might even, stupidly and unprofessionally, have mentioned the surname. The clinic only had one Megan Cotterell on file.

Had Jade played on Nick's fears – that it was because of Kaya that Sarah's feelings for him had changed. All she'd have needed to do was plant the seed, watch it grow, give it a nudge in the Cotterells' direction. And it would have been Jade who'd have convinced them that this was the solution to their problems. Neither Megan nor Andrea had mentioned her involvement. Perhaps it was a case of honour among thieves. Nick was dead, so it was easier to lay all the blame on him. Or perhaps because nobody had asked if there had been anyone else involved.

Sarah remembered Jade accusing her of having organised the abduction. How clever she'd been to muddy the waters. How deviously clever. This was the dark side of her friend that she'd known was there but had never seen in action. It was far darker than she could possibly have guessed. She'd killed Nick, had organised Kaya's abduction. Had she really hoped that a bereft Sarah would turn to her for solace? Or that now Kaya was home, they could play at happy families?

If she had, she knew it wasn't going to happen. Sarah had rejected her. Absolute terror jolted her and focused her thoughts. She needed to get Jade out of the apartment, lock the door, and ring the police. 'A bigger place? Perhaps,' she said, forcing a smile. 'But not right away. There's been so much turmoil recently; to be honest, all I want at the moment is peace and quiet and time to bond with Kaya.'

'But you'll think about it?' Jade staggered slightly as she edged around the coffee table to Sarah's side. Too close, she leaned in and pressed a kiss against her cheek.

Sarah's jerk away was automatic. She tried to disguise it with a laugh. 'Your lips are cold,' she said. Perhaps the words sounded off, her laugh was too forced, or her expression showed her fear, because Jade's face fell. She took a step back and turned away.

'Of course I'll think about it,' Sarah said. Luckily, she didn't need to make a living as an actor, because even to her ears, her response sounded false.

When Jade turned back, her expression was hard, cold. 'Lying bitch.'

Suddenly, Sarah had had enough. Enough of the suspicions, the lies, the hurt and deceit. She glared at her erstwhile friend. 'You tried to kill me. You did kill my husband, and I know you were involved in Kaya's abduction.' She laughed at the look of shock that greeted this but it didn't dampen her anger. 'Yes, I know you were, Jade. How else would you know what the Cotterells' house was like, eh?'

'Ah, now that was silly of me, wasn't it?' Jade screwed up her nose. 'Why did you do it?'

'I told you. I'd do anything for you. Kaya was making you unhappy.

You didn't love her, didn't want her. I remembered the story you'd told me about the sad woman who wasn't able to have children; it seemed the perfect solution to me. Nick was quite happy to go along with it; he could see that motherhood wasn't doing you any good.'

She was making it all sound so reasonable. Sarah looked towards where her daughter was sleeping peacefully. 'I was confused. Nick was making me unhappy. My emotions were tangled so I might have given the impression I didn't love her, but I do. I love her desperately.'

'Well, that's okay. You have her back now.'

Sarah blinked. Jade had admitted to killing Nick, to arranging for Kaya to be abducted, and she was talking as if it was something they could simply forget about.

'There's no reason for you to tell the police, is there? Andrea will have kept my name out of the abduction and if she's confessed to killing Nick, that's perfect. As for Megan, the woman hasn't two brain cells to rattle together so I doubt she even remembers me.'

There was no point in explaining that Andrea had rapidly backtracked on that confession. Anger had pushed Sarah into making the mistake of mentioning Jade's knowledge of the Cotterells' house; she wasn't going to make another. It was time to lie. 'No, I won't tell them. It's not going to make any difference in the end, is it? It was Andrea and Megan who took Kaya, they who kept her for all this time. Telling the police about your involvement won't change the outcome for them. And as for Nick: well, you thought you were helping me; I can't condemn you for that.'

She could and she did. But now wasn't the time. She brushed a hand over her forehead. 'Listen, I'm sorry, but I'm wrecked. I need to have a lie down and rest before Kaya wakes up again, so d'you mind?' She indicated the front door with a nod of her head.

'And that's it? You think you can just dismiss me?'

Well, yes, that's exactly what Sarah thought. Or rather, what she hoped. She wanted Jade gone. As soon as she was, Sarah would ring DI Bilton, tell her that Jade had been responsible for the hit-and-run. '*Please go.*' *Please, let it be this easy.* But it wasn't going to be. She saw it in the change in Jade's stance, the sudden rigidity, the clenched fists, the hard line of her mouth. Sarah tried again. 'I think it's the pain relief that's making me so tired. I need to lie down. Go, and we'll catch up tomorrow.'

'It's why I tried to run you down, you know.' Jade's voice was suddenly eerily calm. 'It was you I was aiming for. That poor fool Nick was in the wrong place at the wrong time. I've loved you for so long, given you so many fucking chances. I can't live without you, Sarah, but I can't leave you behind either. Seems like we've reached an impasse and I can think of only one way out.' She glanced towards the kitchen, then looked back to Sarah with a strange smile. 'Both of us going together. It'll be the perfect ending.'

58

Sarah froze as Jade crossed to the magnetic knife holder set on the wall beside the cooker. The knives had been ridiculously expensive and were even more ridiculously sharp. The first time she'd used them, she'd sliced her finger so badly she'd almost needed stitches.

She glanced towards the door. What if she made a run for it? But, no, she couldn't leave without Kaya. Even if she managed to grab her, with only one arm free, she couldn't hold on to her child and open the door.

Delaying tactics had worked with Megan and Andrea, but there wasn't going to be anyone racing to her aid this time. All she could do was to try to appeal to what was left of Jade's sanity, to try and dip into the past they'd shared. 'I'm going to need you to help me bring up Kaya. When she gets older, you can tell her stories of what we used to get up to. Maybe between us, we'll be able to make sure she doesn't make the same crazy mistakes.' She tried a humorous laugh that didn't quite work.

'The same crazy mistakes, eh?' When Jade turned, she was holding one of the knives. 'You mean like falling in love with the wrong person?' She ran the blade across a finger, eyes widening when it left a thin trail of blood. 'Good knives.' She lifted the finger to her mouth and sucked on it. 'The way I fell in love with you.'

'I'm sorry.' So many regrets. For marrying Nick. For giving Jade reason to believe she ever had a chance. For never having the time to make it up to Kaya. 'I did wrong by you, Jade. Your friendship was so dear to me that I was afraid to lose it by telling you that I would never, ever be interested in you that way.'

'Before Nick came on the scene, you—'

'No!' Sarah wanted to cry for all the stupid mistakes she'd made. 'You were being so kind to me after I split with Clem, and yes, for an infinitesimal period of time, I did wonder if it wouldn't be nice to be with you. I knew how you felt about me and I wondered if it would be enough. But it wouldn't have been. Ever.'

'It would!' Jade took a step towards her, the knife gripped in her hand.

'People keep coming at me with knives.' Sarah laughed because right at that moment, she couldn't think of anything else to do. Her life had become one great big joke.

She had to remember the good things. Her parents – her mother would ring later. She'd be concerned when there was no answer and would ring again. When she didn't get an answer the second time, she'd come over and use her key to get in. Sarah hoped her father would come with her, that her poor mother wouldn't have to face the awful scene on her own. Kaya would be well taken care of. Her parents would love her, as they'd loved Sarah.

She'd almost accepted her fate when the buzz of the intercom startled the silence.

Before Jade had time to react, Sarah did, rushing to it and pressing the release button while shouting into it, 'Help! Ring the police! Help!' Behind her, Jade was also shouting. Sarah felt a hand pull at her shoulder. She pulled back, keeping her finger on the buzzer for as long as she could, screaming with her last breath. 'Help us!' The pain when it came was sharp and her hand fell away. She screamed again, a wordless sound of agony as the knife twisted. 'Jade, don't do this.' Redundant words, the intense pain showed that Jade not only could, but had.

Sarah turned, caught the determined look in her attacker's face, and knew this was the end. She was going to die in the same room as her innocent child lay sleeping. Her final wish was for one last glimpse of her, one last chance to tell her that she did love her, that she always had.

There was never time for one last chance. There wasn't now.

More pain.

And then none.

59

Pain, a wave of it. Sarah welcomed it, embraced it like a saviour. If she hurt, she was alive. There was so much noise. Multiple voices shouting. Hands on her, hurting. A voice mumbling words she couldn't make out as she was rolled and pulled. A jerk as she was lifted. More unintelligible words, the tone reassuring. *Reassuring.* She was alive and now she was safe.

'Sarah?'

A firm voice, one she recognised. She opened one eye, then the other. They'd given her enough analgesia to take the edge off the pain. It also made her thinking processes slow and it took her a few seconds to focus on the face that was peering down at her. She ran her tongue around her dry mouth. 'Jade. She stabbed me.'

DI Bilton sat back on the chair behind her. 'Yes, perforated your lung, but you're going to be fine.'

Sarah's head was clearing. She looked around, took in the small room, the monitor beeping beside her, nodding slightly when she saw that her observations were all within normal ranges. A drainage tube was dealing with that perforated lung. Bilton was right, Sarah was going to be fine.

Her last clear memory was of shouting into the intercom and

pressing hard on the door release button. With her mouth too dry for long-winded questions, she stuck with the simple, 'How?'

'You let us in the main door, but I'm afraid we had to break down your apartment door to get access. Don't worry, though; your parents are getting it repaired. They're also looking after Kaya.'

'How did you...?'

'Know you were in trouble?' Bilton smiled. 'People constantly underestimate us. We interviewed Andrea Cotterell for hours, and whereas she did admit to her part in abducting your baby, she consistently denied she'd anything to do with the hit-and-run despite what she'd told you. With that doubt in our heads, we decided to keep you under police protection and had a car outside keeping an eye on you.

'Luck often plays a vital role.' Bilton shrugged as if it was an admission she was loathe to make. 'This morning, we re-interviewed Andrea and Megan—'

'Megan told you?'

Bilton shook her head. 'No, she's claiming she didn't know she'd done anything wrong, that she simply did what she was told, including taking Kaya from you in the pub in Lynton. I'm guessing her legal team are going to argue that Megan was a victim of coercive control. She'll certainly get brownie points for bringing Kaya out to the police that day.'

'Andrea?'

'Yes. She said Jade was the one who first approached them about taking Kaya and it was she who introduced them to your husband. Andrea said it was obvious that she was obsessed with you.' Bilton heaved a loud sigh. 'The line that divides obsessive love from hate is whisper thin. When the surveillance team reported that a woman had been let into your apartment, a warning bell rang in my head. I told the team to check that you were okay. You were clever to have released the main door and screamed for help. They didn't hesitate and luckily were able to break through your door.'

Sarah remembered the noise. 'Someone was talking to me, trying to reassure me.' She met Bilton's eyes. 'That was you?'

'I arrived before the paramedics and it was all I could do.'

Sarah smiled. 'It was good, thank you.' She shut her eyes, then opened them and looked at the detective. 'Is Zoé-Lee still doing okay?'

'Yes. I'm heading to see her next. She's hoping to be discharged in another couple of days. She'll be pleased to hear you're safe.'

'Tell her I said hello.' Her eyes shut on hot tears of relief. 'God, what a nightmare it's been.' It was time to tell the rest of the sad tale. 'It was Jade who was responsible for the hit-and-run.'

Bilton didn't look particularly surprised. 'I'm assuming she wanted Nick out of the way, to leave you free to pursue a relationship with her. Is that about the cut of it?'

Sarah ran her tongue around her mouth again. 'Is there water?'

'Yes, but are you sure you're allowed?'

'Just a drop.'

Bilton stood and held the glass to Sarah's mouth, taking it away once a small mouthful was swallowed.

'Thanks, that's better.' Sarah shuffled in the bed. 'Jade and I have been friends for a long time. I knew she had feelings for me that went beyond friendship, but I'd told her that I didn't love her in that way.' There was no point in talking about that moment's weakness she'd felt before Nick had come into her life. It had merely been a silly thought; she'd have never acted on it. But had that silly moment's weakness given Jade hope? How much of what had happened was down to Sarah's selfish stupidity. 'It wasn't Nick she wanted dead; he was merely collateral damage. It was *me* she was trying to kill.'

'Ah,' Bilton said. 'If she couldn't have you, nobody was going to. A sad story that unfortunately I've heard before.'

The intravenous line trailing from Sarah's hand clinked as she lifted it to wipe the tears that had started to fall. 'What's going to happen to her?' Jade had killed Nick and tried to kill Sarah – twice. Plus, she'd been involved in Kaya's abduction. She'd spend a long time in prison. Unless they decided she wasn't mentally fit to stand trial. Sarah felt the hot tears build again. She and Jade had been friends for so long. Despite all that had happened, she couldn't simply abandon her. She'd visit if she was allowed. She glanced at the detective, who sat silently, and opened her mouth to ask, shutting it again when she saw her expression. 'Jade?'

'I'm sorry. When they broke through your door, she obviously knew the game was up. The knife was sharp; they didn't have a chance to save her.'

Jade was dead. Sarah dragged a ragged breath in and let it out on a sob. It was a few minutes before she could speak. 'She was my friend, but I couldn't love her the way she wanted me to. Nick was my husband, but I'm not sure I *ever* loved him. Was everything they did my fault? Even their deaths? All my fault.' If only she'd been firmer with Jade, had never given her the slightest hint that she might be interested. If she had seen Nick's clinging love for what it was, and never married him. 'All my fault,' she said again.

Bilton dragged her chair closer and reached for Sarah's hand. 'I'm not saying you didn't make mistakes, but you didn't make Nick or Jade fall in love with you, and you can't be blamed because their love twisted into an obsession.' She patted the hand she held and let it go. 'Pure love is amazing, but obsessional love can be lethal.'

After Bilton left, that final sentence ran in a loop in Sarah's head, until the door opened and her mother walked through with Kaya in her arms.

'I thought you'd like to see her,' her mother said. She moved monitor leads and the intravenous line gently to one side and settled the baby into the crook of Sarah's arm.

Kaya snuffled softly and opened her eyes.

And as Sarah looked down at her, she felt a wave of pure love. Bilton was right; it was amazing.

This was all she needed.

No more mistakes; she was going to be the best mother.

ACKNOWLEDGEMENTS

A huge thanks to every member of the incredibly professional and supremely talented Boldwood team, especially my wonderful editor, Emily Ruston, who is unfailingly supportive.

A special thanks to the Valerie Keogh Supporters Group, many of whose names I've used in this book – I hope you're all happy with your characters.

Keeping me going through it all, are the usual suspects, writers Jenny O'Brien, Anita Waller, Judith Baker, Keri Beevis, Pam Lecky, Lesley Bratspis, and blogger/reviewer Lynda Checkley; and so many other bloggers and reviewers that I'm not going to name any more in case I forget someone – you all know who you are.

And of course – a huge thanks to my family. My wonderful husband, Robert, my sisters, brothers, in-laws, nieces, nephews, and grand-nieces and nephews – a wonderful family, I love them all.

I love to hear from readers. Overleaf you will find a number of ways to get in touch with me.

ABOUT THE AUTHOR

Valerie Keogh is the internationally bestselling author of several psychological thrillers and crime series. She originally comes from Dublin but now lives in Wiltshire and worked as a nurse for many years.

Sign up to Valerie Keogh's mailing list here for news, competitions and updates on future books.

Follow Valerie on social media:

facebook.com/valeriekeoghnovels
x.com/ValerieKeogh1
instagram.com/valeriekeogh2
bookbub.com/authors/valerie-keogh

ALSO BY VALERIE KEOGH

The Lodger

The Widow

The Trophy Wife

The Librarian

The Nurse

The Lawyer

The House Keeper

The Mistress

The Mother

THE *Murder* LIST

THE MURDER LIST IS A NEWSLETTER DEDICATED TO SPINE-CHILLING FICTION AND GRIPPING PAGE-TURNERS!

SIGN UP TO MAKE SURE YOU'RE ON OUR HIT LIST FOR EXCLUSIVE DEALS, AUTHOR CONTENT, AND COMPETITIONS.

SIGN UP TO OUR NEWSLETTER

BIT.LY/THEMURDERLISTNEWS

Boldwood

Boldwood Books is an award-winning fiction publishing company seeking out the best stories from around the world.

Find out more at www.boldwoodbooks.com

Join our reader community for brilliant books, competitions and offers!

Follow us
@BoldwoodBooks
@TheBoldBookClub

Sign up to our weekly deals newsletter

https://bit.ly/BoldwoodBNewsletter

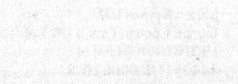

Milton Keynes UK
Ingram Content Group UK Ltd.
UKHW040702150624
444051UK00002B/8